The Abbey Close

STEVEN VEERAPEN

First published in 2018 by Sharpe Books.

ISBN: 9781983298059

TABLE OF CONTENTS

THE ABBEY CLOSE

PROLOGUE

If they found her they would kill her. The words echoed in her head like a motto. The fear sped up her heart, bidding her to move more quickly. If word of what she had done, what she had striven to keep secret for years, got out, they would mock her, beat her and put her to death. There would be an end to a life of pain and misery, but it would not be on her terms.

She battled on through the dense undergrowth, forcing herself to take slow, measured steps. She halted as a hidden branch cracked underfoot, and the stupid beast whinnied. Anyone might hear it, might come upon them there in the woods and drag them back to the burgh, back to death. A light caught her eye and she stood locked in place. It was only the reflection of the moon, which had emerged from the clouds above. In its pale glow, the skeletal claws of the trees seemed to beckon her, silent and dead. She read it as a good omen. The moon was said to be a friend to women who had gone a little mad, and what she was attempting was surely a kind of madness. Still, the sensation of being watched was strong. Sweat burst out in little beads on her forehead, despite the chill.

If she was captured, she would have to face what would be called good men's justice, however unjust it had shown itself. The baillies, the Prior, the monks at the Abbey, all would cast her down. Where? Into a dungeon, perhaps. At first. Wherever she was put, they would want it done quietly, neatly, so as not to bring disgrace upon the damned burgh. And that loathsome creature would torment and make sport of her before breaking her neck. Well, she thought, stopping to let her heart slow, perhaps she deserved to live in fear. She had done things that Christian law judged evil. But courage had brought her this far

1

and must carry her just a little further. Just a little further, and she would be free of her burden. Her nerve could not flee her now. To her surprise, she found her lips moving in prayer. Strange that she should pray to God now, despite all she had done; it would be better to pray to the other fellow. The fellow who embraced her kind. The fellow who made his presence known more than God seemed to.

She had dressed lightly, and she shivered in the cold November air. Sweat prickled on her brow. It was not too far to the river. They had met in a little clearing near it. That had been clever. She could hear the black waters of the Cart tumbling and crashing, still wild from a summer of rain. When daylight came, if she had managed to free herself, she would be able to live at peace. Not at first, perhaps, but in time, when she had learned to live with freedom. If she were to be taken, captured, then it would be better to end her life herself, to dive into the river and turn her back on them all. Still, the shivering.

She trundled on.

It was later that night that a deer, escaped from the Abbey's parklands, froze and pricked its ears at the sound of splashing and laboured, human grunts.

1

Our Cardinal stuff'd up wi' sin
Neglects to tend the poor
Instead he lies abed each day
Astride his arrant whore

was scrawled on the paper in spiky, inked lines. It seemed pointless even tearing it down. Too many people had seen the words. They danced across the ice-flecked page, inviting laughter. It was fixed to the wooden boards of Glasgow's market cross. Some ragged boys were standing nearby, chanting the lines in their west-coast accents, all battering-ram vowels and dropped consonants. Simon Danforth turned to them. 'Get away from here, you wretches!' Despite the cold, colour had risen in his cheeks.

One youth, braver than the others, spat at the ground. 'An Englishman, an Englishman,' he cried, drawing laughter from his fellows. 'Murderin' basturt! English devil!' Danforth's colleague, Arnaud Martin, stepped forward.

'Get out of here, you little shits! Away!' His words came out in a fury of steam. He drew off a glove and snapped it in the palm of his hand. 'I swear before God I'll tan your arses.'

'Aye, right! Mon get us then! Yer fat king's on his way, ye'll wantae make ready tae kiss his arse and burn us oot!' called the spitter. But already the group was skipping away. 'Devil's dogs!' was their leader's parting shot. Martin turned to Danforth, his face apologetic. Danforth had seen the look before. He disliked it, disliked how people had an irritating need to apologise for others.

'Ignore them, Mr Danforth. Wee devils. Lucky for them they ran.'

'They're frightened,' said Danforth, his voice above a whisper.

'Eh? What's that?'

'They're frightened, Mr Martin. Every man, woman,

3

children too – all afraid.' He glanced around at the now quiet cross.

'No excuse. They've no damned respect.'

'The likes of them respect no man,' said Danforth. 'True Scotsmen know not all Englishmen are King Henry's spies.' Martin nodded, his eyes drifting, but Danforth had already turned his attention back to the scrap of paper. That was his business, after all. His fists were balled at it, not at the worthless youths. 'It is another one, for sure. Put up when I was at Mass and you in your bed, when the town was otherwise occupied.' To his disgust, he saw that Martin was stifling a grin. 'Mr Martin, do you find amusement in this … this violence?'

'To be honest, I find it lacking in wit compared with yesterday's,' said Martin, stamping his boots on the ground. The first real cold of the season had set in, the air thick with the autumnal smell of invisible bonfires. The dirt of the market cross had been turned to hard, close-packed grit. Shop doors were closed against the chill. 'Doesn't even call his Grace "Cardinal Sins". Our friend's slipping.'

For week, slanderous little verses, handwritten and anonymously posted, had been appearing in Glasgow's market cross. The libellers were clever. They worked in secrecy. Yet their victim was always the same: Cardinal David Beaton, the sprightly, good-humoured face of the Roman Church, and Danforth and Martin's master. The day before he had been 'Cardinal Sins': the epigram beneath had charged him with 'keeping whores within his doors to satisfy his lust – outside the poor will starve or burn because he says they must'. An older paper had proclaimed that 'all the jades of St Andrews work to delight what's in his trews', whilst 'the commonwealth cries out in shame at men of God who take no blame.' Such insults were not to be borne. An attack on Beaton was, as the Cardinal himself had protested, like a dog raising its leg and pissing upon the hem of the Pope's robes. And here was Martin, smiling.

Danforth turned his irritation into what he hoped was a look of steel. 'If you find wit in violence, you lack wit yourself, you really do. You are like Nero, fiddling as the flames lick at his feet.'

'I don't know any Nero, nor any fiddlers. It's a poor profession, that,' said Martin, wiggling a ring off so that he could replace the gloves and still display it.

'As you are a poor man.'

'Not in his Grace's employ I'm not.' Martin patted the breast of his doublet: like Danforth's, it was the Cardinal's livery, but Martin had decorated his with glittering buttons and slashes. His ring glinted in the pale sun.

'Oh, do be quiet. The Cardinal shall hear of your lightness. I shall tell, you see if I don't.' But in response, Martin widened his eyes in mock horror. Danforth tutted. A strutting peacock was a poor excuse for a partner. The sooner they caught the libellers the better. A hanging would be good. Or a burning. A bit extreme, perhaps, but all the more powerful for it, all the more likely to encourage the crowd to pity the sinner and hate the sin.

Danforth reached up and gripped the paper with numb fingers, tearing it from its nail. He folded it and deposited it in the pocket of his doublet, next to the weather-beaten and faded papers already taken down. He breathed out, as though to shrink his chest away from contact.

'Instead he lies abed each day astride his arrant whore,' sang Martin, a smile on his handsome face.

'Hush your mouth, you ass,' shot Danforth, looking around to see if anyone had heard. 'It is enough that the verse has lain here like … like a naked harlot all day. You think it right that you should quote it?'

'My voice was low,' said Martin, holding up his hands. 'These Glasgow folks have sharp tongues, but I doubt their ears will match them.'

'You are a fool. I cannot think why the Cardinal esteems you; some sudden weakness of the mind, it must be.'

'A fault,' said Martin, 'in our Cardinal? Hold your tongue, sir, or I shall drag you before him as art and part of this business.' Danforth only scowled. Martin's manner was intolerable. Some men were not worth insulting – it just bounced off them.

'I will hear no more of you, sir.' Danforth's nose rose in the air. 'Until we reach the Bishop's Castle. There, I regret, we shall have to appear united.' It was their second day in the town. It was time to confront the Archbishop of Glasgow for his laxity in condemning the criminals. He turned away.

'Hold on. What's this?' Martin reached out and plucked another paper down. It was older, tucked away between a call to muster and a faded note bearing the emblem of the silversmith's guild.

'None of ours. Leave it. Only matters touching his Grace touch us.'

Martin ignored him. 'Says here a girl is stolen away. "Most wickedly handled, ravished, and stolen away by evil persons unknown." Kateryn Brody, from Paisley, the monastic lands. Her father, writing under another hand, asks the baillies and good men of Glasgow to take up any strangers if they be in the company of a strange girl, and to report any such capture to the Paisley baillies. Odd sort of hue and cry. Stolen away.'

'Aye, I saw it yesterday, it is none of ours. Put it back or cast it away. Rubbish.' Instead, Martin slotted the paper into a pocket.

'Strangers, eh? I hope we're not taken up, Mr...'

Danforth was already marching towards their horses, his back poker straight. 'Ho, Woebegone,' he called, clapping the beast's chestnut flank before lumbering onto the saddle. The former plough horse, old and cheap, did not move. 'Come on, come on, you old fool.' Danforth stuck the back of his heel into its side. 'Let us go,' he called down. Out of the corner of his eye, he watched Martin. The younger man let his hand rest on the pocket with the note about the missing girl. Whistling, he sauntered towards his own horse. As the pair departed, groups of people began to converge again. 'Eh Cardinal, stuff'd up wi' sin' echoed. 'Sin, sin, sin'. Hooting laughter followed Danforth and Martin as the residents of Glasgow, bundled in their furs, enjoyed a scandal.

By English standards Glasgow would have been little more

than a village with ideas above its station. All that elevated it were its great Cathedral and its university. The university had merit. During his time at Christ Church – before Henry of England had suppressed it – Danforth had enjoyed three years as a university man, absorbing wisdom and reading for a degree, unachieved, in the liberal arts. That was over ten years past. In that time, he had seen a queen die, a prince born, and England's ancient Catholic faith chopped off with Thomas More and John Fisher's heads. And, of course, he had seen his wife and child die. He turned his mind away before the images took root. Dark memories, he found, were like uninvited guests: once given lodging they wouldn't leave.

Instead he rode through Glasgow, Martin being – for once – silent. Only when they crested the hill on which the Cathedral lay did there seem to be evidence of human activity. Beyond it was the Bishop's Castle, its tall frontage and pointed roof soaring above the walls. As they approached, Danforth turned to Martin.

'I shall speak for us.'

'Ah, so you can speak?' Danforth ignored him and veered Woebegone right, into the crumbling gatehouse. From under the chipped stone arch slouched a liveried guard.

'We come on the Cardinal's business,' said Danforth, producing a letter bearing the Cardinal's great seal from his cloak. He flashed the array of titles before tucking it away again. It was a gamble. The Archbishopric of Glasgow did not have to answer to the authority of Cardinal Beaton. Danforth held his breath as the gatekeeper gaped at them. After a few seconds, he shrugged, scratched himself, and waved them through. Danforth's shoulders relaxed as he shook the reins and spurred Woebegone on.

The courtyard was thronged. Danforth caught snatches of conversation: 'It's getting' caulder,'; 'My fingers are red-raw,'; 'Upstairs floor needs fresh rushes, will you dae it?'. Two priests were arguing in a corner, one of them waving his arms whilst the other tried to calm him. A groom, no more than fourteen, came forward. Danforth and Martin dismounted, the former slipping a coin into the boy's grubby

7

hand. In return he smiled, revealing broken teeth. Danforth looked away.

'Where might we find the Archbishop,' he asked a serving woman – one who looked respectable and orderly. She pointed at the central tower, saying nothing.

'Friendly natives,' remarked Martin. 'Sociable. Merry. You been giving them instruction?'

'I shall instruct you to hold your tongue,' said Danforth. He softened his tone. 'This is a heavy matter. As the elder, I should speak to the man. I think his Grace shall be rather stiff, formal in his manner.'

'Mmm. I can see why that might disturb a wild-man like you.'

'See,' tutted Danforth. 'You cannot be serious for even a moment.'

'Well then let me be. He may have better faith in a Scotsman.' Danforth frowned, and Martin held up a hand. 'I don't mean to offend. God's wounds, was my own father not a stranger? No, but with things as they are, an English tongue might cause trouble. Especially if it tells the man news he'd rather not hear. It's the way of it, no point complaining.'

Danforth thought for a moment. Battle with England was looming, and the English were not popular. Still, Danforth's Scots was impeccable; he had worked hard at it for years, ironing out his genteel London twang. Children were bairns and scuffles were tulzies, his brain always reminded him before he opened his mouth. He had lived in his adopted realm for the better part of a decade. And if being in the service of Scotland's only Cardinal was not a sign of acceptance then nothing was. His hand went to the little medal of St Adelaide he wore around his neck: his talisman, the patron saint of exiles. Clasping it had become a ritual.

'No, Martin,' he said. 'I want the measure of the man. He must see the violence in his parish.'

'They're only bills, papers – they'll blow away in the first strong wind.'

'And that is exactly why I should speak. Papers? Mere papers? They are like bullets fired from a musket. The damage they do is just as bad, no physic can repair it. Besides,' he added, tapping his chest, 'I have the commission. Are we clear?'

'As the noon day.'

'Then come.'

'Ugh, fine. You're so much the elder, after all. But wait, hold on,' said Martin. He straightened his hat, sniffed at his gloves, and shook his cloak open to show more of his slashed doublet. 'There. Better. Onward.'

Danforth shook his head, drew his own cloak tight, and stomped the muck off his boots. Letting his features go blank, he stepped through the open door into an airy entrance hall, dominated by a carpeted staircase. They climbed to the anteroom at the top in silence.

An open horn window admitted weak autumnal sunshine. A dumpy bespectacled man sat at a desk littered with a confusion of papers and inkwells. The desk was a barrier, set before the great doors of the Archbishop's inner sanctum. The secretary looked up, the quill in his hand quivering.

'Timid wee fellow,' whispered Martin. Danforth hushed him with a hand.

'Good morning, sir. We are come to see his Grace the Archbishop.'

'Are you expected?'

'I think not.'

'What is your business.'

'Our business is for the ears of his Grace.'

At that the little man, who reminded Danforth suddenly of a mole, shot them a nasty look. 'His Grace is not at home to unexpected guests. He is at prayer.'

'We come from the Cardinal.'

'Cardinal Beaton? Ah,' said the secretary in triumph, his magnified eyes twinkling. 'The Cardinal has no authority here.'

Damn, thought Danforth, his mouth working as he tried to think of something to say. He did not want to spread the matter around. Secretaries were known for their loose tongues. He should know; he and Martin had begun in the Cardinal's

9

service as English and French secretaries.

'Listen, you little nyaff,' said Martin. 'Do you want burst? We're come on the Cardinal's business, and the Cardinal acts on behalf of his Holiness in Rome. And our sovereign lord, too. I might tear your name from your lips and carry it back to the Cardinal. And he might carry it to the king.' To Danforth's horror, he was sliding a glove off. 'Bampot,' he uttered.

'I,' began the secretary, his eyes flitting away, 'I shall inform his Grace you men are come.' He scraped back his chair and stood, turning towards the tall doors that marked the entrance to the Archbishop's privy chamber. He rapped before pushing them open and sliding in. Danforth turned to Martin, a grudging respect in his eyes. 'Bampot?' he asked, an eyebrow arched.

'Am I not half a Scot, born and reared? Insults and oats for breakfast, Mr Danforth. Part of my nature.'

'As behoves an ass.'

'Ah, comme c'est drôle! I like that very much, my friend. Yet it roused the fellow, did it not? I suspect his lugs will burn for a while.'

'I was raised to believe that Scotsmen and the French were louts to a man. I can see why, now. Put those reeking gloves back on.'

'Ha! I was raised to believe all Englishman have tails.' Before he replaced his second glove, Martin wagged it behind himself. 'I own I'm glad he took fright. I'm all talk, in truth.'

'That, at least, is something,' said Danforth.

Clasping his hands behind his back, he looked around the entrance hall. Tapestries hung on the walls, all religious scenes. He smiled up at the Virgin, a dove in her hands. Inside her halo golden flowers blossomed. He ran a finger over it. All at once it was rough, soft, smooth, warm, cold. A guttering wind invaded the room, making the bottom of the tapestry ripple, and a candle on the desk flare before dying. He strode to the desk, his lip curling. In his own offices – at home in Edinburgh and in the Cardinal's various lodgings, his papers were neat. Some men didn't deserve the office of secretary.

'What's keeping that damned whoreson?' Martin had crept

up behind him and was eyeing the desk's clutter. 'As lax in tending his office as he is unfriendly.'

'I daresay the wretch is telling his Grace that we handled him a wee thing roughly. It is an offence to threaten a man of the Church.'

'Not, I reckon, if the threat is of one higher in degree. Stung by the rebuke, so I am, sir.'

'No sting is so sharp as that which gives us which we seek.'

'Hmm. Is that from your reading at the university? A quote?' Martin had lowered his voice. Danforth almost smiled at the sudden earnestness.

'Of course not. It is ghastly, of my own sudden composition. That, Martin, is extempore.'

'If you say so. I'll own though, I wish I had real learning.'

'You speak French, and Scots, you read and write passing well. His Grace would not employ you otherwise'

'That's not learning, not really. I wish I'd been a university man, I mean.'

'There are divers paths to knowledge. I was a poor student, apt to retain only what pleased me and not what should. Yet–'

Danforth was cut off by screeching door.

'His Grace bids you enter', said the secretary, his eyes fixed on his seat. Danforth gave him a little bow before stepping towards the privy chamber. Martin did not. Instead, he stepped in front of the little man for a few seconds and appraised him with a hard state. Then he made a sudden jerking motion with his head. It sent the secretary scurrying for his desk. Danforth averted his eyes from the little scene, fighting another uninvited smile, and stepped inside.

2

Gavin Dunbar rose from his high-backed chair, gripping the neat desk before him with slender hands. His rich robes, cream and gold, swirled about him. Danforth inhaled the flat, stale smell of incense, picturing old churches, his father's smile, childhood summers. Dunbar proffered his ring for them to kiss.

'Gentlemen of his Grace the Lord Cardinal,' he said. 'And come on his Grace's business. What news? Sniffing out heretics? Looking for books to grace St Andrews' libraries? Or does the master not tell the dogs why they must retrieve the stick?'

'Good morning, your Grace,' said Danforth, removing his hat and bowing. 'I am Simon Danforth, English secretary to the Cardinal. Here is our commission.' He handed it over and clasped his hands over his stomach.

Dunbar slit open the seal. His bushy eyebrows rose and fell, his lips moving soundlessly. When he had finished, he looked up at them without expression. 'Slanders touching the estate of the Church, eh?'

'Yes, your Grace,' said Danforth.

'The Cardinal bids me trust in you fellows.'

Danforth bowed his head, but his heart fluttered. He hoped Dunbar would not read pride. 'Danforth … Danforth,' said the Archbishop, touching a finger to his lips. 'You are, I believe, the tamed Englishman come out of that hell-blasted realm.' His hand danced over his chest in an abortive attempt at crossing himself. 'Aye, I've heard of you.'

'The same.' Danforth frowned, deflated. He had not expected warmth from Dunbar, but he had hoped there might be some recognition that they had a common enemy. Instead the Archbishop seemed to be sneering at him. 'And with no loyalties to the kingdom that bore you, I trust? Nor to its king'

'None. The antichrist Henry has shown himself rather an enemy than a friend to Christendom.' Danforth had seen the king once. It was during one of the great progresses through London – a tall man sitting astride a charger, arrayed in rich velvet and jewels. Rings of noblemen, retainers and guards had surrounded him. All that had really been visible over the throng was a sturdy arm waving high in the air, sunlight glinting off a multitude of rings. Danforth had also seen the coronation entry of the king's concubine, Anne Boleyn – a thin-faced, unsmiling shrew with black hair and large, haunted eyes, dressed as a maiden queen despite the bastard in her belly. He shivered inwardly at the memory, unwelcome and unwanted.

'It is so. And now the great whale declares himself supreme sovereign of this nation.' Dunbar shifted his gaze to Martin. 'Your name?'

Danforth was pleased to see Martin bow, only ruining the effect with an open smile as he rose. 'Arnaud Martin, your Grace: French secretary to the Archbishop.'

'I see: Danforth the tamed pet Englishman and French Martin, the half-frog.' Danforth sensed Martin's spine stiffen but was grateful he kept his jaw taut. 'Pray tell me, gentlemen,' said Dunbar, amusement on his wrinkled, aquiline face as he sat, 'how fares our ... most *worshipful* father in Christ in keeping good office, when he sends his secretaries out of his lands and into mine? Perchance he has no other use for your toil. I understand he has flown south.'

Danforth cleared his throat. Dunbar was fishing for gossip, and he would not be the one to give it. 'The Cardinal has gone to the army, your Grace, to better serve the king. Yet before he did, he had news of these bruits. About the appearance of slanderous bills attacking his Grace, and so attacking the Church and realm. Your Grace might see from our commission we are to stop it.'

'This,' said Dunbar, jabbing a finger at the letter he had dropped to the desk, 'speaks of slander ... of defamatory bills in *my* lands.'

'It is so, your Grace. The Cardinal would have you take action against the malefactors.'

'Would he now? I hardly require counsel in tending my own

garden.'

'Yet his Grace thinks it right that the great men of the Church work as one in stopping the spread of the Lutheran heresies. And their agents.'

'Oh, you have knowledge of the slanderers, eh? You think Lutherans have made their home in Glasgow?'

'I ... well ... I can think of no others. No others who might gain by bringing the faith and its leaders into hatred, the hatred of the people. Lutherans, Lollards, any of that rabble, you – your Grace sees?' Danforth felt himself faltering. It was not going how he'd hoped. His voice sounded hollow, whining even. Had Martin noticed?

'I must say, these bills sound most wicked. Hatred of the people, eh? Deliciously wicked, indeed. What is their nature?'

'Oh, they are vile, unseemly things, your Grace, vulgar. Such filth sucked out of Christian pens! Neither Juvenal nor Horace: I think our friends might finish a jug of ale before they finish an alexandrine–'

'I did not ask for a study of their *style*' snapped Dunbar, thumping his fist on the desk. 'What matter touching the Cardinal was contained within them? What did they *say*, man?'

'They ... They touch upon his private affairs, and his friendship with Mistress Ogilvy.'

'Ah, that. It makes easy prey for prating tongues.'

'Indeed, sir. The Cardinal's friendship with the lady is spotless. Their children are legitimate, born before he was ordained; they are faithful servants of the Church, acknowledged by the Holy Father.' Danforth's Adam's apple jerked like a marionette. He didn't like to dwell on the subject of the Cardinal and Marion Ogilvy. But, as he reminded himself, the great Wolsey had kept Joan Larke as a mistress. Few men's private lives could stand up to scrutiny. His own could not. He pushed away the thought of fumbling, of hitched skirts and dropped breeches.

'Indeed. Would that his Grace was not so strong in condemning the like fault in others, eh?' The corners of Dunbar's lips twitched. 'Where are these bills?'

'We have destroyed them, your Grace,' said Danforth, ignoring the odd look he drew from Martin. He felt his heart speed at lying to a churchman and prayed again that his face did not betray him.

'You've done what? What possessed you, man? This business falls within the cognizance of my courts; you have destroyed evidence, you and your master.'

'Your Grace, the bill that we took yesterday had lain for some days; it was near frozen in place. Others were set behind it. No wardens had acted. The people laughed. This has been happening for some weeks, as we understand, unchecked. We do not know how many more have been and gone. You have the power to stop it, your Grace. Help us stop it.'

Dunbar fixed a curtain of grey hair behind an ear and eased back in his chair. 'You and your master will allow, I think, that the times carry weightier business than this. Across the kingdom men are preparing to fight for the Church. Leave this matter with me.'

'You ... your Grace will take action against the Lutherans?'

'There are *no* Lutherans in my lands. I would know. It is the Cardinal who takes up men who have their roots in foreign lands, not I.' Danforth's chin jutted. 'His Grace has more enemies than hairs upon his head, alas. I would that it was not so. Of course, I also wish he was as zealous in matters spiritual as temporal. It will be some of the university men grown bold.' He nodded. 'Aye, that'll be it. As their Chancellor, I shall take the lusty fellows in hand. When the times allow, I shall begin a commission of my own. You are right in one thing: it does not befit the Church to have men within it who bring disgrace. I'll dig 'em out. You might carry this news back to his Grace, with my ... reverences.'

'Yet ...' faltered Danforth, 'surely Your Grace could do morely.' Morely! Not even a word. He bit his tongue, hoping Dunbar hadn't noticed.

To his credit, the Archbishop did not laugh. 'I am not,' he said instead, 'so fallen in my wits that I need the counsel of clerks. I've burned more heretics than you've had new boots. Off you trot.'

'Uh, the Cardinal bid us tarry until the matter is concluded, until the perpetrators have been brought to task or the bills ceased.'

'Tarry as you wish. None of my concern. But the inquiry, when I bring it, will be none of yours. And you need not think your meddling will be forgotten. If my courts find no libellers to answer for their crimes, you'll have the blame of it. For the moment, I shall order the market cross watched. You may go.'

Danforth and Martin bowed in unison, ignored by the Archbishop, who was already looking down to his desk as he reached for paper and a quill. Together they left the privy chamber. Dunbar's secretary tilted his head up at them, balancing his spectacles. There was a sheen of sweat on his forehead. Danforth realised he had been listening at the door. 'It was a pleasure, sir,' said Martin as they strode around the desk.

They blinked out into the light. The sun was making an effort for November, but it was a losing battle. 'Why,' asked Martin, 'did you not pass the bills?'

'Wheesht,' replied Danforth, looking around. The courtyard was still mobbed. Although the servants did not seem interested, one never knew which ears were listening. 'Later.'

Regaining their horses from the shoeless boy, Danforth mounted Woebegone and led them back to the highway. 'The Town Council maintain this roadway passing well,' he said. 'Would that all of the king's highways were so well attended.'

'Never mind the roadway, sir! Why did you not pass the Archbishop the verses?'

'The Cardinal should see them. I think the Archbishop is no friend of his.' That was diplomatic, he fancied. 'He might hold an inquiry, for the sake of form, but our naughty verses would then be read in open court. That would rather magnify their slanders than bury them. We must deal in this matter privately.' He spoke as though lecturing a schoolboy.

'Sir, you're quite a cunning wee agent beneath the airs.'

'Well,' said Danforth, feeling generous, 'I shan't forget that it was your rough tongue gained us an audience. He cannot now deny knowledge of these bills, nor let them spread.'

'A fine job of work, if you ask me.'

'A fine beginning.'

'But who in hell's name is doing this? Someone's writing these things, they don't just grow – some creature moving unseen, behind our backs, mocking us.'

'That is what we must discover. I might almost think it is the work of some demon.'

'Surely not.'

'Not unless demons write in ink on scraps of paper. No, this is some mortal man.'

'Or woman.'

'Some man, with a little learning, and a hatred of the Church. Or an affection for England's treatment of it. He cannot –'

'An Englishman?'

'Can I finish? I did not say an Englishman. A man who cannot –'

'I do love it when you lecture, just as a note to you,' Martin interrupted again, with a smirk. 'You should do it morely.'

'He cannot speak openly,' said Danforth, raising his voice, 'for he would feel the flames. And so he moves, as you say, unseen. Or he has done.'

'So we tarry in Glasgow,' sighed Martin. It was more statement than question.

'No. I have business elsewhere. You stay in Glasgow if you wish.'

'Alone in this little corner of the world? I think not. Where are we going?'

'For the moment to our inn and bedward,' said Danforth, nonplussed. 'Above all else, I crave rest.'

Darkness had fallen by the time they arrived – the days were growing meaner. The sky, Danforth noticed, seemed very low, the stars emerging from behind cobweb clouds. The inn stank of ancient beer, and crane flies danced around the candles, unaware that their time was past. They fought their way between tables of card players towards the bar. 'Watch where yer gawn,' one hissed as Danforth jostled him. 'Tryin' tae play cairds, for Chrissake'.

'My apologies, sir, I meant no offence.' The man shook his head, mumbling oaths.

The pair commandeered a circular wooden table. Martin ordered bread and cheese. Danforth refused. It was a Friday.

'You might eat of the man's table,' said Martin. 'The Church allows it.'

'My customs are my own,' said Danforth, drawing in his cheeks.

'And welcome you are to them. Pour l'amour de Dieu.'

'I do wish you would not speak in that devilish tongue.'

'And I wish you wouldn't speak as though you were in your first year at college and keen to let the world know all about it,' snapped Martin. Danforth opened his mouth to argue but shut it again. Better to let the man whine, and say nothing, than rise to a fight. He pursed his lips. 'Besides,' Martin continued, 'you speak Scots and live in Scotland. French is the realm's favoured second tongue. I can't seem to shift it since being in France. And I'd be loath to lose the nickname "French Martin". Makes me sound much more gallant than I am.' He rested his chin on a hand and fluttered his eyelashes.

'Ach, chase yourself,' said Danforth. His eyes nipped. Martin had recently accompanied the Cardinal to France, to drum up support for a Holy War against England. They had only returned in August. Danforth had been left at home. The Cardinal had called him his watch-candle: burning with intensity, seeing all. He didn't mind. Who cared for France? Yet still there had been a shameful little sense of jealousy, of being unwanted and unvalued. It was nonsense, of course, the stuff of schoolboys – but it remained there, secretive and niggling. Somehow Martin had sensed it.

'You know I've got the right of it,' smiled Martin. 'Sir, something's been preying on my mind.' His tone had turned serious with the speed of a candle being snuffed.

'Concerning the Cardinal's business?'

'No. Jesus, do you ever –'

'Do not blaspheme.'

'Do you ever turn your mind from toil and work? I've been thinking about the current broils, the war with England. Although I suppose they might yet become our work.'

'Oh?'

'Well, with the war and all … You lodged in London some years, didn't you?'

'My family were from Surrey,' he said, knowing it wasn't an answer.

'But when you were a university man, and when you were a … what was it?'

'Assistant to the London coroner, and discharging most of the lazy fellow's duties.' Danforth's lips turned down at the memory. He had taken up the position in the short years between leaving the university and fleeing England, but the unpleasant memories were never far from his mind and had become uglier with time. Dead bodies, broken limbs, hysterical people dragged off to be hanged.

'Aye. Coroner. And your father was a servant of the old Cardinal. His Grace told me.'

'He was a gentleman usher of Cardinal Wolsey.' A little pride coloured Danforth's tone.

'Yet you never speak of London. I've been in his Grace's service for,' his lips moved as he counted, 'four years, and yet in all that space I've never had a word out of you, not about your life. You're a closed book.'

'His Grace has never thrown us together,' said Danforth. He did not like the direction of the conversation. It was threatening to become personal, the precious knot of a professional relationship in danger of being loosened. He straightened his back and crossed his arms.

'No, he hasn't. Did you not like England?'

Danforth became very interested in his hands. 'I did not like its religion, or what it came to.'

'Ho, here's my supper!' Danforth blessed the reprieve, as Martin's interest shifted to the innkeeper, who set a loaded wooden trencher before him. 'What a feast, sir. I'll give it a good home.' Danforth watched as Martin's fingers danced around the food. 'This is good,' he said, his cheeks blooming.

'Sure I can't,' he swallowed, 'tempt you?'

Danforth paused before answering, to allow a chorus of cheers to dampen. Someone had a good hand. He hated taverns. 'Indeed you cannot,' he said, cursing at his mewling stomach. 'I am not so weak.'

'Nor I,' said Martin. He swallowed again, before dabbing a napkin to his lips and glaring at Danforth. 'I'm as strong in the faith as any man standing in this realm or without. Though I don't need to advertise my religion and virtues to the world.' With that, he picked up another wedge of bread and shovelled it into his mouth, defiant. A morsel of cheese fell onto his doublet. 'Ah, shit,' he mumbled. 'My good doublet. And me a gentleman.' He brushed at it, his mouth a little moue.

'More dandiprat than gentleman, for all your airs,' said Danforth. Martin narrowed his eyes, but continued to eat. Danforth felt the need to lighten the mood. He uncrossed his arms. 'Did they starve you in Paris?'

'Rather I reckon they increased my capacity. Better food in France, though.'

'You shall become unwell, eating at such a pace. And there might be no apothecaries where we go on the morrow.'

'Is that so?' asked Martin, with a little interest. 'And where might that be, O wise one?'

'Not far. By my reckoning some ten miles or so to the west. Perhaps less. Paisley.'

'Paisley?'

'The same. I have a mind to see it. It is one of the four great places of pilgrimage in this realm. I have seen Melrose, and Scone. Dundee too.'

'There's no bruit of the slanders in Paisley. The Cardinal might wish our attendance upon him. He gave us no freedom to go and play.'

'His Grace has given me leave to visit the town, knowing my desire.' Cardinal Beaton was always sympathetic to him. Fatherly, almost. 'And we are not to return to him until the matter of the verses is settled. As well you know. It might be that our shaking the Archbishop will now put fear into the rebellious churls. We shall return in a week and see if his inquiry has borne fruit. Or even if it has been convened. I suspect it will be dilatory.'

'If that means half-arsed.'

'At any rate, you need not accompany me,' said Danforth, sensing his chance. 'By my truth, I think it better that I make pilgrimage alone. Aye, that's best, for sure. You can tarry here and make your presence known.'

'Non. Paisley's a busy place, from what I've heard. Any news out of Glasgow will reach it. I prefer company, sir, even if you don't.' Something illuminated Martin's face. His hand wandered to his cloak. 'Aye, I knew I'd been thinking about Paisley. That paper, the one I took. A missing girl. From Paisley.'

'What has that to do with anything?' He felt a groan coming on.

'Nothing. I might make some enquiries whilst you make your obeisance, is all.'

'Enquiries? About what?'

'This little kitty. I've heard nothing about strangers turning up here – save ourselves, and we've seen no stolen lass. It excites my mind, that's all.' Martin's voice had turned defensive. 'I might learn something, and the girl might be discovered, and we might win the friendship of the Abbey. Or our master might.' He shrugged.

'Kitty … I think I prefer not to know how your French blood heats. She shall be already found, or run off for a whore, or dead upon some ditch, you mark me.'

'You have a black mind, sir. Sick.'

'My mind inclines towards business, not trifles. Our business is this crime, this writing. Some stolen girl is of no consequence. Some feud, she'll be an heiress taken for marriage, or some such nonsense.'

'You're hard, Mr Danforth, a hard man. Which is the greater crime, attacking the Church in words or stealing away one of its flock?'

'Ugh, I want no debate. But I will say this. You mention sickness? The whole world, Mr Martin, is a sickly patient, sick since the great fall. And God is the physician, the clergy his

21

apothecaries. But He deals with a stubborn patient who turns to tricksters, who feed him heresy, Lutheranism, whatever you call it, instead of honest medicine.'

'Fuck physicians,' spat Martin. Danforth cocked an eyebrow. If Martin had some grudge or other, that was his business.

'I shall ignore that. Me, I have had business enough for this day. My back fair aches from the saddle.' That seemed to happen a lot. Whoever said spending a lifetime in the saddle accustomed one to it was a liar. 'I am retiring.'

'And I'll finish my supper, and perhaps keep these gambling fellows honest.'

'Goodnight to you, Martin. Keep your mind on business, and off missing lassies.'

'Goodnight, Danforth.'

3

Danforth's wife had died again. It had been that damn Martin who had done it. He lay on the soft pallet bed, gazing at the indistinct blur of the ceiling. It had been Martin who had forced his mind into dark places. It had been Martin who reminded him of his own great sin, the one that no amount of pilgrimages seemed to erase.

The dream had not come upon him for some time. Months, perhaps years – he couldn't remember. He'd trusted that his devotions had banished it, that his silent pledges to God that he would complete his Scottish pilgrimage had been enough to keep it at bay. Somewhere, however, he must have slipped. It had returned and roused him, as familiar as a scar, at whichever dark and breathless hour it was.

As always, he was back in England. None of the foulness of London was present in the dream: no fetid airs; no noise; no sense of fear. Nor was there plague. He would be reading by candlelight when Alice would come through the door, rosy-cheeked and blonde-haired. She still had the snub-nosed look of youth. Alice, dead and gone for years. Alice, pretty, needy, childlike, entrancing. 'No,' she said, 'there's been some mistake. I am alive, I'm well, Simon. I've come home.' She was carrying their daughter in her arms and all was well. 'What death? What curse of God? I'm here, don't tease me.' He would stand, his book falling to the floor – a valuable thing, but no matter. He would embrace his wife, their child between them. 'Thank you, God. Oh, thank you, God.'

And then he would wake up. His grief would be fresh. The mind was cruel. Alice, he realised, had now inhabited his dreams longer than she had lived by his side. He had loved and been loved by her so briefly, and yet it cast a long shadow, her face and voice never far from his mind. That was her home now. He had laughed a great deal when she was alive, when he was young. He didn't need to be reminded of it. And it was all that wretched Martin's fault.

He turned on his side and stared at nothing until the blackness began to change in quality and thin shafts of greying light broke through the gaps in the wooden shutters, announcing the morning.

After Mass at the Cathedral, they took the highway south, through Glasgow's fields and orchards and across the Clyde. South of the river the highway turned to the west, dotted here and there by spittals. Despite Martin's protestations, Danforth insisted they stop and pray at each of the little wooden lean-tos. He didn't care to repeat the nightmare of the previous evening.

'I find the labour of journey a great comfort,' he said, by way of explanation. 'Do you know, I considered taking holy orders myself when … in the past.'

'Oh? What prevented you?'

'Well,' Danforth sighed, looking upwards 'it came to me that I did God's work better in more active service.'

'Christ's cloth, you're a pious old bugger,' said Martin, smiling. 'I hope you did not consider taking the monk's robe. You have a fine head of hair, not best suited for the tonsure.'

Danforth turned to him, but said nothing. He prided himself on being a serious-minded fellow: deserving of respect, not ridicule. 'You are a grave and solemn lad,' his father had often told him, one paw on his shoulder, 'fashioned for grave and solemn business.' He had never questioned the prediction. Henceforth, he decided, he would not speak so freely. It was labour enough to work cheek by jowl with Martin until the job was done.

As they rode in the cold sunlight, they were joined by fellows on the road. Their companions were a happy assortment of pilgrims and country people. Coming the opposite way were grinning chapmen, their packs filled with goods that they hoped to hawk at profit in the outlying districts. All talk along the road was of war. Making for the Abbey also was a rabble of itinerant vagabonds, the men unshaven and wild, the women coughing and shivering in rags. Exiles too, thought Danforth, but in their own country. Many of them leant on sticks. Some had skin infections so grotesque they were difficult to look at. Danforth turned his face from them; they would be moved on by the burgesses if they lacked license to beg. In summer, he thought, this journey, this pilgrimage, must be a thing of beauty. But now it was ugly, the ground damp and cold, the trees signposts declaring the way to winter. The smell of wet woodland rose from the ground. It had been a bad summer.

Long before the burgh came into view, the spire of the Abbey was visible over the treetops, reaching heavenwards. The road passed outlying tanneries, the corn-mill of Seed Hill, and wound around the tall, grey Abbey walls before forming a bridge over the River Cart. The narrow skein of roiling pewter, in high spate, cascaded over a low waterfall, full of dead leaves and brambles. Danforth was disappointed. He had hoped for still, clear waters. He had wanted the place, he realised, to resemble a picture in stained glass. In the surrounding hills and braes, the Abbey was supposed to resemble a jewel in the cupped palm of a hand. His shoulders slumped as he crossed the Bridge Port.

The crowds of people melted away to attend to their own business. The Tolbooth, municipal courthouse and gaol, caught Danforth's eye. Paisley's was surmounted by a squat tower with an enormous clock displaying a time far later than the sky suggested. He started when a gnome-like face appeared next to the clock. It was the knock-keeper, hanging out of a shutter by the clock-face. Danforth looked away, surveying the town with a traveller's eye. The towns and villages he knew better paraded through his mind: the Canongate, St Andrews, York, Surrey, London, London Bridge, home, Alice... He shook the cobwebs and refocused.

Though it lacked the ancient grace of Edinburgh and the neat lines and dramatic vistas of St Andrews, Paisley had a vigorous, earthy vibrancy, like a brash and uncaring musical score, composed more with a desire to make itself heard than to soothe and delight the ear. No doubt, thought Danforth, that is what conditioned its people's accents.

'And so we arrive,' Martin announced. 'And hours later than we need have. Ought we not have announced our arrival at the

Abbey? We're on the Cardinal's business, we might lodge in the guest house.'

'No. I am not minded to lodge there.'

'Why not? There'll be good beds, good wine.'

'I wish to stay in the burgh, near the people. News will carry here out of Glasgow before it reaches the monks, I fancy.'

'News of the bills, or news of the war?'

'Both.'

'Then we must find some inn. Jesus, another inn. So much for good beds and wine. Do you see one?' Several signs hung from the wood-and-stone buildings: a butcher, with bloodstained table in front of the building; a draper, who displayed lengths of colourful cloth; a fishmonger, table glistening. But no inn. Danforth peered down the streets and vennels converging on the cross. Each spewed human waste and sewage in brownish streams to meet and continue the journey to the river. His breathing slowed. Even the smell of Martin's perfumed gloves would be preferable. He struck off for the broad High Street, Martin following at a trot.

They passed a variety of tenements and frowning, close-packed houses in the lower High Street, all crumbling stone foundations and heavy thatched roofs. The stones used on them must, thought Danforth, have come from the same quarries as those which built the Abbey, but here they were put together without care. The road widened to allow a series of finer houses, the burgesses' and prelates' mansions. None of them were attractive. Only colourful front doors and gallons of whitewash proclaimed wealth. It was not until the end of the High Street that they spotted an inn sign. The place itself might once have been a fine, small private home. Now it had fallen on hard times, despite the prosperity of the burgh. Its thatched roof was a few feet from the ground, the whitewash on the low walls flaked and peeling. The sign, in contrast, was bright and gaudy, like a jewelled ring on the finger of a rotting carcass.

'Might we now reconsider approaching the Abbey?' asked Martin.

'No. This will suffice. I did not come to these lands to be

cosseted like a new born bairn.' Already Danforth was dismounting and removing his saddlebag. He threw it across his back. Beside the building was a gated stable with a grey palfrey and no ostler. Danforth rattled the gate. Eventually a boy appeared, stretching.

'Whit ye after, sirs? Ah'm busy.'

'Mind your tongue, you saucy whelp,' said Danforth. 'A poor excuse for an ostler, you are. Take these horses and see that they are attended well.'

The sulky child took the horses, closing the gate behind him with a disgruntled bang. 'A labourer, that one,' said Martin.

'If he proves not, he will feel the pain of it.' Danforth opened the door of the inn and led the way, his spare frame bending under the low lintel.

Inside was a bare and neglected asylum. No one had bothered to make even a pretence of attracting business; the only concessions to comfort were some wooden chairs facing an unlit central hearth, and the entire building stank strongly of burnt peat. Danforth started at what looked, in the gloom, to be thin, trailing columns. As his eyes adjusted, he saw that they were ropes, tied around heavy stones lying on the floor. The other ends disappeared into the low part of the ceiling. It was an old trick, used in the houses of the very poor. The ropes and stones would keep loose patches of thatch from blowing off in heavy winds. It was a strange sight in what once must have been a good, two-storey house.

'Good morning?' called Danforth, wrinkling his nose. 'We seek lodging.' Beyond the hearth a crudely-built wall divided the room. No answer came. Martin made a move towards the passage through it.

'What do you mean, sir?' hissed Danforth, raising an arm.

'I mean to find our host.'

'He may be from home; you cannot just intrude.'

'It appears that I'm doing so. Can't seem to help myself.' Martin stepped through, his own arms held out like a sleepwalker.

Muttering, Danforth followed him. In the back the ceiling was higher, its beams crossing above them, and there were some odds and ends of furniture – a washbowl, another chair, a trestle that looked like it might once have been valuable. Some scattered account sheets lay neglected. One of the walls appeared to have once held panelling, but it had been torn or fallen down, likely to be burnt or sold. A good flock bed with a battered mattress took up one corner: an unkempt sign of better days. Light poured through an open door leading to the garden, and already Martin was making for it. Danforth plucked at the back of cloak. 'Stop! This is not your house!'

Outside was an overgrown yard, littered with denuded trees and felled stumps. Midway down some chickens scratched at bare patches of soil, and at the far end was a stout woman, a stained cap on her head. Her back was to them. She stood on a low box, affixing an assortment of brambles and nettles to the top of her fence. Beyond the fence loomed the uppermost branches of countless bare tree limbs. Danforth shivered at the sight of the wet, black confusion. It was not by chance, he thought, that when poets turned their pens to the woodlands they wrote of the sweetness of summer airs.

'Good morning, mistress,' cried Martin cheerfully, swaggering towards her. The woman jumped and almost toppled. She turned a granite face towards them, throwing her thatch of jagged foliage to the ground.

'Who the hell are you? What do you mean by comin' in here?'

'My apologies, mistress,' said Danforth. He cursed at Martin, and gestured behind him. 'We are looking for lodgings.'

'What? Who are you?' Suspicion and fear mingled in her protuberant eyes, which ran over their travelling cloaks. Her hair, escaping its cap, was the colour of rust.

'We are gentlemen of his Grace the Lord Cardinal.'

'The Cardinal? Then you lodge in the Abbey. Guests of quality lodge in the Abbey, always they lodge there. Why are you here?'

'We are minded to stay in the burgh, mistress.'

'We are come on matters touching the Cardinal's honour, some crude bills in Glasgow –' began Martin, Danforth silencing him with a stare.

'We have seen no better lodgings than your own,' he said. It was true, in its fashion.

'I … I don't take much business, no' these days,' she said. She caught Martin's wandering gaze. Then something dawned in her eyes. 'But neither can I refuse custom. Cardinal's men? Come away ben, sirs. I apologise. I was securin' the limits of the burgh. We're wantin' for stout town walls. Not that there's much worth savin' here.' Danforth did not ask if she meant the house or the town. No sense prolonging her blabber. She marched across the garden, black skirts trailing in the mud and grass. As she passed, she attempted a welcoming smile. Behind her back Martin made a sarcastic, lustful face, and Danforth raised a warning fist in return.

Following their hostess, they listened as she chattered over her shoulder. 'I'm no' used to guests these days. Forgive me, gentlemen. My name's Euphemia Caldwell, wife to Kennedy.'

'Your husband runs the inn?' asked Martin.

'My husband's abroad on business.'

'Oh right. We saw your boy at the stable. Your son, I presume?'

'That lazy creature's no son of mine. He's the orphan of a bondsman bound to serve my husband. Uh, but the boy's good wi' horses,' she added, catching Danforth's look. 'I'll say that for him.'

'I see,' said Danforth. He had seen women like her before, full of complaint. Enduring her grumbling might be a fitting penance in itself. 'Yet you might lodge us, Mistress Caldwell?'

'Wi' gratitude, sirs, wi' gratitude. I meant you no offence. There have been troubles of late, and when I saw two fellows, strangers, I …'

'Troubles?' asked Martin.

'It's nothin', sir. Nothin' to trouble a Cardinal of the Church.'

'Is it the lost girl?'

'What?' she asked. 'Angus Brody's girl, you mean? What of her?'

'We heard tell of her in Glasgow, a placard said she had been stolen,' he said.

'The news went to Glasgow?'

'Aye. The paper said "ravished", it said "stolen away by wicked persons".'

'Aye, right enough, she's away. There are men in town, sir, that would have been pleased to see her gone by some means. It might be better no' to ask questions. She was badly used. By men, of course. But I trust you gentlemen are no' like that.' Her tone was almost accusatory.

'Like what?' asked Martin.

'Enough.' said Danforth, crossing his arms. 'I will not listen to idle gossip. Mr Martin, I can see no use in pursuing this matter.' The lives of monks should be beyond reproach. The Abbey of Paisley was the final holy place in Scotland he had to see. It must be sacrosanct. Martin and his new friend would not spoil it.

'I forgot myself, sir,' said Caldwell. 'It's no' often there's news, no' often there's a scandal here. And of course, with the nation at sixes and sevens wi' this war...'

'Times are unsettled.'

'Indeed. And so ... well, forgive me, sir, but when I heard you speak, and I thought of England, well ...'

'Quite.' An awkward little pause drew out.

'Well, you'll lodge upstairs,' said Caldwell. 'The rooms are kept as well as I can manage wi'out my husband's guidance.' Her tone became business-like. 'You shift for your own meals, pubic oven is down the town.'

'These arrangements suit us,' said Danforth, as Martin's face fell.

'And payment, sirs?'

'We shall pay you in full when we take our leave, and with generous gratuity.' Delight and disappointment fought for control of her face. Danforth enjoyed the battle.

'Very good, sir. Your rooms are upstairs.' She gestured to a rough, narrow wooden staircase on the right of the room. 'If you'll excuse me, I'll continue the fortification.' Her chin jutted up at the last word. 'No pissin' in your rooms, by the way, or the halls.'

When she had slouched back through the passage, Martin exhaled. 'I don't much like staying in such a scabby place, nor being starved by that stewed prune. There's a face that I'd bet seldom sees a smile. I wonder how such unhappy people find the will to continue living. Must be overflowing with black bile, don't you think? Swimming in it, I reckon.' He looked at Danforth directly, amusement in his eyes. 'Anyway, it ... well, doesn't it reflect poorly on our master to stay in such a mean place?' Danforth caught the upwards inflection of hope. He dashed it.

'You are at liberty, Mr Martin, to take yourself to the Abbey and beg lodgings from the brothers.' He didn't care for the jibing. He liked to think of himself as a phlegmatic man, calm and reasonable: the temperament associated with cool, clear water.

'Peace – I've no wish to cloister myself with those holy fellows either, even if you'd rather make submission to them on your knees. No, I'll make do. Reckon I can have the old bat serving us, to be honest, though I'd doubt her fare. Old women love me. It's lassies my own age who don't.' He gave a little laugh, half serious and half sad. Danforth gave him a half-smile in return. 'Here, what do you think of this business of the girl and the monks, though?'

'I do not think of it. Neither should you. But I might well raise it with the Prior when we visit. The Cardinal will want report of any breath of scandal, and he shall not have it from the Cluniacs.'

'Shall we go now?'

'No. This morning's ride has tired me. I have something else in mind.'

'Well, mon ami, you're not the young man you once were. Past forty, are you not?'

'I am not yet thirty.'

'And yet so serious of mind.'

'As a man of my years ought to be.'

'Perhaps. Perhaps not. Do you want to go in search of a meal? Sure as fate we won't find one at this lady's table. She's only a poor woman unable to do for herself, you know.'

'No,' said Danforth. 'No, I had my fill on the road. I should like to take to my room and think. You go and scout the town if you wish.'

'I'll find a barber,' said Martin, rubbing a hand over his jagged neck.

'Ugh. Busy, listening fellows, barbers. Read your Plutarch.'

'They know everyone's business in any burgh, I'll give you that. Couldn't hurt to ask some questions. Then I'm going to eat. Well, Mr Danforth, enjoy your think.'

Danforth's unpacked his possessions: a rosary, cutlery, inkpots and paper, and his Book of Hours. The book had been a gift from Cardinal Wolsey to his father, and passed from his father to Alice, to be given to Danforth as a wedding gift. Its illuminated pages gleamed and sparkled in good light. Here they glowered.

He wrote a letter to the Cardinal informing him of their whereabouts, straining his eyes in the half-light. He tucked his own mall, neat signature at the bottom and smiled. It was unobtrusive, the perfect marker for a good servant. Then he turned to the Book of Hours. Inside, an inscription from Alice read, 'plees excuse mine bad wrytting in thes my furst attempt in my hande. Rember your love in yr gud prayers'. Underneath he had written, 'I thank you humbly and pray continue, for letters are lasting'. He ran a finger over the words, and then flipped through the pages, stopping when he found what he wanted. A tiny coloured drawing of a bearded man surrounded by a golden halo frowned at him. 'Saint Odon de Cluny'. Venerated by the Cluniac monks of Paisley. Patron Saint of rain. Feast Day, November 18th. Taking his pen, Danforth wrote in minuscule script, 'With the forgiveness of God I did miss this blessed Saint's Day, on this day of November 1542'. He was a day late to Paisley, but he would see the Cluniac Abbey soon enough.

That done, he dozed a little in his chamber – a bare room with a rough, horsehair mattress on the floor and a sagging desk – until he was woken by Martin's light tread along the passage outside. The steps paused outside his door, and then came a soft rap.

'Come.'

'You thought, sir?' asked Martin. He had had his shave, and his black stubble had been arranged into the whisper of a fashionable beard, more neck than face. It was the style the king wore. Seeing Danforth appraising it, he passed the back of his hand across his chin. 'Did the barber do a job of work? I never know whether to trust a strange one. It's a risk.'

'Indeed he did. I shall have to pay this fellow a visit myself. You appear much more a Cardinal's gentleman. What news from our nimble-fingered friend?'

'Of the war, not a scrap. I also cast about for bruits of the Cardinal. In Paisley his name and credit are clean as a whistle. They know, of course, about the troubles in Glasgow, but only of those bills we've already taken. The common voice holds it's the work of the university men, at some jape or other. Always someone else's fault.'

'A jape to abuse a Cardinal. Yet it is fine news that they do not listen.'

'Aye. But sir, what a people are these! They're so damn full of pride. One would scarce think any other burgh had been chartered, nor any place in Christendom quite so blessed. "Oor burgh" this, and "oor burgh" that.'

'And you know what they say about the sin of pride.'

'I fished also for some news of the monks and the girl.' Martin ignored Danforth's tut. 'The young wench was of no great reputation, but no one blames her for running off, if she has. She has made her escape with her father's savings, right away she got, on his horse too. The old lout's turned to drink, and no longer respects his service to the Abbot. His behaviour has been strange. Leastways that's what the barber said, anyway.'

'The Abbot. He has been in France some years now.' Danforth knew that Abbot John, of the noble Hamilton family, left his lands and Abbey in the care of a Prior. 'It will be their Claustral Prior who must keep the Abbey's tenants in order.'

'Aye, the Abbot ... His Grace dined with him in France. I

had no news of the Prior. No one seemed much interested in him.'

'Well, we shall see him tomorrow, perhaps he shall be obliging.'

'He's no need to speak with us.'

'I know that, sir. But I believe in community in our Church, not division. Remember the folk of Jerusalem, fighting amongst themselves as Vespasian pressed their walls. Have you any other news?'

'None.' Martin looked down at the palm of his glove. It was stained brown. The scent had faded. He touched it to the wall of Danforth's room, and it came away black. 'Jesus, what a place. Ever look at something and think, "what am I doing with my life"?'

'When I find myself on business with you? Yes, Mr Martin. Frequently. If you have no more news, then you might retire to your own room.'

'As you wish.' Martin turned to go.

'Wait, Mr Martin.'

'Yes?'

'Did you eat?'

'Yes, sir.'

'Good. I hope you sleep well.'

Martin closed the door behind him and Danforth settled down in darkness. He left the pages of his Book of Hours open:

Oh Lord my God, I love Thee above all things and love my neighbor because of Thee, because Thou art the greatest, infinite, and most-perfect Good, worthy of all my love. In this charity, I resolve to live and to die. Amen.

He could feel his rosary by touch. His routine of counting seven prayers – his lucky number – would not be interrupted. Tomorrow he would see that last holy place of Scotland. Perhaps he would discover some little abuses or slackness, gently rebuke the Prior – who would nevertheless be thankful for the correction. Then he might bring about God's forgiveness for his great trespass. He did not dream that night.

4

Danforth awoke famished. It occurred to him that he hadn't eaten since the previous morning, during the ride west. He really would have to take meals more regularly. He scrabbled for his boots. At his touch, one fell on its side, and something raced from it. Danforth let out a little shriek as a small, grey blotch flew across the floor. It was a mouse. He cursed, embarrassed at making a spectacle of himself, even though there was no one to see. He nudged his head out the door and into the gloomy hallway, and spotted what he was looking for: a narrow garderobe with a high window at the end of the hall, past Martin's room. Inside was a washbowl of clear, cold water. His face wobbled in its still, stagnant depths. He attended to his toilet and used his own handkerchief to polish his teeth before returning to his room to dress. Martin's light knock interrupted him.

'Good morning, Mr Danforth.'

'Martin,' he said. His gaze fell to the man's bare hands. 'No perfumed gloves today? No aping your betters?'

'Eh?' said Martin, looking down. 'Oh. No. You know, I had them in my hand, breathed deep of this rank Paisley air, and thought, who's this for? Who am I looking like a gentleman for?'

'I see. I intend to hear Mass before we impose upon the Prior.'

'Me too.'

'Very well. Only … where is our nearest chapel? I did not think to ask Mistress Caldwell yesterday.'

'A surprising omission,' smiled Martin. 'Fear not – I asked my barber. The main parish altar is apparently across from the Tolbooth. We both missed it yesterday, so intent were we on finding a meal.'

'So intent were *you* on finding a meal,' said Danforth, his stomach warbling at the suggestion. My mind was fixed upon …' He remembered the hairy little knock-keeper attending to the clock-face. 'Upon finding this lodging. Come, let us go, and then we might find somewhere to feed. Although it is Sunday – the people of the town will not be selling.'

The little chapel stood across from the Tolbooth, on the south side of the high street. It was not surprising they had missed it. It was a small building of grey stone, lacking the beauty of greater religious houses. It was a strange trade-off, the great religious house on one side of the river and the upstart town cresting the hill on the other.

'You needn't have worried about the town folk refusing work, sir. Look how they prepare already for a fruitful day.'

Martin was right. Despite the early hour – the sky was still an impassive slate – people were moving to and fro, conducting business and shouting to one another across the street. In the porch of the chapel a crowd of young men escaping the cold were throwing dice. 'Gies a song, hen' one shouted as a woman passed by them.

Danforth shouldered his way through, his face turning a blazing red as he smelled strong liquor. The louder folk seemed to be recovering from revelry. Martin followed. Inside the church the wizened chaplain was muttering 'Pater Noster', whilst his congregation chatted in huddles. He nodded at Mistress Caldwell, who stood bent, her beads wrapped around thick fingers, her eyes on a statue of the Virgin. They took Communion, Danforth finding that it did little for his physical or his spiritual hunger, and then allowed the chaplain to draw the Dismissal to a weak close. When they left, still more people were playing and carousing in the porch.

'An outrage!' shouted Danforth when they were outside. 'In this holy place, these holy lands, to behave so … so …'

'It's the same up and down the kingdom,' said Martin. Whether his words were meant as a consolation was unclear. 'It's what leads to disaffection. Although I've not seen so merry a bunch as these.'

'The Church must take a stronger hand, a *much* stronger hand in these matters. It has been altogether too timid against these abuses and against the heretics. A little burning,' said Danforth, removing his hat and running a hand through sandy hair, 'is what is needed to remind the people of what lies before them in the next life if they persist in abusing God's word. Otherwise the Church is as Epicurus, the people fallen in hedonism. I will not have the Church of Rome follow the Empire of the same, falling into bacchanalian excess.' Her heart was racing. He knew he was bordering on a tantrum and didn't care. 'They do not behave so saucily in Edinburgh, nor St Andrews – else the courts ecclesiastical would have them. There we have good faith, uniformity of –'

'Quiet, sir. We have a guest.'

Danforth turned and looked into the faded blue eyes of a tiny old woman, dressed entirely in blue. She smiled. Danforth thought of grandmothers and gave her a bow. 'Mistress, might we help you?' asked Martin.

'Strangers in the burgh,' she said in a papery voice that slobbered slightly on the letter s. 'I couldn't help but hear you, talking in the street like that. You're officers of the king?'

'No, mistress …?'

'Mistress Clacher, sir.' She held out a hand, bone-white and corded with blue veins. Danforth took it. The grip was strong, the little nails sharp. 'You're then perhaps men of the Church?'

'In a fashion,' said Danforth. He shivered, wiping his hands on his cloak. There was something unpleasant in the woman's eyes. On the heels of that, he thought he was being unfair. He was only annoyed at being thwarted mid-rant. 'We are the Cardinal's men. But,' he added before she could speak, 'we are in the burgh on simple pilgrimage.'

'That's good. It's good to know that the young still make the pilgrimage, and that you condemn all this.' She gestured towards the chapel. 'So many young folk these days devote themselves to pleasure and vice, ever since money raised up the town. Every night you can hear them at it, in every wynd, laughing and singing, and the *drinking*! Gives the place a rotten name. Gives the country a rotten name. You're so right, young man, all the whores and whoremasters ought to die; the streets need cleansed of sin as the rain washes away our waste.' Martin took a step back, his eyes wide and his bottom lip jutting. 'I'm forever telling my husband to do something. And so you have nothing to do with the Brody girl, that sad little bitch? Oh, but the life she led. Nor yet the war?'

'Nothing.' Led? he thought.

'Oh.' Her eyes dimmed, and then brightened again. 'Has the queen taken to childbed yet, is it known?'

'Those are women's matters,' said Danforth. 'I cannot say.'

'Och, she'll have a new prince soon enough. And where are you lodging, sirs?'

'At the inn of Mr Kennedy.'

'Is that so? Well then, we're neighbours, so we are. She's on the Oakshawside, I'm in Prior's Croft, over the road. Euphemia Caldwell's place, eh? She's an odd duck.' As she spoke, Mistress Clacher jerked a knotty thumb up the High Street, where Mistress Caldwell's grey back and slumped shoulders were ascending the hill towards her inn. An unaccountable little chill of sadness ran through Danforth at the sight. Caldwell was an outcast. 'Still, watch what she charges you. She's not as green as she's cabbage-looking. Is her house still falling into sluttery? On the inside?'

'Yes –' began Martin.

'The inn is a reasonable establishment suitable for our needs,' said Danforth, cutting Martin off. 'Mistress Caldwell governs it well, though her husband's business has carried him abroad.'

'What's that? Oh, business abroad! Mercy, but she's yet playing upon that harp! More to be pitied, I suppose.'

Confused, Danforth and Martin turned to one another. As though scenting easy prey, Mistress Clacher went on. 'Her husband has no more gone to business abroad than Queen Marie has gone to Normandy, unless whoremongering's his business. He ran off with a whore – pardon, young widow Blackwood – must be, oh, two years back. Took the whole lot, horses, everything. Off in Ayr, if the bruits be true.' She smiled broadly, revealing a few nubs of teeth. 'And his wife reduced to taking in strange men, like an arrant whore. Ha!'

'Grissell Clacher, you'd better no' be bletherin' gossip,' cut in a new voice. It belonged to a fat, middle-aged woman in her

Sunday dun. 'Forgive her, gentlemen, for she's mistress o' the art o' gabbin'.'

'You hold your tongue, Mistress Darroch,' said Clacher. 'And come and meet these fine young men. They seek to root out the rabble from the Church.'

'King's men, are they? Any news o' the war?'

'No, they're in the service of the Archbishop.'

'The Cardinal,' said Danforth, exhausted.

'So you boys will ken, then, news abroad – news fae ootside the burgh?'

'We travel,' offered Martin.

'You woudnae, by any chance, have knowledge o' the news oot o' Glasgow?'

'What news do you seek?'

'O' the Brody lassie. Kate.' Danforth sighed. He was sick of hearing about the missing brat. Martin, however, leaned forward.

'Only that she's missing, mistress. Why do you ask?'

'For ma son. He's up at the university. He was quite taken wi' that chit. I widnae have let a marriage take place, o' course, no' wi' how little she could bring tae it. But since she disappeared … She's no' run off tae Glasgow then? Nor naewhere else you've been?'

'Alas, no.'

'Ach, I didnae think so. She'd want tae get further away fae that father of her, the vicious brute, fae all o' them. Well, she's gone right enough. It was all for nothin'.'

'What was all for nothing?' asked Martin. Danforth spoke over him.

'It has been a pleasure to make your acquaintance, ladies, but we have much to do, and little time here. We must away.' He bowed again, as did Martin, more reluctantly, and the pair retreated down the High Street. After them Mistress Clacher's voice sounded like a tin drum, 'You gentlemen come to me if you wish to know anything about the burgh. Seventy-four years of it I've kent!'

'And you lads ask they monks aboot the queans who ride aboot the burgh at nightfall! They think we don't see them but

God gave us eyes tae see and ears tae hear!' called Mistress Darroch, unmindful of the stares her words drew.

When they had escaped, Danforth exhaled a long sigh of relief and Martin bent double with laughter. 'Is there a town in the kingdom that does not have creatures like that?' he asked when he had recovered.

'Idle, prating old crows? I should think most of the large burghs have a good many.' He had seen no town, village or hamlet in either Scotland or England that did have a resident fishwife. Creatures like that could be lush fields of information, if one was willing to sort the wheat from the chaff. Or they might be all chaff. Often men were the worst for it. The image of Archbishop Dunbar, with his curtain of greying hair and his sharp, bright eyes floated into his mind. 'Anyway, we have done it now. That shall be the word out, who we are and what we're about. We shall have the petitioners at us from dawn till dusk, making nuisances of themselves.'

'Oh aye? Well, maybe we can make some money out of that, then.' He winked at Danforth's knitted brows. 'Still, that was news about Mistress Caldwell, wasn't it?'

'Do you think it? I do not.'

'Why not?'

Danforth tilted back his head and crossed his arms. 'What business do you know of that takes a man from his inn and leaves it in the governance of his widow long enough that it falls into disrepair? Her tale did not hold. Yet, having heard the sordid nature of her circumstances, I can understand her clinging to it. Without doubt she will fall into arrears and her house revert to the Abbot.'

'I hadn't thought of that,' said Martin.

'And so you are come to esteem the value of thinking.' He tapped his temple. A look of grudging respect dawned on Martin's face. Danforth smiled. 'Now let us hope that it may provide us with more useful knowledge than the state of our inn and its mistress.'

Full of passable mutton pies, Danforth and Martin began

their trek through the Bridge Port and over the Cart. Ahead of them loomed the Abbey complex, and they followed its walls around to the great entrance gate. At intervals were recessed statues of saints, looking through sightless, gentle eyes at the monastery's visitors, offering guiding hands. The wall itself, nearly a mile in circumference, stretched behind and ahead of them, encircling the Abbey's buildings in a protective embrace.

To their surprise, the gates were open, and no one was in the gatehouse. They passed through, Danforth feeling as though they had wandered into some chivalric land of the past. The Abbey church lay not far into the enclosed monastic lands, surrounded by satellite buildings, each of neat grey stone. Around all were clipped lawns, small deer parks with neatly placed trees, and fenced orchards that stretched off to the left of the buildings. Once again came to Danforth the strange idea of how much more beautiful it all must appear when summer was at its peak, when a blazing sun illuminated all without a veil of thick, louring clouds. Despite knowing what the weather would be like he had imagined a grand building – which it was – bathed always in glorious sunlight – which it wasn't.

'A quiet place,' whispered Martin.

'A place of peace, a place of constancy, as unchanging as Polaris.'

'I dunno know how a few monks keep it up. Places like this, I've seen them in France. There were always heaps of monks at work. Same in St Andrews. In France –'

'In France, in France! In France it would be this, in France they do that. In France the fountains spout wine and men chew through metal! Well here they do not, Mr Martin. The Cluniacs forbear toiling with their hands. They employ servants and poor folk of the burgh to maintain all, so that they might spend their own lives in silent prayer and gentle learning.'

They struck out on a little path, brushed clear of dead leaves, that curved through the moss-green parklands and past the towering entrance door – closed, to display its carved effigies of St Mirin – to the Abbey church itself. The path passed under the stone arch of a wall leading from the cloister on their left to the outer wall. The peaceful silence of the place was shattered by some loud guffaws, and a stocky, red-bearded man emerged from an out-building, his cheeks glowing. In one hand he carried a large, stoppered jug. He saw Danforth staring. In return he gave a belligerent look and swaggered past them, arms swinging, in the direction from which they had come. 'Something is slack here,' said Danforth, when the man had gone. 'Something is not right.'

'Aye, the smell.'

Danforth wrinkled his nose. A sour smell caught in his throat. 'Eurgh. You are not wrong, Martin.'

'It's worse than the burgh, Jesus. Is that the river?'

'It must be the drain. If Paisley follows Melrose, one of these buildings must lead underground. To a great drain. Then the river.'

'Great, my foot. Swollen with monk shit. Backed up with bile. Let's go.'

They found the doors of the Abbot's House, or the Prior's House, as it was serving, open: a Romanesque building reared up in provincial self-importance. Inside, another monk sat reading at a lectern. He looked up as they approached.

'Brother,' said Danforth, 'we are in the employ of his Grace Cardinal Beaton and would speak with the Prior.'

'It's Sunday, sirs,' said the steward-monk in gravelly tones. 'The Prior is upstairs at prayer and would not wish to be disturbed.'

'Then we are sorry that we must disturb him.' Already Danforth was rifling under his robes for the Cardinal's letters of authority. 'Kindly request us an audience with the Prior. We shall not detain him for a long space.' The monk slouched from his stool, stretched, and padded up the stairs. When he had gone, Martin turned to Danforth.

'Odd fellows, these monks, to sit and read with want of company to listen.'

'This is true,' said Danforth. He wandered over to the lectern and began scanning the pages. He ran a finger over the doodles in the margin and smiled at the whimsy.

A slight cough brought his attention back to the room, and he stood back from the lectern, folding his arms over his chest as he realised the monk had returned. 'Pray attend on the Prior, gentlemen. He has broken with his prayers to speak with you.'

They climbed the stairs. 'The Prior shall not feel the cold in this place,' said Martin, running his hand over the tapestried walls. Danforth nodded. The building was surprisingly warm, its wall sconces making wavering patterns on the carpeted staircase.

The door to the Prior's office was open. Inside he stood, his head cocked on one side, the light from a roaring fire playing on his tonsure. No smelly peat fire burned here, but good, clean wood. Crumpled papers were curling in the flames. Beyond the Prior the door to a bedchamber lay open, and a four-poster bed was visible. Danforth saw Martin eyeing it with envy.

'Gentlemen. I am Alexander Walker, Prior of this blessed Abbey. Brother Adam tells me you are the Cardinal's men. What news? I can have no commissioners here without the foreknowledge of the Abbot, and will not submit this house nor any of its order to any authority, for none in this realm have authority over us.' The speech almost seemed rehearsed, stiff. Walker was not an old man, but the fire was merciless in picking out the deep worry lines which scratched their way from the corners of his eyes, and made twin tracks over his lips.

'His Grace,' said Martin, putting a hand on his hip, 'is Primate of Scotland, with full powers of visitation. We can go wherever we feel the urge to go.'

Do not push it, thought Danforth. The Cardinal was not *legate a latere*, however powerful he might be. Besides, they had come as friends, not enemies. 'Forgive us, Father, we come not on the king's business, nor, in faith, on that of the Cardinal.' This threw the Prior, confusion raising the black slashes of his eyebrows. 'We are pilgrims, like any other.'

A speculative look crossed Walker's face. 'Yet not like any other, I think, when his Grace the Cardinal is your master.

What business then brings you to the west? Do you seek lodging here? I have nothing sweetened. The guest house is yet being restored since our fire. The expense of it... the stewarding... You gave no warning, we need warning.'

'We were brought to Glasgow to seek out the matter of some seditious verses against his Grace, Father; that is all. We are not here to meddle in your affairs, and we lodge in the burgh.'

'I see. Yes, the news out of Glasgow has carried hither. None here had foreknowledge of it. I promise you, in God's faith.'

'That I do not doubt.'

'Yet there is,' said Martin, 'some other matter touching the Church, isn't there, Mr Danforth?'

'Yes, sir. Father, by my truth we have been distressed by the behaviour of the people in this burgh in matters pertaining to the Church. Only this morning, at the Mass, we found gamesters at play in the porch of Our Lady. Business was conducted as though there were no sanctity. Your people are ... well, they are wantons.'

The Prior's face began to flush, and he crossed to his desk, overflowing with papers. Danforth could see that most of them were covered in numbers. Walker leant on it, knocking over an inkwell and hissing. 'Ugh! Damn it! This the Town Council's business, sirs, and the Abbot appoints them. I cannot do everything, I am not an Abbot. If it offends you, I suggest you speak to the burgesses. Nay, more, I suggest you take your devotions to the chapel of St Nicholas, or St Roque, where you will not be offended by the boisterous. Blast it, find solutions, not problems.'

Danforth took a deep breath. 'Peace, Father. We came in good faith, not to make trouble for you or this Abbey. We are all of us in communion. We raise this matter only in case it should bring disgrace on the Church.'

'And what would you have me do?' said the Prior, collapsing into a chair. 'We are a small order, fifteen monks, and without our Abbot. I cannot ... I cannot maintain order over the entire burgh in right of the Abbot without seeking permission, and he in turn from the Holy Father. The Pope, sir, is the true master of this place. The Abbot and the Pope are our only sovereigns.'

'And so you send letters from here, naturally?'

'Naturally.' Walker looked at them with contempt, and cast an arm over the papers. 'What gave me away, sir? We have a boy rides with haste up and down the kingdom. Bills, account papers, bequests, contracts, I must keep it all going. Our lad knows every fast post rider from Carlisle to Aberdeen.'

'Then perhaps you will allow us to impose upon you a letter to the Cardinal,' Danforth reached into his pocket and extracted his letter, 'advertising that his servants lodge in the town, and that we might likewise be reached through your office. Your good office. If your boy is well hooved, he shall have no trouble finding the army and its messengers. This letter may invite news of the war in return. We lodge at the end of the Oakshawside, along the High Street. Mistress Caldwell's – or rather Kennedy's – inn.' The Prior took the letter in his fingertips, as though it was something unclean.

'More work, yes? I shall, trusting that it does not contain matter prejudicial to the Abbot's rights.'

'I note, Father,' said Martin, drawing the Prior's eyes from the letter, 'that you keep a free house.'

'What?'

'Only that we were allowed to come right in without stop or check. The gates lay open.'

'The gates are locked at night. The Brothers of the order here are not prisoners, sir. I am no gaoler.' As he spoke, the Prior's hand curled into a trembling fist. Danforth had the impression of fear. He should have anticipated it. The presence of a great man's men in distant parts was apt to cause anxiety and suspicion, and suspicion bred jealousy and dislike. When he had first come to Scotland he had met the Prior's expression every time he opened his mouth.

'Nor should you be, Father. My colleague mentions this only for your better knowledge.'

'You'll be aware also,' said Martin, 'that a girl from the burgh, a daughter of the Abbot's tenant, has gone missing? Angus Brody. Kateryn is the daughter.' The Prior's fist fell to the desk. More papers fluttered to the ground.

'What do you know of this?'

'Only what I've had from my barber.'

'Barbers! Hmph. A gossiping trade. Stopper your ears.'

'And more, there was a paper pinned up on the market cross in Glasgow, advertising that the girl had been carried off, not run.'

'Carried off? What paper, when?' Martin produced the placard from his pocket. The edges were blunted and the writing faint. 'Let me see that.' Martin held it up, but did not hand it over. Walker leant forward, his eyes darting over the page and his lips moving soundlessly. His voice, when he spoke, was strained. 'Who wrote this?'

'I can't say.' Martin shrugged. 'She was a servant of yours?'

'... yes. She was.'

'And yet you didn't write this?'

'Indeed not! No!'

'Why not? If she's your servant, or your master's, you must seek her return. This note says that her father entreats it, and that her discovery is to be reported to the townsmen. The townsmen. Not the Abbey.' The Prior sat back, silent, staring into nothing. 'Have you any notion as to the girl's whereabouts, Father? Alive or ... or otherwise.'

'No, and nor do any of the order. Why should I? Why should any of us? I know only that her father has turned to drink and neglects his duties here and on the land the Abbot leases him. He will be evicted, the dirty old monster. I have written the Abbot telling ... asking him for advice on how to proceed.'

'And this girl was happy here?' asked Martin.

'What has that to do with the matter, sir? She was here to do a job of work, and that she did with little skill. If she's gone, good riddance to her, for she was naught but an arrant whore, a temptress. Better she were dead than continue the life she did.'

'Is that so?' said Danforth. His arms were crossed, and he drummed his fingers. 'Hard words.' An uncomfortable thought had come into his mind: temptresses tempt. Whom did she tempt?

47

'Yet the girl has not been spied in Glasgow,' said Martin. 'And there is nothing to say she got away at all. She might be kept somewhere, kept close. A prisoner.'

'What nonsense is this, sir?' asked Walker. 'Who would gain by keeping a little jade enclosed? Gone is gone. And she is gone. You said you are pilgrims. I say guests. She is none of your business.'

'Again,' said Danforth, holding up a hand, 'we sought only to enlighten you, but see that the matter is already known. Only fifteen monks, you say ... a small order indeed, for a land of such revenues.'

'We were founded, sir, by only thirteen. We were of course a greater number until your fellows in the Cardinal's inquisition burned three of our company for heresy, when the young novice informed against them back in '39.' He delivered this without expression. 'I ... I must return to my devotions, my business.' He put his hand to his forehead, kneading it. 'Pray get you gone, gentlemen. You may look over the grounds. You will find everything in order. There is nothing here which could bring disgrace on our Mother Church, nothing. Lend no ear,' he added, his voice turning silky and vicious, 'to any slanderous words that the people of the burgh might say about our community. The lass is neither murdered nor harmed, and there is no proof to the contrary. I would not have our monastery pulled down for idle rumours, as they were wont to do with the great houses of England.'

5

A frowning Martin turned to Danforth. 'He's a tart fellow. Not at all what I pictured. I thought he'd be a jolly old fat man, old and doting, all cheerful and scatter-brained. Not a skinny, tart one.'

'Nor a worried one.'

'You saw that too?'

'I could not do otherwise,' sighed Danforth. They were out in the Abbey's grounds, the smell of rot drifting towards them in the breeze. 'The man governs weakly in want of the Abbot, and he knows it. Yet all men of the Church live in fear, every monk and nun from Melrose to Monymusk. The tales of the plunders in England blow northwards.'

'I'd wager he knows something also about the lass who's departed.'

'An arrant whore … familiar words, eh? Yet who did this young jade make free with, I wonder.'

'And who wrote the placard about her loss?'

'Some friend of the father's, I should warrant.'

'A monster, the Prior said. Doubt he lacks unfriends.'

'Well, that hardly signifies anything. Some friend of hers.'

'It can't have escaped your notice, though, that the paper about this Brody lass was brother to the verses against the Cardinal. Perhaps they're connected.'

'Aye, and perhaps that paper from the silversmiths signifies that they collude in some great conspiracy that involves breaking the Church and stealing away tempting wenches. I note you did not take that one. You are at it, sir. Clutching at straws, as Sir Thomas More said.'

'Maybe. Maybe not. But you'll allow a crime has been committed.'

'Aye, and the girl is the criminal, running off from her duties, robbing the Church of service.'

'Or abused, taken by force,' said Martin, halting and putting a hand on his hip. 'To God knows what end. You say criminal,

49

I say victim.'

'Well, the Prior was right in one thing – as I have said from the start, she is none of ours.' He kept walking. 'I daresay the Abbot will recommend some punishment for the father. The sot neglects the labour he owes and must pay for the labour lost by his bairn.'

'I say the Prior is concealing something,' mumbled Martin, before skipping after Danforth. 'Here, d'you wish to look upon the Abbey, sir? I admit I'd like to see it, have a proper look.'

'Yes, let us do so.' Danforth very much wanted the comfort of the Abbey, the smell and the peace of it. The Prior's words had pinched, his parting shot struck home. He might never be anything more than an Englishman, a defector. He bore his identity like a cross and had done ever since coming into Scotland. He could remember his flight as though it was a fevered dream, out of London and its growing horrors, up through the wild north, sleeping at mean inns and fearful that he would be followed, or reported to the local lords of each new district. He had been half-mad when he had run, crazed with grief, feeling that the last standing pillar of his life, the Church, was falling. England seemed to have gone mad. Scotland, he felt, would welcome him as an ally, and might offer him a new life with the familiar comforts of what England considered the old religion. Here his fat purse had been worth far more than in England. Here he had found a strange but exciting mix of poor, feuding common folk and stuffy, hard-nosed intellectuals. And, after settling himself in, making himself known, David Beaton, then ambassador to France, had taken him up, impressed by his writing, his earnestness, and eager to adopt an Englishman.

Now his Englishness felt almost tangible, as the old enemy of Scotland once more sought to ravish her and cast down her people. Within the open arms of the Catholic faith, there was no Englishman, no Scotsman, but only the purity of the true religion and the wickedness of those who sought to damage it. But within these ancient walls there could be no damage, and he would be a true son.

They found an elderly monk, the white hair around his

tonsure sparse, looking up at the sky outside the open door of the Abbey.

'Good morning,' said Martin. 'We're looking for a guide.' The monk only looked at them, cloudy eyes set deep in a seamed face.

'You may speak, Brother,' said Danforth. 'I fancy you have dispensation. The Abbot has given us liberty of the Abbey. We are servants of his Grace the Lord Cardinal.'

The monk's face split in a smile. 'I think we shall have more rain this week. It does get into the bones.' He arched his back, cracking it. 'But good morrow to you, gentlemen,' he said. 'If a guide you seek, I am he. Brother David, almoner of the order. And so,' he winked, 'not unused to speech. I know every brick in the place. On pilgrimage, are you? I think I hear English in your voice, my son? You're an Englishman?'

'I am, Brother.'

'Well, that's a good thing. This Abbey was founded by men of the order from Shropshire. Do you know Shropshire? It lies near Wales.'

'I am afraid I do not. My family came from Surrey.'

'All come to Scotland, are they?'

'No,' said Danforth, his eyes falling to the ground. He didn't mind speaking freely to a monk, but Martin was watching, amused. 'I no longer have any family to speak of.'

'I'm very sorry, sir. Family's a grand thing. Still, if you've suffered grief, or loss, let it be a comfort that you're then one of God's chosen ones. Pray come, gentlemen, follow me. You haven't riding boots on? No spurs?' He glanced down at their feet, smiling at the soft leather. 'That's good. Rules. It is usual that the guest-master should show the Abbey and its buildings to visitors, but … look, there is the fellow yonder.' Danforth followed his outstretched hand, to one of the buildings along the path. Outside it stood a young man, his hands buried in his robes. He was staring at them, and on meeting Danforth's gaze, he started and turned back through the door. 'Damaged his hand. That's the infirmary. And so, of late, access to the Prior has been too easy. Oh, but it is good to use the voice. Come.' They followed him.

The ceiling of the cavernous Abbey church soared above them, lost in the gloom. They genuflected, dipped their fingers in the stoup, and blessed themselves before looking around. Fluted columns climbed upwards, meeting in arches of stone, and at the far end stained glass refracted soft autumn light. Dark glass, too, reached upwards along the aisle walls, and the aroma of ancient incense – of sanctity and refuge – perfumed the air, sweating from stones that had absorbed it for centuries. But no monks were present, no bald heads and black-robed backs bent at any of the altars.

'Your brothers all at prayer?' asked Martin, his voice low.

'Eh?' asked David. Martin repeated his question, this time letting it bounce around the room. 'The brothers are in our dormitory, adjoining the south transept.' He gestured ahead and to their right. 'Over in the quadrangle. You say you are the Cardinal's men?'

'Yes, Brother David.'

'I hear he has been having troubles in Glasgow.'

'Yes. We are putting a halt to them.'

'Good. I can't understand this division, this schism.'

'Nor I,' said Danforth.

'Are you to lodge in the guest house? The west range of the cloister has fine lodgings.'

'No,' said Martin. 'We lodge in the burgh.'

'A pity. So few people remain, and the older of us do not meddle with the servants unless it is to give orders, and those seldom followed. Come, regard this, sirs.'

Brother David led them around the transepts of the Abbey, giving them as he did its history, from the role it had played as birthplace to the first of the Stewart kings through the more recent fires that had plagued it, to the rebuilding and restorations of the previous Abbot. Much of it Danforth knew already, but it was a pleasant thing to hear it from the mouth of an old man who had lived a life in the place.

As they strolled around the nave, with its profusion of altars each dedicated to different saints, Danforth began to note the hint of decay that tainted the place, like a spot of dirt in the ruffle of a clean, white shirt. The offerings on each altar, the candles and plate, caught the eye, but they provided only a brief distraction. Fire had destroyed the choir, and masons had walled it off, replacing the rood screen before it. David made no comment on the destruction, but instead showed them the makeshift high altar in the northern transept, groaning under a glittering array of damask, candlesticks, gold and silver plate, and jewelled crucifixes. There was enough, he thought, to bury a person. 'Such riches, a goodly sight.' He was gazing at a large pile of gold offerings.

'More than we're used to seeing out in the burgh, or back in our lodgings,' said Martin. Danforth said nothing. Riches belonged locked up in religious houses, piled up by the only people who could be trusted not to covet them. Throw one gold font out amongst the braying mob, and the only survivor would use it to pursue vice. He turned to Martin, eager to point it out, and tutted as he saw the younger man holding the end of a red tablecloth up to his shoulder, and admiring the effect in a silver dish.

Eventually they were led back to the entrance.

'Well, sirs,' asked David, his eyes shining, 'what think you of our Abbey?'

'It is a most grand construction, Brother David. A true tribute to God's glory. Perfect order, perfect,' said Danforth.

'It is that. A fine thing,' said David, mollified. 'And you gentleman will not ... well, you will not speak ill of the place to the Cardinal? Nor the king?'

'Brother David, you misunderstand us,' said Danforth. 'We are here as pilgrims.'

David exhaled his relief. 'And glad I am to hear it, sir. One never knows when that devil King Harry will convince our king to embrace this reform.'

'There is no reform. There is only destruction.'

'That's the truth of it. And we of the order, we are good men and true to the faith.'

'Brother David,' said Martin, a frown appearing between his brows. 'Forgive me, but you said the older brothers don't meddle with the servants. What did you mean by that?'

'Did I, sir?' asked David, looking away. 'I had not realised, I

53

… well, you are good men, loyal to the Church. I only mean that if one of number errs, what of it? Any man might fall in error, and be forgiven for it.'

'And has one of yours?' pressed Martin.

'I cannot say.'

'Perhaps with a girl from the burgh, a servant?'

'Sir, I … I have no knowledge of that. If there has been slackness it is … rectified. If any man has done wrong, he can yet repent. Forgive me, sirs, but the hour draws near for our supper.' All three looked up as the spire began to toll, followed by the echoing simulacrum of the Tolbooth. 'I've been here so long I need no bells, you see. It has been an honour to escort you. You will come back before you leave Paisley, and take Mass in our pilgrim's chapel? It is the true measure of a pilgrimage, the crowning glory, as it were.'

'That would be my honour. God be with you, Brother.'

'And with you, sir. And thank you. I enjoyed my talk.'

'As did we, Brother David,' said Danforth bowing. He then took Martin roughly by the arm and they blinked back into November's answer to daylight. There he fixed him with a warning look before stamping off for the gatehouse, Martin trailing him.

When they were outside the walls, Martin called, 'what ails you, Mr Danforth?'

'See you, you are determined to start something! You shamed us both vexing that old monk.' High colour streaked Danforth's pale cheeks and his green eyes flamed with self-righteous anger.

'I did no such thing; or if I did, it wasn't my intent.'

'There was no need to press him like that. The old fellow meant only to treat us as guests, to do us a service, and you harried him as though he were a criminal. I am ashamed of you, sir, ashamed.'

'Yet we know by him that there was some error on the part of the monks. That this missing girl was meddled with –'

'Leave off, will you?' snapped Danforth, stopping as they reached the bridge over the Cart. He hated raising his voice, but he could not control it. 'We have informed the Prior that we will not meddle in the Abbot's business. This foolish jade is none of our concern, nor is her traffic with those of the Abbey. Why can you not let it lie?' Beneath them the waters roiled and raced, intent on keeping pace with the human argument above. 'Whatever fond fantasies you have, Mr Martin, of being a knight errant, or rescue, or, or, I don't know what – leave them!'

Martin scuffed at the ground, frowning. 'Very well,' he said at length. 'How long shall we tarry in this damned burgh?'

'Until I feel that my soul is cleansed,' said Danforth, and began his march back to the inn, leaving his colleague in his wake. As he stomped, an ugly premonition ran through him. The stupid, irritating missing girl, he suddenly felt, would not let his soul be shrived so easily. Martin's obsession had begun to infect him.

Danforth could scarcely wait to be alone. He opened his Book of Hours to November. 'Today,' he scribbled, 'I did see the last of the Holy Places of Scotland. It was a goodly sight. Bid me free of these terrors. Shrive me of distrust, for I do distrust some people here. Sit laus Deo in sempiternum.' As he closed the book, the edge of a page sliced through his finger. 'God bless it,' he hissed. Before he could pop the finger in his mouth, a few droplets of blood had splashed onto his cuff.

Monday was Paisley's market day. Danforth rose early and, without waiting to see what Martin was doing, took himself to the chapel of St Nicholas, its churchyard lying on a steep wynd that snaked its way uphill parallel to the lower High Street. The ground was still dusty with a thin lattice of dawn frost. Though the muddy wynd had been scattered with gravel, and stones and planks of wood had been hammered into the sloping ground at intervals, it was perilous going.

There he heard Mass in more subdued surroundings. They reminded him of the little parish chapels of Surrey in the old days, and he could feel himself a child again, led by his parents and grandparents into the cosy surroundings. They were all gone now, buried hundreds of miles from him. Idly he wondered if all men and women, as they approached thirty, sought refuge in hoary memories.

When he re-entered the High Street, he found it transformed into a fury of colour. The smell of roast meats was heavy, covering the customary smell of waste. He might even, he decided, enjoy himself that day, make some purchases. The memories St Nicholas had stirred had left him eager for gaiety. No dream had troubled him. Besides, the market would bring even more people to the burgh, and any news of libels and evil epigrams.

'Good morning, stranger,' said Martin, and Danforth started. He had, he knew, been rough the previous day, and he had avoided his colleague's company since. Luckily, Martin's manner did not register ill feeling.

'Mr Martin. You intend to make free in the market?'

'Indeed I do, sir. If you're to cleanse your soul, I'm going to enrich my wardrobe. Shirts, I fancy. I wouldn't buy breeks anywhere but Edinburgh or France.'

'Now that is a strange thing. I was minded to do the same.'

They began picking their way through the stalls, looking over fruit – Martin bought them some apples, which both wolfed – cheeses, wine and fish. Household goods too were being hawked, from cheap crockery to sturdy pots and pans. Men bartered over saddles, boots and latchets, with the burgh's officers keeping watch. As they went, Danforth turned a jaundiced eye and Martin two appraising ones on the young ladies. The Paisley women had on jaunty French hoods made of ersatz materials, wide sleeves and skirts that trailed through the mud. Martin hooted laughter at one girl whose train, unbeknownst to her, was soaked with spilled ale. Even Danforth managed a tight smile.

A young man in a leather jerkin and fashionable breeches caught Martin, still grinning, looking at the girl he was escorting. 'Whit-ye-lookin'-et?' he asked. Martin held up his palms in the age-old gesture of apology. 'Aye,' said the youth, his chin high, 'ye know better.' He grasped his lady's arm tighter and tried to pull her away into the crowd. She shook him off with a cry of, 'I can shift for masel, 'sake.' Again,

Martin broke into laughter.

'Ho, gentlemen,' cried an old man in particoloured breeches. Danforth and Martin turned to him. He was carrying a stick, and his stare denoted blindness. A little distance from him stood a girl, also in peasant's clothing, keeping an eye on him. 'I can see ye by yer voices, sirs,' he explained. 'Come, see a great jape.'

Danforth made to move off, but Martin stayed him. 'What is it, a trick?'

'Gie me but a coin, a single coin. Here.' He pulled out an empty purse. 'Drap it in. Ye'll have it back in a moment.'

'That *will* be right!' said Danforth, but Martin obliged.

'Now, now,' said the old man, whirling on the spot. 'Who else'll gie me a coin?' Not to be outdone, several other men stepped forward, eager to show their own solvency. When the man's purse was filled, he stepped back, into the centre of the circle of people that had formed. He launched the purse into the air and caught it, to a few muted cheers. He then shook it vigorously, jangling the coins together. 'Now behold,' he said, loosening the string. Heads craned forward.

Methodically, the old man took out each coin in turn, held it up to the crowd, and passed it to its original owner. 'An' this was yours, sir, was it no'?' he said to Martin, who held the coin close to his face and rubbed it between thumb and forefinger.

'Aye, it is that. Here, Danforth, look, it is mine, for sure.' Danforth nodded, impressed in spite of himself. 'Here,' said Martin, passing it back to the old man. 'For your pains, for your art. It was a good trick, that.' The old man nodded his thanks, muttering, 'no trick tae it, no trick.' The other men, groaning, also handed back their coins, none wishing to look mean.

'That was good,' insisted Martin. 'Do you not think so, Mr Danforth?'

'Hmph. There must be some cunning skill behind it.' In truth, it had unsettled him. Blind men seeing things, feeling things. He looked at the girl who worked with the man. She was pretty, her face veiled. Criminals often worked in pairs, one to distract and the other to steal, or stab.

As though reading his mind, the old man croaked, 'ye see, folks, dinnae trust yer eyes alone. They deceive ye. I've been wi'oot mine for fifty year, and yet can see better for it. Whit's before ye, that's whit's false.'

The pair found their way to the burgh's draper, on the corner of the High Street and Moss Street. Inside the wooden-fronted shop they found a harassed young apprentice, no older than sixteen.

'Good gentlemen, I see by your clothes you are of quality, and wanting only for the better things.' The boy had an affected, well-heeled-for-the-customers voice. 'Come, come, please, regard: I have silks and linens. What are you after?'

'I should like some shirt cloth,' said Danforth. His current one was feeling looser than ever. His doublet too.

'Good, good. You'll be for some good linen, the best? And hose to match, I should think, you must have hose.'

'Your cheapest woollen, thank you.' The boy was not good enough an actor to hide his disappointment, nor to mask his delight when Martin spoke.

'He'll take that because you don't have hair ones,' he smiled. 'I shall have enough linen for a shirt. Two shirts, in fact.'

'Very good, very good, sirs. He appraised both, and made an unsuccessful attempt to deepen his voice. 'For a good price, I can have your linens, and your,' he said turning a sour look to Danforth, 'cheap wool made into a shirt this night. If you pay me now. In coin, sir. No credit to strangers.'

'And we shall collect them on the morrow?'

'If you wish, sir. Are you here for the market?'

'No,' said Martin. 'We lodge in the Oakshawside. Kennedy's.'

'I know where you are,' said the apprentice. 'I'm Jardine, son to the elder. I can have the tailor make them up, and run them to your lodgings tomorrow. If you pay me now. It will not be,' he added, turning again to Danforth, 'an extra cost. It is a … gratuity.' He laboured over the last word, his voice cracking.

Danforth and Martin paid. 'You're very young, Mr Jardine, to be in service here alone on the market day,' said Martin. Distracted by the money, Jardine added, 'Aye, sir, yes. My father is away. He goes to the western ports, puts our cloths aboard ship to be sold across the seas. Foreign ports. Europe.' Pride had come into the boy's voice.

'And we'll have fresh shirts tomorrow?'

'You shall, sir, no delay. Those who lodge in the Prior's Croft and the Oakshawside never wait.' He turned his back on them and busied himself locking the coins into his strongbox. They left him to it, leaving the shop and pushing past two women who were arguing over a bolt of royal blue wool. Their colourful insults turned the air bluer.

Finding a vendor who was selling ale – which had to be gulped under his distrustful eye, and the battered wooden cups returned – and some chunks of roast meat, they settled down to watch the rest of the market unfold. 'Ugh, what I'd give for a capon, a bloody great capon,' said Martin, eyeing his food with distaste. 'Swimming in a rich sauce.'

A balladeer had taken up residence by a chicken coop, and he fought for attention. 'Come all you constant lovers,' he called, before launching into his first warbling tale of a woman who rejected her lover for his poverty.

The crowd laughed at the tale, and Danforth clapped a hand to his knee. 'Very true, lad,' he called to the balladeer. 'For more courtships hang on money than love.'

'Have your humours improved, then, since yesterday, sir?'

'They have, Martin. My conduct was poor.' He paused to wipe his fingers. 'I can say only that things have weighed heavily upon me of late. Being an Englishman is no easy thing when that tyrant to the south makes false claims on this kingdom. And this business with the verses, not knowing when they might again spring up–'

'I've heard no whisper of them today.'

'Nor I, and that is good.'

'And you're more at ease in your soul, sir; this pilgrimage providing relief?'

'I think it is, yes. In faith, Martin, I have carried with me a

59

burden since before my coming out of the old realm and into this.'

'Mon ami, if you've some, I don't know, some burden of conscience for abandoning your loyalty to England, you shouldn't.'

'Peace, no – it is this unpleasant business of a young girl behaving wantonly and then running off, it cuts–'

'Murder,' screeched an excited voice. 'Murder!' It was taken up by others, some bellowing it, some questioning. The original rose to surmount them. 'Foul practice o' murder!'

At that moment the clouds opened and a downpour began in earnest.

6

The rain began to disperse the market. The voice, which continued to cry 'murder', was found to belong to the boy employed by Mistress Caldwell – or, rather, never unemployed by her husband. Some townsmen took a grip of him, slapping at him until he stopped screaming. Danforth moved towards the furore, heedless of the rain. The balladeer fled, as did the younger ladies, mindful of their market day hoods and skirts. The young men of the town – and some who had come in from beyond it – followed them to shelter in doorways, hoping to make them swoon with beer-scented kisses. It was mainly the burgh elders who stayed to find out the news.

'You boy, what is this? What murder?' Dazed from a smack to the side of his head, he took a few seconds to focus on Danforth.

'It's yersel, master. Help – help! Someone's done murder!'

'Who has done it? What is it you speak of?'

The boy seemed to realise that he was being held, and began to wriggle furiously. 'Murder,' he cried again, and Danforth began to sympathise with the man who had struck him.

'Listen to me, you little fool,' he said. 'Cease your crying and tell us what has happened, else you'll be thrown in the Tolbooth for a tale-telling knave.' The boy swallowed and looked up with huge, frightened eyes. Spots of high colour sat on his prominent cheekbones.

'I saw it, sir, wi' ma own eyes.'

'What did you see?'

'Murder.'

'We rather gathered that,' said Martin, and a few people chuckled.

'Where? Who?'

'Up the Moss.' Danforth looked blankly at Martin, who shrugged.

'The common, north of the burgh,' explained one of the

boy's captors. 'Beyond the woods and meadows there's common land where anyone might gather peat and chestnuts and moss.' The tattered old shoes on the boy's feet were caked in mulch, dead leaves and spongy greenery.

'We understand …' Danforth paused. 'Boy, what is your name?'

'Archie, sir.'

'We understand, Archie. Tell us what you saw, that we might the sooner be out of this rain. Do not say murder.'

'It's the Brody lassie, sir. Done tae death, she wiz, and oan the bank o' the river by the Moss. She's been murdered, sir, smashed tae pieces. I've never seen such … such.' He cast around, trying to find the right word. 'Barbarosity.' He looked almost pleased that he had managed it.

'Murdered,' whispered Martin.

'Pray do not *you* start,' said Danforth. He looked up at the men holding Archie's scrawny arms. 'You men, you are burgesses?'

'Yes, sir.'

'Then you know the baillies; who are they? They must be here somewhere, tending to the market.'

'Pattison and Semple are the baillies of this great burgh. They'll see this little rat questioned properly.' The burgess laid emphasis on the final word, which came seasoned with roasted meat and the tang of ale. Danforth ignored it.

'Where are they?'

'We are they. Now if this wretch speaks true, sir, who are you?'

'I am Mr Danforth and my colleague there is Mr Martin. We are secretaries to his Grace the Lord Cardinal, here on pilgrimage. We have no hand in this matter.'

'You are right, sir, you don't. Though it would have been right proper for you to inform us of your coming into the burgh. You know better than to lodge yourselves as strangers – and may count yourselves lucky we don't fine your host for taking you in without our consent.' His fellow grinned. 'We shall go and see if this little slave is an honest rat, and if it be so, we shall know who has the guilt of it.'

'Not he, nor us, surely,' said Danforth. He was seldom surprised by the officialdom of burgesses and ballies, nor their suspicion of strangers. He still did not like it.

'No, sir.' They looked at each other, then threw the hapless Archie towards Danforth, who shook him off. The heavier, a red-nosed and thick-bearded brute – who announced himself to be Semple – then said, 'Well, we'll go to the Moss. And if there's no corpse and my boots get ruined in the jest of it, that whelp will wish he lay smashed to pieces.'

'Hold a moment, gentlemen,' said Martin. 'Was it yourselves wrote to Glasgow, begging the folk there to report if the girl was taken there?'

'We beg Glasgow nothing. We conduct our own affairs.'

The baillies marched off, heads down against the driving rain. They slid and lurched through the melting street. 'What do we do with him?' asked Martin, pointing at Archie.

'Return him to Mistress Caldwell and ensure he does not leave, I suppose. Come, let us away before we are drowned.'

As they half-dragged Archie, who threatened to begin wailing again, back up the High Street, Danforth caught sight of old Mistresses Clacher and Darroch, holding court amongst a crowd of ladies in drenched dresses. Each seemed eager to hear Paisley's duumvirate masters of gossip. Clacher was soaked, a fine black shawl glinting with rainwater, but she appeared to be enjoying herself far too much to care. To Danforth she looked like one of the evangelical preachers he had sometimes seen in London, tending a flock of wild-eyed acolytes. He and Martin skirted the group, ignoring the pleas for news, and continued up the Oakshawside.

Throwing the door wide, Danforth called for Mistress Caldwell. She appeared from her rooms, a jaunty ribbon laced through her cap, and her face fell.

'Sirs, must you trail that in here?' Danforth looked down at his sodden boots, before meeting Caldwell's eyes and realising that she meant Archie.

'Mistress,' said Martin, 'the boy has borne witness to a murder.'

'What,' she asked, her mouth falling open in shock as her

eyes began to flame with interest. 'It's the Brody lassie, isn't it? What is this, boy, from your mouth. Gentlemen, dump him by the fire.'

A drab peat fire was burning, and they set Archie in one of the old chairs. He looked in to the flames. They danced in his hazel eyes. 'The baillies beat me, mistress.'

'No' hard enough, I'll wager, you imp. What's this about murder?'

'The Brody lassie,' he said, his voice detached. 'Deid.'

'How, dead?'

'Beaten. Broken. It wiz wickedly done.'

'If you're lyin', if this is some jape that brings trouble and shame on this house—'

'The baillies are searching the Moss to prove if he speaks true,' said Danforth.

'And what were you doin' on the Moss,' cried Mistress Caldwell, crossing the room and bending over Archie.

'Ev'dy uses the Moss.'

'Ev'dy?' asked Danforth.

'Everybody,' said Martin, under his breath.

'For fuel,' Archie continued, 'fur the fire.'

'We've a surfeit of fuel, you wretched little liar. If you had some tryst there, or if you were hopin' to steal fuel meant for this house and sell it – I'll skelp your arse raw myself.'

'Ah swear, mistress, Ah meant nothing dishonest. Am a pure honest Archie.'

'I apologise for the wretch, gentlemen.' She turned her attentions on them and patted the ribbon in her cap, her voice softening.

'No need for apology,' said Danforth, glad the awkward little scene was at an end. 'Perhaps you could find the boy something to eat.' She opened her mouth to object. 'Just on this occasion, something small from your own stores. And then he might be sent to wherever it is that he dwells.' She shuffled off, returning with the barest husk of mouldy bread. Archie gobbled it. The side of his face, thin-skinned, was starting to bruise.

'The Brody girl,' said Mistress Caldwell, addressing

Danforth and Martin. 'Run off, my foot. She's been killed by some lover, hasn't she?'

'It's possible,' said Martin.

'If she has been killed at all,' said Danforth. 'If this boy is no liar.'

'Ah spoke truly,' protested Archie, crumbs flying. 'Truly Ah saw her, a' smashed to bits, like … like,' he struggled, 'a boiled apple, thrown doon a vennel.'

'Lord have mercy,' said Mistress Caldwell, crossing herself, 'Let her be laid to rest quickly, then, poor lass.'

'Soft, madam. The baillies shall have the truth of it,' said Danforth. 'You will attend to this little baggage?'

'Aye, sir.'

'Handle him gently, mistress,' added Martin. He looked at Archie with a doleful smile.

'You're no' leaving?' she said. 'You're no' going back into the rain?'

'It cannot continue so heavily. Already I think I hear it slacken. I wish,' said Danforth, 'to find the truth of this.'

'As do I,' said Martin.

'But … but there may be a murderer abroad. I'm alone here, and this is no help.' She jabbed a finger at Archie.

'We shall be about the business with haste.'

They departed, closing the door as Mistress Caldwell wrenched Archie out of her chair. The rain had slowed to a persistent drizzle. 'If this weather stays as it is,' said Martin, 'we shall certainly be trapped in Paisley some time.'

'Aye,' said Danforth. 'Yet I think I should tarry anyway, and find out what has truly become of your friend.'

'My friend?'

'This Brody chit who has exercised your mind these last days.'

'Oh. You have changed your tune.' Danforth did not reply. Privately, he felt that the note about the girl's disappearance, so close by the paper that was their business, was a sign. He had intended to come to Paisley anyway, and in His wisdom, the Lord had provided labour for him. He had been wrong to try and ignore it. God, it seemed, must have guided the hand which placed it where he would see it. But who, who did that hand belong to?

The merriment of the market had moved indoors, and music could be heard over the roar of rushing water, drifting out from the windows in which lights blazed. The people appeared loath to put an end to their good cheer. It was odd, thought Danforth, how towns developed their natures. Rather than absorbing the sanctity of the nearby Abbey, Paisley seemed to have sought an independent identity by embracing revelry.

The various shops, including the drapers, had brought in their wares; only the butcher and fishmonger had left their tables out. The only stragglers were a few drunks. Above them the sky had turned the strange grey-black favoured by November – the colour that marks both daylight and darkness, without conceding to either.

For some time they waited, illuminated by the cold glow from the window of the tailor's shop, asking news of people who hurried by. Eventually they struck lucky when a burgess passed them, the pin on his cloak proclaiming him a spice merchant.

'What news, sir?' In return, the pug-faced spice-man eyed them suspiciously.

'It seems we have a murderer in the burgh. Who are you gentlemen?' Danforth rolled his eyes, wondering if every conversation would follow the same course. Rather than respond, he produced his papers, showed them to the burgess, and then snatched them back before the mizzling rain could spoil them.

'My apologies, sir. Yet you understand my suspicion.'

'Do I?'

'Yes,' said the burgess, his eyes bulging. 'There's murder here, oh, most rotten indeed.'

'Who is it,' asked Martin. 'Is it this Brody girl who has been thought flown?'

'It is, sir. Not that you'd know it to look upon her, even had you the stomach for it.'

'Where is she?'

'She lay upon the Moss, by the Nether Common. It seems

she had been in the Cart some days, thrown like a bundle of waste.' He crossed himself. 'They say she was no better than she ought to have been, but I shan't say nothing of that. There are none deserve a death so unkind. And to happen here, in these holy lands.'

'Have they brought forth the corpse?'

'The baillies have had some free men of the burgh carry it to the old tithe barn beyond the Tolbooth. It is used for keeping animals, sir, but then I doubt the lady shall mind. The smell shall not offend from there, sir.'

'And where are the baillies? I should like to speak with them.'

'You think the Cardinal will have an interest in the matter?' he asked, trying his luck.

'None. We do. The process of right justice always interests those who work for the Church and the king.'

'I see. The baillies are gone to take in the murderer, that he might repent for his crimes before he is hanged for a beast.'

'The murderer, you say? Whom?'

'Her father, sir, Angus Brody. The old drunkard. If you'll excuse me, gentlemen. This rain ...' He bowed and scurried away.

It was only a short time later that Pattison and Semple, macabre grins on their faces, came towards the Tolbooth, walking the bellowing Brody as easily as Danforth and Martin had carried Archie back to his own prison. Brody was deeply in his cups, and seemed unaware of what was happening; yet he walked with the determined gait of the practised drunk.

'Am no' so drunk,' he yelled. 'It's market day, Christ's sake! Ah'll no' work for the monks who took ma daughter, and nae man oan this earth kin make me, damn them! Accursed bald beasts! Perverse hoormongers!'

'Shut your filthy mouth,' said Semple, his jowls quivering. His stringy colleague brought the edge of his hand down on the prisoner's neck.

'Peace, Mr Semple,' said Pattison, squinting through myopic eyes. 'He won't have the use of his tongue for long. I'll wager you an abbey crown the bastard bites it off when the rope tightens.'

Danforth and Martin looked at each other and then strode towards the trio. Brody looked up at them from red-rimmed eyes. The smell from him was pungent: sweat, urine and alcohol. His ragged clothes hung on him. What had once been a powerful man, thought Danforth, had been lost to alcoholic ruin, the world's most effective creator of scarecrows.

'Youse again?' said Pattison, exasperated.

'We've no need for you,' added Semple. 'Be about your own affairs. We have taken up our murderer, we have his confession.'

'This man confessed?'

'He did. As though confession was required. The whole burgh knows of this old dog's treatment of his daughter, foul and shameful though it is. He has now confessed to it, yet still the drunken animal rails against the monks.' At the word, Brody began again.

'Ma lassie's shame-faced chastity taken by the pious pricks! Ma money robbed and ma mule taken! Ah'm undone! They've a' undone me!' Danforth felt a wave of dislike for the man. His daughter was dead and yet he wept for his property. Some men did not deserve children.

'Worry not,' said Semple. 'You'll not live long enough to suffer it.' Confusion crossed Brody's face. 'You are taken up for the murderer you are.'

'Whit's that, murderer? The monks hae killed her?' He began to cry – loud, racking sobs.

'Enough of this,' said Danforth. It seemed that Brody did not even comprehend that his daughter was dead. 'This creature is incapable. What is to be done with him?'

'Hanged,' smiled Pattison. His face was gaunt, collapsed over missing teeth.

'At what verdict, sir?'

'At our verdict.'

'That cannot be. He was not caught red-hand.'

'Then the Abbot's courts will have him,' said Semple, shrugging.

'These lands are only a burgh-in-barony. You cannot give a

free man the penalty of death.'

'Free man? Brody scratches out less than a yardland in the common field – he is a poor husbandman. A nothing.'

'Yet free he is, and entitled to justice. You overstep your privilege. This matter must be remitted to the Sheriff's Court, and brought before the Assize. Where is your Provost?'

'We have no Provost here, sir, nor are we inclined to elect one. Two baillies might manage without a fool to lead us. And who are you, sir, to order us? Are you a lawyer? An assessor? A ... a forespeaker? Mighty suspicious to appear out of the blue sky all of a sudden and ask questions.' Anger, in its red and trembling glory, had begun to blaze a trail across the baillie's face.

'I am no lawyer, sir, nor in any wise inclined to that fractious and avaricious profession.' Danforth raised his nose in the air. He disliked lawyers on sight, recalling their wild training grounds by the whorehouses of London, their festive guisings and their loathsome profiting from neighbours at war with neighbours. A profusion of lawyers meant a community at odds with itself.

'You're an Englishman. We are at war with you fellows, and in times of war the niceties of your courts don't matter. Or perhaps you're come as a spy?' Danforth bit his cheeks, his face a stony mask. He had worked hard to master Scots after growing tired of explaining and excusing his English. He fancied he could pass for a native when he put his mind to it.

'There's no need,' said Martin, 'for that. You may attempt whatever you wish, but I don't think that the Abbot will wish to hear of lawlessness. It may be that Prior, Cardinal and king will take an interest, should this man be found innocent after unlawful execution.'

Semple and Pattison wore matching scowls but contented themselves with roughly handling Brody. 'Ach,' said the latter, 'the filth may rot in the Tolbooth then, until the next Assize. It makes no odds to us. He'll hang as well at Yule on the Sheriff's verdict than now. Aye,' he added, 'let him suffer for his crime before he meets his end at the end of the rope at Yule. They can shove the Yule log up his arse for all I care.

Good evening to you, gentlemen.'

'We have made no friends there, I'll be bound,' said Martin when the baillies had dragged the weeping Brody into the Tolbooth.

'No,' said Danforth. He was looking sadly at the clock. Now its hands would be counting down the time until a man lost his life. 'No, once again we meet hostility. Do you not tire of it?'

'Of what, sir?'

'Of finding every man who might be an ally to us suspicious and full of mistrust. It should not be so.'

'It's the nature of the world, sir.' Martin wore a dubious look, and scratched at an eyebrow. 'Each man grasps after what he feels is his own by right, and feels wary that another will try and encroach upon it. I can't say as I like it, but I see it.' Danforth sighed.

'So young, and yet a cynic. I prefer to try for a better world. Do not roll your eyes in your head; they might become stuck there. Did you think him guilty, Martin, that woeful old ruin in there?'

'No.'

'Nor I.'

They found Mistress Caldwell sitting before her fire; Archie was nowhere to be seen. She began to rise when they entered.

'Please, mistress, do not get up.'

'What news, gentlemen? she asked, kneading her hands. 'Is the girl dead, truly?'

'It appears so,' sighed Danforth. He knuckled his forehead and shook water from his earlobes. Mistress Caldwell's eyes danced and glittered.

'And all as Archie said?'

'Yes.'

'Do they know how it's come to be? Some stranger come in for the market, I shouldn't wonder.'

'They have taken a man.'

'Who?'

'Her father.'

'No! Old Brody?' she gasped, clapping a hand across her

mouth. She settled back in her chair, digesting the revelation. 'That wastrel. That worthless Abbey-loon.'

'You have some grievance against the Abbey, Mistress Caldwell? You have some complaint, or difference in opinion?' Danforth's back straightened.

'Ah … no,' she said. 'Why, it's only that he's no better than my Archie – a common servant. Worse than a low servant, come to that, for the whole town knows he drinks and beat his own child. Some say he did worse wi' her, but then people will say anythin' about a pretty young girl livin' alone wi' a drunken man, father or no'.'

It was Danforth's turn to sigh. Unspeakable acts were like magnets to the ghoulish. Well, perhaps Mistress Caldwell, having been the subject of gossip for so long, felt it was now her due to revel in the misery of others. 'Will he hang?' she asked.

'Perhaps. It is unclear. It must be remitted to the Assize. If it is and he is found guilty then I think that yes, he will hang.'

'Then God have mercy on his damned soul.' She crossed herself, gazing into the fire as Archie had done. At the same time both she and Danforth shuddered. The man would die: of that Danforth felt certain.

The Book of Hours was open at the Act of Hope. Danforth took his pen in a shaking hand.

Let her pass unharmed through the gates of death
to dwell with the blessed in light

he wrote in Latin. Then, in Scots, he added, 'A murderer undiscovered. Much suspected by me.' He contemplated writing more, but his hearing disappeared, and a continuous ringing sounded in one ear. He shook it off, and tried to sleep.

As Danforth and Martin fought discomfort that night, the clouds over the town continued to shift and thicken. As the night wore on, Danforth felt one certainty. Under one roof, one mind must be seething and boiling. One mind, at least, knew exactly what had happened.

7

Danforth awoke full of resolve. He washed in the icy bowl of the garderobe – he was beginning to suspect Mistress Caldwell never refreshed the dirt-flecked water, and he had to flick away some dubious fluff that skimmed its surface – checked on the horses, and joined Martin for Mass. They took it at St Nicholas again, Martin agreeing that the service was more rewarding and the company more agreeable. No drunken louts thronged the little chapel; perhaps, Martin suggested, even those who usually used the Lady Altar as their gambling den would be too weak from the market day's revelries even to trouble that place.

As they puffed down the wynd, wind whistling at their robes, Martin slipped, Danforth catching him by the elbow.

'Thanks. Jesus, the muck in this place.'

'Yes, there is little point in washing.'

'Aye, that's true enough, especially in that damned inn. Christ, you wouldn't see a dump like that anywhere in France. I swear the clatty water in that garderobe still had my belly button dirt in it from yesterday morning. Jesus, to have to live like this. Reckon I was made for better things, to be honest.' Martin nearly stumbled again as Danforth jerked his hand back and wiped it on his breeches. 'Here, what are we to do now?'

'I intend to inspect this corpse,' said Danforth. Martin wrinkled his nose in response. 'You have never seen a body after death?'

'Of course I have,' protested Martin. 'I'm as much a townsman as you, sir. I've seen many bodies, stacks of them. It's only that … it's only that they have been very recently dead. Fresh, you know. Or even boiled clean and strung up, the criminals. I have never seen one which has lain any time, nor in any place in which it might be abused by the elements. And Mr Danforth: I have never seen a girl after death, nor have I ever cared to. Yet if it must be done then let's get to it quickly, and the sooner it'll be over. It will not be a pleasant morning's work.'

'No, but it is all that I might do. I have some experience in these matters.'

'You're no justice, sir, if you don't mind my saying so.'

'No, but I was close to a coroner. The office is different in Scotland, and so the Cardinal put me to better use.' He could recall the delight on Cardinal Beaton's face at having an Englishman who had turned his back on England. 'Despite what is bruited of me,' Beaton had said, 'I bear no hatred towards the men of England. Be my friend, Mr Danforth – do me service and together we might defend the faith not as Englishman and Scotsman, but as God's warriors.' Those words were always a comfort. Danforth's mind recited them like a Hail Mary.

'Our coroners,' said Martin, 'are the king's servants. They seize goods for the sovereign. Yet I own I've never met one, nor even a coroner as was, save yourself.'

'Indeed, though I was but the city coroner's right hand. I was an appointed officer until the murders of Sir Thomas More and Bishop Fisher bade me flee. When suspicious deaths were reported I would investigate them. In case,' he added, 'there might be some chance of enriching the coffers of the crown. It was work I found I could no longer do when it meant bringing further wealth to King Henry and his familiars. I was only young of course – younger than you are now, and I could not stomach it long. Yet I have seen death. I know it, in its many hideous guises. I am aware of the evil man can inflict on man. It holds no terror for me.' He only half-believed his own words, but saying them, he hoped, would make them true. He could already smell the old smells.

'I say again: it won't be a pleasant morning's work.'

Silence fell between them for a time as they made their way along Moss Street, which connected the bottom of St Nicholas' wynd to the High Street. Here they paused. 'We need not become part of this matter,' said Danforth. 'We can even yet look through our fingers.'

'I wouldn't, sir. If this fellow's innocent, his name despoiled and his life lost, I would think justice for the girl unserved.

And there's something more here. Something strange. I've felt it since I saw that paper, on the same cross as the libels.'

'Aye, well, I meet you in one thing. I am reminded of the words of Antiphon, sir,' he said, quoting: 'We know that the whole city is polluted by the killer until he is prosecuted, and that if we prosecute the wrong man, we will be guilty of impiety, and punishment will fall on us. The entire pollution shall fall on the burgh,' he added, 'if this man proves innocent.'

'A wise fellow, this Antiphon. We should all be so wise. What became of him?'

'One of Athens' goodliest orators. He was condemned for treason and put to death.'

'That's a comfort.'

Danforth knocked on the door of the Tolbooth and found it open. Inside the wide main hall sat a chubby man, the burgh's disinterested gaoler, idly cracking his knuckles. He half-rose, putting a hand to the dirk in his waistband. His piggy eyes raked them, before fastening on their smart, mud-splattered, secretarial robes. The sight seemed to sober him and the pudgy hand fell. With surprise Danforth and Martin each recognised him as the tipsy oaf who had come charging out of the Abbey's brew-house. There was no answering flicker of recognition on the ruddy face.

'Soft, sir,' said Martin. 'There's no cause for alarm.'

'Who are ye?'

'We are men of the Lord Cardinal,' said Danforth. Before he could continue, he was cut off.

'Oh aye? I'm Logan, the gaoler. I've heard tell o' you fine gentlemen. Stayin' up in the Oakshawside wi' the Caldwell wench. Damned fine wummin that, though nothin' to look at. Were she a widow I'd no' mind joinin' ma name to hers. Haughty, though, like most o' them.' His eyes, drifting, refocused. Danforth wondered if he had drank much the previous night. 'Busybodies, as the baillies say. Wherefore are ye come?'

'We would speak with your prisoner.'

'That you will no'. He's locked in his chamber.'

'Then you will allow us through.' A sudden light flared in the gaoler's eyes.

'Cardinal's men, eh? Ye might provide the condemned some spiritual comfort at that. Of course, I shall need some surety o' yer good office.'

Rolling his eyes, Danforth produced some coins, of the lowest value he could find in his purse. The gaoler took them, bit them, and then put them in his own pocket. He jangled the keys from his belt and unlocked the door to a tiny room. 'Ye'd better no' tarry. He's a dangerous swine.'

'We shall have caution.'

Brody lay on the floor of the chamber, on a pile of soiled straw. As they entered he looked up at them in fear before raising his arm to protect himself. He bared broken, painful looking teeth and gums.

'Peace, Brody. We are come to have answers from you. We are your friends.'

'Ah huv nae friends. Ah huv nae daughter. Ye're come tae hang me.'

'We know of what you are accused,' said Martin. 'We saw you taken up yesterday. The baillies say you've confessed to the slaying of your daughter.'

'Ma daughter slain! Ma mule stolen! Ah confessed nothin', sir,' said Brody, furrowing his brow in an effort to remember, 'save that Ah confessed tae beatin' the wean, tae givin' her right Christian discipline. Though no' harshly enough. Oh, but Ah should hae boxed her the more; Ah should hae broken her.'

'You beat your girl?' Martin's lip curled downwards. 'Then is it any great wonder she fled, and met her end?'

'Ah didnae spare the rod, but that's a', nor forbore tae skelp her as often as wiz needed. Ah didnae meddle wi' her otherwise, Ah swear before the saints. It wiz they bastardin' monks. She neglected her duties and fell in close wi' they cowled devils, giein' her body to one. An' noo they're engaged in conspiracy, in a plot, the whole pack o' them. Ma name slandered, an' their crime buried wi' me an' ma daughter, ma poor Kate! It's one o' they monks has slain her, sir, by St Andrew his'sel. An' the murderer has escaped wi' ma mule.'

'Cease your prattling on the monks,' snapped Danforth, not meeting the man's eyes. 'Else you are guilty of defaming your betters without proof or cause.'

'But she telt me, sir, she telt me she wiz taken up wi' a monk, that she meant tae flee wi' him. They made a common stewed strumpet o' her. An' now she lies deid. They made me look upon her, though it sickened me.' He gestured to some of the straw, sodden with vomit. 'They made me look upon the corpse.' Tears pricked out in the red eyes. It was difficult to feel pity for him.

'Listen, Brody,' said Martin. 'Did you write, or cause to be written, a bill advertising your daughter's loss, her vanishing, some time in the last week? Did you cause it to be set up in Glasgow?'

'Whit?' Brody sniffled. 'Ah cannae write, man, nae mer than ma sign.'

'And you know of no one who would write on your behalf?'

'Naw. Naeb'dy.'

'If you speak the truth, Brody,' said Danforth, 'and I have my doubts that you do, then the truth of the matter shall come to light. If you lie, then the fires await you for the violent drunkard that you are. Come, Martin, leave the wretch.'

'Gladly. Sick of him pouring pity on himself.'

Danforth turned his back on Brody, disgust trouncing pity. Pathetic boor. The image of the stately old William Danforth swam into his mind, kind-eyed and smiling, as he had been before grief at the death of his wife, Danforth's mother, and his master, Cardinal Wolsey, had driven him into his grave. He had died in 1530, after turning his back on life. His was another death to be laid at the door of King Henry. Danforth thought of him often, wondering if he would have understood his turning his back on England. He thought – he hoped – that he would.

They re-entered the lobby of the Tolbooth. Logan took the opportunity to spit into the cell before closing and locking the door. Danforth eyed him with distaste, wondering which was the more repellent, gaoler or prisoner. 'Rails he still against the monks, then, aye? Monks meddling wi' maidservants, eh? Well, they're bent over anyway,' he grinned.

'Ah, the monks,' answered Danforth, crossing his arms. 'I understand you have cause to do business in their brew-house, sir. Mr Martin and I visited the Abbey, and I confess myself surprised that you do not recall us.' Logan's face turned from pink to a deeper crimson.

'Whit do you mean, young fella? Ma business is ma own. I pay ma way. If ye think to make trouble wi' me, sir, ye'll be the one that's the worse aff for it.' Again, his hand hovered towards his blade.

'I have no desire to make trouble in a burgh that has troubles enough for a century, and such men as you to handle them. Where is the corpse?'

'Ye want a look at it?' asked Logan, his teeth showing in a sneer. 'I should warn ye, gentlemen, it's no' a goodly sight, though the wee jade was a damned fine thing when she lived. I wouldnae have minded takin' her masel, but ye'd no' know why, to look at her now. I've had some fiends already this mornin' begging sight o' it, for a fee. Looky-loos. An' this will be your only chance, gentlemen. It'll be put to the soil directly.'

'She is to be released for burial?' asked Martin, getting close to Logan's face, his fists clenched.

'Certainly, sir, before it brings foulness to the burgh.'

'Where?'

'I don't care. St Nicholas, if Abbey servants can be found will haul it up the wynd. The Abbey shan't want it, though it's their property. Yet their good hearts and rich purse will see it planted. No' that she deserves Christian burial, the daft wee harlot. The likes o' her are the worst type o' women, always trying to tempt men intae inconstancy. Now, to the matter o' that fee.'

'You shall have nothing more by us,' said Danforth, drawing his eyes away, 'but if you refuse us access you shall be reported for obstructing the king's justice.' Thankfully the gaoler looked confused and doubtful enough to frown and nod his acquiescence. 'As ye list. It lies beyond the kailyard in the back. I warn ye again,' he added, smirking, 'she's nothin' to look at anymore, if ye hope to peep.'

He led them through the postern of the Tolbooth, where he stopped. 'I'll come no further. The reek's unsavoury. She lay in the river some days.' Across the rain-blasted grass was a small wooden outbuilding, low-roofed and ugly. To the right stood an old gallows, weathered and without a rope. As they crossed to the shack, Danforth became conscious of Martin falling behind. He turned.

'Forgive me, sir,' said Martin. 'I ... find I don't wish to see her. To see this ... Kate.' An expectant little pause drew out between them, before Martin spoke again. 'I never saw her, but she lived in my mind, I confess, a stolen girl awaiting rescue, you know? And all along she lay slain.'

'It is no matter,' said Danforth, cutting the air with a hand. 'I have no great desire myself. But the condition of the corpse may tell us something. You might wait here, where the air is fresher. Somewhat.' Martin nodded his gratitude, and Danforth turned to the flimsy wooden door.

When he had begun in the service of the Cardinal he had hoped mangled corpses were a thing of the past, and yet now he found that he had a hunger to know, to see the truth unmasked. But there was always a thrill of terror prior to viewing a body. It would, he knew, dissolve when more scholarly senses took charge. It was the anticipation of horror that was sharpest and most keen. He did not want to step through the door. Before he had become a green young coroner's man, before he had even considered such an office, his father had always told him, 'what a gentleman has to bear he will bear, because he has no choice.' It was useful advice, even if the old man had not taken it himself.

He swallowed one last gulp of cold air and entered. The smell inside hit him like a cruel wind – the stench of water and rot, mingled with the unforgiving, bitter tang of a tannery. To the right of the barn a sheep was penned, its back to him. Closer by, he forced his eyes to a low table. A filthy sheet, raised here and there in crags, sat on it. With one swift movement he yanked it back and threw it aside.

He drew back, his stomach lurching. The whisper of the sheet had cast up a concentrated wave of the foul air, and he drew a hand before his nose to protect himself. The girl's body had been beaten beyond recognition. Cringing from the touch, he gently turned the head to one side, finding the killing blow. She had been struck in the back of the skull with something heavy, something sharp. He pulled the head back so that what must once have been a pretty face looked upwards again. Whoever had done the deed had not been content with striking her down – they had used their weapon to smash in her face, hacking and chopping wildly. This was a person of strength, or of supreme hatred and fury. Bits of shattered skull glinted in the dim light, mingled with jellied grey matter and strands of blonde hair. There was little blood. It must have been washed away by the river's current, leaving the corpse even more denuded.

He looked away from the desecrated face. The swollen arms and legs were mostly bare. He narrowed his eyes. The tattered remains of clothing were odd. The girl had been dressed in men's breeches and a blousy shirt. The breeches were as drained of colour as the body was of blood. In places the had been shredded by rocks, revealing more mottled grey flesh. He felt bile rise, attracted by the stench. Bending down, he picked up the sheet and replaced it.

A familiar, unwelcome feeling washed over him. Deep melancholy. It always came when he looked upon brutal death, at the wreckage of humanity. This place, this burgh, had been created to provide protection to its denizens. Yet this woman had found only violence and death. Why, he wondered, should it be that man grasps for fellows, for comfort and community and then, on finding them, resorts to violence and enmity? He crossed himself returned to life beyond the decaying walls.

Martin was waiting for him, chewing on a thumbnail. 'What did you see?'

'Our man,' he said, surprised at the choke in his throat, 'is a wicked fellow indeed. This was not some robbery, nor any murder of opportunity. This was done by one known to her, one who hated her enough to desecrate her body in some fit of passion. I could see no marks of defence.'

'The father, then, after all,' said Martin, looking towards the Tolbooth.

'I think not. What do you think of the condition of the man?'

'Most sorry, sir. He's an imbecile, if you ask me, a weak waste of breath and skin.'

'And our killer is one of strength and fury. Do you think yonder fellow could wield an axe, or the like, and strike from behind one taller than he?'

'I rather think yonder fellow might be blown clean away by a fart.'

'Apt,' said Danforth, arching an eyebrow. 'Of course, he might have struck her whilst she kneeled. She was dressed as a man,' he added.

'The better to make her escape, I should think. Might it be,' volunteered Martin, hope lighting his face, 'that she fell in the river when trying to make a run for it, and died without any pain, just her body striking the rocks?'

'No, sir. I do not see it. Her extremities would not escape the violence of nature, and they bore no marks. And then the mule might have been found.'

'God damn it. I always think of death by accident being painless.'

'Aye, I meet you in that. It is a strange thing. Death comes so easily by accident. By design, it is harder. A person fights, struggles, rages against it when they see it coming. But one can fall from a great height, or stumble on a flight of steps, and give way to it unprotestingly – unknowingly, even. Like Aeschylus by falling turtle, or the French king Charles, who hit his head on a door lintel, and fell down dead many hours thereafter. Murder is hard; accidents are easy. But this was not an accident.'

'Could you say where she entered the water? I mean, if she entered by the Abbey, or nearer where she was spat up, or –'

'She did not sit up and speak!' snapped Danforth. 'My apologies,' he added, kneading a brow. 'I … no, I cannot tell that much.'

'And so we have murder.'

'I fear so. Yet, Martin, the killing blow appears to have come from behind, as I said. I do not doubt that she felt little, suffered little, at least in the manner of her death. A rare kindness if it was the lamentable creature in the Tolbooth. He admits freely that he wielded the rod against her with license.'

'A feeble father, indeed.'

'A detestable brute. But that is no reason to be hanged. Someone battered that lassie to death. Someone hated her, wanted her silenced. Why might that be?' Martin said nothing. 'It might be that she offended someone, or she knew something that our killer did not wish her to repeat. Martin,' he asked, giving him a curious look. 'Of what nature was your father?'

'My father, sir? The old Frenchman? A jolly old gallant, to be sure, and an adventurer to the bones of him.'

'And how did he come to be in this kingdom?'

'For a time he was a merchant. Wines. He was in Scotland when he heard of France being attacked by that leopard Henry, who hasn't changed his spots. He joined the old king's forces to fight against the English at Flodden, when the present king's father was slain, and was more fortunate than most. And then, of course, he met and married my mother, and got seven of us on her before God took him. He left her quite a fortune, mind, from his trading after the war. And now she is alone.'

'She lives?'

'Lives? My mother? She reigns, sir. Holds court in grand style in one of the finest houses in Stirling. Until lately,' he said, a cloud crossing his smooth brow, 'attended upon by the baby of our house, my little sister, Christian.' He pronounced the name in the French fashion. 'She died when I was abroad with the Cardinal in the summer. She was always a timid little thing. Gentle. Now maman lives with only her maidservant and the others as companions.'

'I am sorry for it, Mr Martin.' Danforth felt a little ashamed. How easy it was, he thought, to wrap oneself in a veil of sadness, to make oneself blind to those worn by others.

'Thank you.' He brightened. 'And your own father, sir, since you are disposed to conversation?'

'A good and grave man. Now in his own grave. But let us not dwell on the past – it is an unhappy enough business in which we find ourselves. It seems we were luckier in our fathers than that poor young bairn.'

'Shall we question him again?'

Danforth, raised his face skywards. The clouds were low, streaked with dark greys and blues. He wanted above all to be out of Paisley. His holy place, his pilgrimage, had become an unpleasant imprisonment; the sensation of being locked in a charnel house was strong. But he had now looked upon the worst of it. He was involved, and would receive no rest, nor dreamless sleep, until he had seen order restored. 'No, I have nothing more to say to the creature at present. Nor do I wish to hear him rant and rave against the monks. Alas, the task which must befall us now is no more pleasant. Now, I think, we must have the truth of these Brodys from one will know, though I am not cock-a-hoop about it. That tedious old neb Mistress Clacher.'

Danforth rapped on the polished door. They had found Mistress Clacher's home in the Prior's Croft with ease; when they asked at the market cross, their request was met with amused glances and directions to the broadest mansion house on the left side of the road. A dishevelled serving girl answered. Two voices drifted towards them, one querulous and the other boisterous. Before she could ask them their business, the reedy voice called out from behind her. 'Who is there, Madge, who calls? Bid them enter and return to your work. You're all behind today, like a hog's tail.'

The girl stood aside, before putting her back to the wall and trying to appear invisible. Mistress Clacher was sitting at a desk in a cosy drawing room, writing letters. Leaning on the side of the desk was Mistress Darroch, her prominent bosom shelving out. Unlike the Kennedy inn, this house in the upper High Street was a study in modern luxury. The trestle table was stacked with plate, polished serving bowls and trinkets, all arranged neatly on a clean tablecloth. No fire sat in the middle of the room, but instead one was housed in a grate, some good cooking utensils lined up on hooks above it. Its cheerful blaze illuminated a gaily painted ceiling, all blues and reds.

'The king's men,' she said, moving a chunk of rock on the desk to weigh down her papers.

'The Cardinal's men,' said Martin, whilst Danforth's tapped clasped his hands, turning them white.

'Oh yes, and here on the matter of the war.'

'On the matter of slanderous writings against the Cardinal,' said Martin, and the old woman's eyes gleamed.

'Oh, is that the purpose?'

'We are here on pilgrimage, Mistress,' cut in Danforth. Already he was weary of the little crow. He could almost envision her pecking at carrion, blood dripping from her furry, pointed chin, her watery eyes shining with malice. 'And we would speak with you.'

At that moment, the maidservant stuck her head forward. 'Do ye need anything for the guests, mistress?'

'No, Madge. Go away.'

'Ah'm Janet, no' Madge. Madge ran away; that's why Ah've started.' She gave Martin a brief shake-and-smile, as though to suggest her mistress's mind was slipping.

'Shut up! You're whatever I call you, slave,' snapped Clacher. 'Get out.' The girl obliged, dragging her feet as she disappeared through a low archway and into the back of the house.

'She's new?' asked Martin.

'Yes. Our last girl left us, ungrateful little traitor. Can't get good help from the young these days.'

'I can't imagine why,' said Martin.

'Why indeed. They're all rebellious, the young ones, all know everything and none want to give an honest day's work. No offence meant to you, young sir. Well, the jade won't work for any good Paisley family again.' Colour rose in the thin skin of her cheeks. 'Anyway, what brings you to me?'

'Is it news o' the war, gentlemen, the battle?' Mistress Darroch gripped the desk with chubby fingers.

'No, we have not had news of any battle. We have some

questions about the burgh,' said Danforth.

'I recall,' said Clacher. 'You are staying with Mistress Caldwell. You would like to know perhaps about her husband abandoning her for the widow Blackwood? Or perhaps you wish to know about the laxity of the Church, allowing vice to prosper?'

'Och, Grissell, whit are ye like. Like as not they want tae know aboot wee Kate and the men who abused her.'

'Wilza Darroch, you're in my house and you'll let me speak.'

'Then speak sense, hen, 'o the times, o' the real rottenness.'

'I'll speak,' said Clacher, sitting back, 'to my visitors privately. You can find someone else to do your little scribblings.'

'Oh, it's like that, is it? Well, Ah willnae stay where Am no' wanted.'

'Peace, ladies,' said Danforth, but Mistress Darroch was already flouncing for the door, fixing her mob cap with affronted fingers.

'Naw, gentlemen. Ah see how it is. Good day.' She swept out of the room. The front door slammed.

'Mistress Clacher, we have no interest in gossip,' said Danforth. She looked disappointed. 'You said that you have seen much in the town, that you have resided here long.'

'Past seventy years,' she said, smiling her gummy smile.

'And you mentioned also that the Brody girl had a ... a difficult life. "A sad little jade", you called her.'

'She was at that. Oh, but I can't remember the last time we had a murder here, even with all the dirty gypsies and beggars and poor country folk who infest the place on market day. Even with all the drinking the young ones do. And all the business that leads to arguments, and arguments to fighting. No murders. Accidents, many; fires and drownings, aye. But no murders. What do you wish to know?'

'Was she a pretty girl, mistress, likely to inflame the passions and intemperate lusts of a man who might then regret it?'

'A married man, can you mean?' she asked, batting her

eyelids. Danforth shrugged noncommittally. 'Aye, she was a rare beauty, unlike to spring from such a glaikit father. Though Brody was not always the shipwreck that time and a love of the drink has made him. Some malady of the humours must have brought him to more outrage than usually he visited on her.' Martin and Danforth exchanged glances.

'It is true he beat her often, then?' asked Martin.

'Aye, he did that. They were nothing, of course, mere chattels of the Abbot. But that girl would not have said boo to a goose, and let him do it, though he went beyond what Christian correction requires, as the town knew. Black and blue she was, always, poor jade.'

'And was she a good girl,' pressed Martin, 'was there ever any bruit of her dallying with anyone?'

'Perhaps,' said Mistress Clacher, waving a hand in the air. 'Yet I cannot think what you drive at.'

'Plainly, Mistress Clacher, you can. Was there any bruit of the young girl meddling with any from the brotherhood of the Abbey?'

'Ah, there it is. As it happens, gentlemen, there was. Though,' she added, ruefully, 'I never had a name. It was mere rumour that she had lost her honour, and cast her bonnet after a monk. Not that that would bother a monk, eh? The things I have seen over the years, gentlemen, would turn your hair white.'

'Your friend, Mistress Darroch, spoke freely about "queans" riding about the burgh under cloak of darkness.'

'Pah!' said Clacher, her wrinkled face turning sour. 'Wilza Darroch is no friend to me. Her husband's great-grandfather was but a villein who bought his freedom. No quality to her, as common as a cock-crow, and not a scrap to her own name. I've brought property of my own to every marriage. There have been Clachers in Paisley for centuries, master masons who were art and part of the construction of the monastery. To our eternal credit and fame. My father was granted the old Abbot's second-best alb, a token of his Grace's esteem.' She raised her little nose.

'You have been much married?'

'Six times,' she announced, splaying, inexplicably, the fingers of one hand. 'The Clacher name I've kept throughout, and it has served me well. And my husband now twenty below me in years.'

'Well done,' offered Martin. He was rewarded with a gracious nod.

'These ladies, though, riding the town at night?'

'Oh, I hear bruits, but I don't indulge in such idle gossip. Darroch fancies low women, whores, use the Oakshaw woods to enter the burgh, for the entertainment of the monks. It would not be the first time such things have happened, though the harlots have not made their presence known to me. They would not dare take to the streets, even at night. The burgesses would not have it. The woman havers. Fond, low-born fool that she is.'

'Well, Mistress Clacher, you have been a help to us,' said Danforth.

'Then I'm glad.' Her eyes darted downwards, following Danforth's. 'You admire it?' she asked, jabbing a finger at the paperweight lump of stone.

'I –'

'A true piece of the Abbey, recovered from the last fire. A blessed stone, given me by the Prior. You may touch it.'

Danforth reached out a finger and traced the sign of the cross on the soot-stained chunk of rock. 'Thank you, madam.'

'My pleasure. When shall the murderer be hanged, sir?'

'That I cannot say. Good day to you.' Both men bowed to her and showed themselves out. Her voice croaked after them, screaming at the 'Madge' who wasn't called 'Madge.' It had begun to rain, soft and intermittent. When they were clear of Mistress Clacher's house, Danforth fetched a sigh. Not for the first time, it occurred to him that it was as well such people as she lacked the Bible in their own tongue. If they were provided with it, they would only spend hours discussing the sexual escapades of Jezebel and debating whether or not Rahab was a prostitute.

'I would speak to that Darroch woman,' said Martin. He had turned his attention to another nail.

'Then here is your opportunity.' Danforth pointed across the street, to a red-painted door on the right. Mistress Darroch, a shawl held over her cap, was standing outside a window next to it, stuffing rags into the gaps in the shutter.

'Mistress Darroch!' cried Martin. She turned, a vague smile on her open face. It did not fade at the sight of them. Danforth returned it.

'Gentlemen. Yez finished wi' yon auld nyaff?'

'Our discussion with Mistress Clacher is concluded, aye,' said Danforth.

'As ye like it. Yez wantin' a wee word?'

'My friend does,' said Martin.

''Mon in.'

There was no serving girl in the Darroch household, which was just as well-appointed as Mistress Clacher's. 'Kin a get ye anythin'? A little ale, or bread? As sure as fate that prune didnae offer ye a scrap. She was ay a tight-fisted auld shite, even in her day.'

'I'd love–' began Martin.

'Nothing, thank you, mistress. We would not trouble you, nor long detain you. To the matter, Mr Martin?'

'Mistress,' began Martin, drawing resentful eyes from Danforth. 'You spoke of something rotten in the burgh. Of men – men – who abused Kate Brody. What, who, did you mean?'

'Och, it's a sad thing, so it is. That wee lassie had a rotten father, nothin' tae her name. Else I'd hae let my boy take her tae wife.'

'Aye, you mentioned yesterday that your son was taken with her.'

'Well, we're only a wee toon. They knew each o'er as weans, they were always the-gither. She got pretty, he got hair on his face, and he fancied her. I wouldnae have it. He's got a future, y'see. Whate'er happens wi' this war, his learnin'll see him prosper. He'll go for a scholar, get oot o' Scotland. Write books, ma wee Jamie will.'

'Of what nature was the girl, Kate?'

'Och, she wiz a good wee thing. Sweet.'

'No wanton, then?'

'No, an' ye should cry shame on any who say it. She wiz gentle. Jist a wee lassie. A bit daft, ye know, given tae dreams an' stories. Used tae let her play wae Jamie when they wur baith in skirts. She wiz ay tellin' him stories aboot how she'd get away fae her da, how she'd get married tae a man o' means. Ah think that's whit made Jamie want tae be such a man, such a scholar, an' for that Ah owe the poor bairn.'

'A worthy calling. You must be proud.'

'Aye, Am are that.'

'About this "abuse", though,' said Martin.

'A' her life. Auld Angus wiz handy wi' his fists.'

'We have heard. You said "men".'

'Well it wisnae jist him. He abused her wi' his hands, left her wi' the bruises. We a' seen them. Since the maw died, he took his bad humours oot on the daughter. Ah kin tell ye, ma boy was for kickin' his arse up and doon the High Street himsel, but Ah wouldnae let him get intae trouble. That's the end o' a boy, the fightin'. As bad as the drink.'

'And?'

'Aye, sorry. Well, the faither wiz violent. But when she began tae work for the monks ... it wiz common report that she was bein' led intae sin by them. When she came intae the burgh she had that look. Ye know thon look – a lass that's gone moon-minded o'er a lad? Well, there wiz nae other lads near her but the monks. They take their pleasure an' they keep the silence o' the lass that gies it.'

'You have no good opinion of the Brothers?' asked Danforth. Mistress Darroch hesitated.

'Ah don't speak ill of the Church, sir. No' at a'. Ah go tae Mass, an' Ah avoid meat an' keep Lent.'

'How about your boy?' At this, a frown crossed the woman's face.

'He's away, Ah telt ye. Glasgow. The university.'

'That is not what I asked. What are his opinions on religion?'

'Good. He has good opinions. He debates. It's whit they learn tae dae up there, is it no'?'

'It is. He has not been back to Paisley of late?'

'Naw, o' course not. It's Michaelmas term. Ah've only written him, and him me.'

'Ah, yes,' smiled Danforth. 'Mistress Clacher encouraged you to do your own scribbling. Mistress, did you write your son news of his … friend … young Kate's disappearance?'

'Well, Ah cannae write letters. Tried, mind you – Ah'm no' stupit – but cannae dae it. So Ah keep Clacher as an acquaintance. Ah talk, she writes. Then ma man takes the letters aff on his business. An' d'ye know, the auld boot asks payment for her labour? Some linens here, fine papers there.'

'And you had the lady write a notice of Kate Brody's sudden disappearance, and caused it to be taken to your son, where he might advertise the matter abroad?'

'Aye.' She paused, her eyes darting to Martin in appeal.

'Thank you, Mistress Darroch. You have been more help than we can say. The question of who wrote and placed that placard has vexed us both some time.'

'Yet it is strange, I think,' said Danforth. 'You wished the girl found and returned to a hard life?'

'It wisnae that, sir, naw.' She shook her head in frustration. 'Ah wished for ma boy's sake that some news' o' her wid be heard. Ah didnae believe she'd come tae good. An' a wiz right, God rest her.'

'I see.'

'Jamie's no' in trouble for it, is he? Ah've no' got Jamie in trouble? Ah telt him she was taken, and said he might put the notice up in case she was driven tae Glasgow, or taken there tae be oot the way. Ah didnae know she'd been kilt. Ah didnae think anyb'dy would want her tongue stilled like that. That wiz a'.'

'Peace, no. You did good service. I am only sorry it did not bear better fruit. In fact, I think you did more than either the baillies or the Abbey in reaching a hand out on the lass's behalf. Let that be a comfort to you.'

'Pfft. Ah did what any good Christian ought. The baillies and Abbey would be glad to be rid o' her. The town's secrets are theirs tae keep.'

'One more thing,' said Danforth. 'You spoke of queans coming into the burgh at night. Be it so?'

'Ah've heard it,' she said, nodding. 'An' word passes at market. Only queans ride alone, an' women have been seen on horses, flittin' aboot under the stars. Hoors for the monks, is ma guess. You tend to that garden at the bottom o' the hill, or see what his Grace might dae. It's choked wi' weeds. It's whit's hurtin' the whole realm. More than any debates might.'

'Very good,' said Martin. 'Again, we thank you.' They left the Darroch house, its mistress's distracted smile seeing them out.

'There is one mystery solved.' Martin clapped a hand over his breast. 'She had it written, and the son put it up.'

'A university boy, given to debate.'

'All Scots are friends to debate. Pretty name for a wee scrap.'

'Perhaps. I should like to know more of this lad. Aye, I think it was you, sir, who said that the papers might be connected. The libel and the notice of Kateryn Brody's loss.'

'Aye, well … I think less on that now. I was perhaps, uh, overeager to investigate the girl, and so said anything that might make you help me. They are in different hands, for one thing, and for another I doubt old Clacher writes verses against our master to please some schismastic student. Leave the boy to his studies, sir. Mistress Darroch think the Abbey-men are art and part of this girl's sorry tale. And so we're back to the monks.'

'All roads certainly lead back to the Abbey.' Danforth looked down the High Street, where the spire was visible even through the misty rain. There was something about the place that both attracted and repelled him. The image of a shiny red apple with a maggot buried in its flesh flashed into his mind. That spire now seemed almost to be trying to reach upwards and out of the sinful world of man.

'Shall we take these rumours to the Prior?' asked Martin, cutting short Danforth's musings.

'Yes. But I cannot today.'

'Then we might eat? She was after feeding me, you know.'

'Sir, does your mind run on nothing but food?' Martin smiled impishly. 'You may go and eat. I cannot stomach anything, I fear.' The maggoty apple had led to the image of the bloated corpse. The girl must be given justice, or something worse would happen. If God provided a mystery and he were to neglect it, He would ensure some greater evil would fall out. 'Take yourself into the town. I shall return to our lodgings. I should like to see if our shirts are come.'

8

The shirts had not come. So much, thought Danforth, for the gratuity of Jardine the younger. But he was too tired to care. His thighs had taken a racking from the recent trips up and down the wynd to St Nicholas. His eyes nipped. Even walking up and down the hill of the High Street and market cross had taken a toll. He began to wonder if he really was becoming an old man. He had always imagined that the middling age began at thirty – he would pass that in a few months – and then old age made its presence felt at forty.

He waved off the barrage of questions from Mistress Caldwell: 'is it true Brody is to hang? Has he confessed? Are you gentlemen engaged in the affair? What news o' the war?' He had had enough of fishwives for a lifetime. He climbed the stairs leaving a disappointed Mistress Caldwell at the foot of them, went up to his room and slept. He woke only at a knock from Martin, who delivered some fruit, much of it dried. He ate everything but the apple, and then turned to his Book of Hours. His father's favourite thing about the book had always been its selection from Proverbs. He turned the pages, finding what he wanted:

20:19. He that goeth about as a talebearer revealeth secrets.

11:13 The gadding gossiper is sure to let out any secret entrusted to him; therefore, it is implied, be careful in what you say to him.

'Or her', he added in thick lettering. But should some secrets not be known? He lay back on his lumpy mattress, intending to think about what he had seen, to go over the details of what he had heard. Instead he counted his seven Hail Marys and drifted back to sleep.

He dreamt that night, but not of Alice and little Elizabeth. Instead he pursued a headless girl, her body marked with bruises, through the grounds of Paisley Abbey. In the deer parks, strange shapes loomed, wild and lumbering, never showing themselves. He chased the girl past them. Watching the pursuit, their faces pressed against the dark glass, were the monks, their mouths making 'o's against the murky glass. And then he felt himself awaken and spotted a length of rope jutting from beneath his mattress. When he pulled on it, it was yanked angrily by some unseen force bent on engaging him in a strange tug of war. A terror came to him that he would be dragged under the bed with it. He opened his eyes then and knew it was only another dream – the dream of a child.

A little knot of dread had taken up lodging in his stomach. He knew that he would have to go to the Abbey again, and he did not relish the thought. He must confront the Prior, draw the truth out of him with threats and terror. He was suddenly very glad that Martin had accompanied him on the pilgrimage. The man's laughing, easy manner – though undoubtedly infuriating – was a remedy to the bleakness that had wrapped itself around his heart. Somehow, he hoped, proving the guilt or innocence of Brody would release it. Then he could take Mass in the pilgrim's chapel and feel free. Either the man was guilty and the Abbey free of taint, or some corruption would be found, pulled out by the root, and tranquillity restored.

Fancying their shirts would last a few days more – and they would have to, until they frightened what they were due out of young Jardine – the pair attended St Nicholas in what was settling in to a ceaseless day of rainfall. If the same weather persisted down south, he thought, the fighting when it came would feel the brunt of it. Men and horses would meet in a marsh, hacking and shooting from uncaring, sucking sludge. In the churchyard lay some freshly turned turf: the hastily dug resting place of Kate Brody.

In the market cross afterwards they scouted, as usual, for news. Following their visit, Mistress Clacher had evidently spread the nature of their business, and they were informed by new arrivals from Glasgow that the only news of slanderous bills was a commission against them being undertaken by the Archbishop. That was welcome. The king, Cardinal and army had been in the troubled borders, trying to draw ordnance, sheep and horses, but met resistance and, it was said, found few vassals willing to muster. That was unwelcome.

'Shall we now attend on the Prior?' asked Martin after their noontime dinner. He wiped his fingers gracelessly on the cuffs of his shirt. 'I would as soon be out of this rain, and the days have grown so short. It seems not long ago I was in France, where the sun seldom retreated.'

'Not yet. First let us speak with young Jardine.'

'Yes, that's an idea. I've fair ruined the rags that young fool has left me in.'

Danforth led Martin towards the shop, eager to delay confronting the acting head of the Abbey. Inside the draper's they found the younger Jardine chatting with a friend, whom he introduced as their erstwhile tailor. Both looked frightened at the petulant faces of their unhappy customers.

'Young Jardine,' said Danforth, crossing his arms in a pose of solemn disapproval. 'We were due our shirts yesterday, and yet in our lodgings we find no shirts. How, I ask you, can this be?'

'Sir, I – we – there has been but a delay. I had news of my father, old Jardine, he is due to return later this week, perhaps Friday, perhaps Saturday, it shall depend on the weather; you can see how much it delays things– '

'We don't care a straw for your father, young sir,' said Martin, 'but for our shirts. You, tailor.'

'Taynne, sir.'

'Taynne, then. You were to cut the cloth this lad provided you into shirts, and to deliver them to our lodgings yesterday, and yet here we stand as vagabonds, not gentlemen in the employ of the Lord Privy Seal. Regard my cuffs, sir. Would you put a villain out in such weeds?'

'Young Jardine, sirs,' explained Taynne, 'is but a prentice. He spoke in haste, eager for trade.' Jardine cast his eyes downwards. 'It cannot be done so speedily, or else you will have poor shirts and be the worse for it. But I and my own prentice are hard at work, gentlemen, on what you have ordered.'

'Yes, very hard at work, as my eyes tell me,' said Martin. It was Taynne's turn to look sheepish. 'When shall we have that for which we have paid?'

'Tomorrow, possibly the day following.'

'Tomorrow.'

'Aye, sir.'

They left the sour merchants to their world of bolls and spools and stepped back out into a washed-out market cross, its complement of argumentative goodwives already settled into the apparent routine of fighting each other for the best of goods. 'Mon dieu, what a people,' said Martin. 'How their minds run on trade. They will say anything to procure it. What a bootless little tinker is young Jardine.' Danforth mumbled in response, already turning down hill towards the Bridge Port, and Martin ceased trying to distract him.

They took the familiar path, the saints now weeping rain. If Cromwell had seen them, thought Danforth acidly, he would use the weather as an excuse to get out the hammers. He thanked God daily that he had left England before King Henry had reduced the religious houses to dusty piles of rubble, or sold them off to grasping courtiers.

Feeling their way along the wall from the other direction were the usual assortment of beggars, eager to seek alms at the gate from Brother David. Danforth cast his gaze downwards. The poor he accepted, as readily as he accepted the role of the Abbey in tending to them. But looking at their pleading, defeated faces, seeing them as individuals, was even harder than looking upon corpses. The dead had lived and lost their lives, were beyond suffering. The itinerant masterless that tried their luck at every burgh and town were suffering alive.

The gates were still open, although a porter emerged from the gatehouse, asking their business before disappearing back inside to record it. Recognising them as the Cardinal's men – their fame had certainly spread through the burgh – they were bid welcome. Unlike on their previous visit, the Abbey precincts were alive with activity, bedraggled servants squelching to and fro. In the park, one was chopping a tree for firewood, the handle slipping in his grasp. In an enclosed space an old woman, her cap sodden, was chasing chickens, mud-soaked sacks tied around her ankles. They followed the path around the Abbey church and Danforth spotted the young monk, perhaps in his early twenties, again looking at them from the door of what Brother David had indicated was the infirmary. His hand was out of his robe this time, lightly bandaged. When the boy saw them looking at him, he stared back hard. The others, thought Danforth, must have had their midday meal and prayers, and be back at their books in the Chapter House. What a strange life they must lead, eating, studying and praying within their sturdy walls whilst outside them a town full of revellers, gamblers and traders loomed, drinking life to the dregs.

The Prior's lieutenant nodded them upstairs, and they began to climb without acknowledging him. They found the Prior seated. He looked, thought Danforth, more harried than before.

'Good afternoon to you, Father.' They received only a tight smile, as the Prior's eyes slid down to the marks their muddy boots were leaving on his Turkish carpet. 'Have you received letters from your speedy messenger?'

'The Cardinal has written you, gentlemen,' he replied, rifling the desk. 'Here.' He passed Danforth a folded and sealed paper. 'I should have had it sent by one our servants directly. You need not have come.' Danforth took the letter and folded it into his robe.

'That was certainly fast,' he said.

'Not so very surprising, sir. Our boy had passed through Glasgow and the letter awaited you there. He has only just taken your own.' The prior reached down again and picked up a leather purse. 'This was sent also. A purse of money from his Grace, less the post riders' fees. A generous man, your master. As long as you are in the burgh I repeat there is no need for you to come down to the Abbey for your correspondence.'

'It was our pleasure,' smiled Martin.

'But not all pleasure, alas,' added Danforth. The Prior raised his brows, the wrinkles on his forehead deepening. 'You know, I think, of the murder of Brody's girl, your Abbot's tenant?'

'I do, sir. And we have prayed ceaselessly for her wretched soul.'

'And you know, of course, that her father stands accused.'

'Indeed, and I am sorry that we have harboured such a vile creature in our holy place. He shall swing for it, I trust shortly, and be cast upon God's great mercy.'

'The man pleads innocence.'

'As do they all. Then he is doubly damned for a murderer and a liar.'

'You do not believe that a man is innocent unless caught red-hand, as he was not, or proven beyond doubt to have done the deed?' Silence fell between them, the only sound the crackling of the logs in the grate. The door to the bedchamber beyond was closed. Walker apparently wanted his secrets better hidden.

'A very English manner of thinking,' said the Prior. 'The matter is regrettable. A servant dead, and another servant soon to be. Most regrettable. I shall have to provide another report, move funds.'

'Brody protests his innocence with great passion,' said Martin, hand on hip. 'He claims that his daughter was molested by the monks here, that she had conceived some fondness for them herself.'

As on their first visit the Prior's glacial composure appeared to falter, the first tendrils of fear creeping into his face. 'That is a slanderous lie. There is no truth at all to it.'

'Yet you called the girl a whore.'

'And that she was, little better than a hobby horse.'

'Is that so, and ridden by your monks?' Danforth sickened at his own words. For one terrible moment he thought of Cromwell and his commissioners. This had been their work: threatening clergymen, throwing sordid gossip and hearsay in their faces. He reddened. Even Martin had turned to look at him, his eyes wide.

'No!' The Prior had begun to tremble. 'Never. I merely heard rumours of her conduct about the burgh, never within these walls. You are wicked, sir, to even speak of such things. In seeking to defame my monks, you slander yourself as the one possessed of a foul mind and tongue.'

'Peace,' said Danforth, 'we are all servants of the Church, and would protect it well. And for that purpose we would know of any troubles concerning this girl and the brotherhood here.' Again, he was conscious of how unctuous his words must sound. How much like a honeyed trap. He wondered if, had he been the Prior, he would have believed them. If only the man was honest, if only he shared all he knew with his coreligionist rather than seeing enemies, this unpleasant scene might not have been necessary.

'There was – there is no trouble. A murder has been undertaken, and the murderer will be rightly hanged.' He gave them a malicious smile. 'Our tenant – this vile creature – is no clergyman, and his evil deed was not committed on hallowed soil. His death shall be at the king's pleasure, and none of my house. And that shall be an end to the affair. And you have no authority here, sir, Cardinal or otherwise, to pry into the working of the monastery and its divines. By the raising of this place to an Abbey we were assured that we answer only to the Holy Father in Rome. And at the present time, with the great battle to commence in very few days …'

'You have had news of the war?'

'I have heard bruits, sir.' The Prior avoided their eyes. Our messenger has picked them up on the road. You will allow no one knows when the battle will come who does not know the movement of the English. And it is on that business that I must apply my mind to silent prayer. You have your letters, gentlemen, and I think we are done. You have your own affairs and those of your master to get in order.' He flopped down and made a show of busying himself, but he could not disguise the tremor in his hands.

Danforth turned to Martin, who shrugged. They bowed without much deference and left. On the staircase Danforth pocketed the purse of coins, but kept the Cardinal's letter out. When they were out of the Abbot's House, he opened it, the seal sliding off. He read aloud to Martin. Beaton had written from Haddington. The king was to attempt seizure of Carlisle on the western march, against only a small English force. 'The army has mustered munitions from the shires as best it could,' said Danforth, handing the letter to Martin and crossing himself. 'The great thrust that will thwart Henry's enterprise of Scotland is likely to take place as soon as the king judges it best. Perhaps it is even now being fought. May the Lord protect us.'

'He's read this,' cried Martin. 'The Prior opened this letter, the corrupt ass. That's how he knows of the battle.'

'I do not doubt it.'

'And the rents and tithes the place earns – yet he deducts fees for the post, can you believe the tightness?'

'Ah, taxation of the Church is heavy under the present king. Yet I agree that this Prior is a hard man. I have no liking for him, though it grieves me to say it.'

'Yet his Grace doesn't recall us.'

'No. I should think he has other matters to attend to. We must tarry here. It will do neither us nor his Grace good to miss each other's letters upon the highway. It is happening, Martin, do you realise it? Somewhere far from here, there is to be a great battle against the heretics. No mere scrimmage, no tulzie such as have plagued us, but a battle.'

'Aye. I confess I'd divert my mind from that knowledge. We can't influence it.'

'Can we not? Cannot our little movements and words and doings play their hand?'

'No.'

'I wonder.'

They were approaching the archway under the wall from cloister to outer wall. As they passed under it, a hooded figure detached itself from the shadows, like a gargoyle come alive. Danforth started as the hood was pulled back. It was the young monk who had watched them so intently from the infirmary.

'What do you mean, Brother, hiding in shadows to accost strangers?' snapped Martin. The monk cast down his head, revealing his tonsure. Danforth placed him at about twenty. When he spoke, it was in low tones.

'Forgive me, gentlemen. You are the Cardinal's men?'

'We are that.'

'I would speak with you, sirs, touching affairs here. I would find friends to help me, and whom I might help. I have fears, grave fears.' The little monk had a curious voice; it sounded like it came from a much older man. That is learning, thought Danforth. He approved of it. Speech, he had been taught from the knee, should be adorned with learning's ornaments. It kept the world at bay, making agreeable inferiors of everyone save his betters.

'Pray do, Brother …?'

'Brother James, sir.'

'What fears are these, Brother James?' The monk raised his head and they read the fear in his eyes. Danforth found himself becoming inured to the sight.

'I cannot speak freely here. Meet me tonight, beyond the Abbey's walls. Eight o'clock, by the Bridge Port.'

'You have liberty to leave the Abbey at night?' Danforth's mouth turned down in a frown. Again, the Abbey was revealing itself to be a disappointment.

'The Prior,' said Brother James meaningfully, 'cares little for our comings and goings. We are free to do private business, to hunt and fish in the burgh as we list. The great gate,' he sniffed, 'opens and closes more freely than the legs of a whore, that the burgesses might wander hither and thither, buying beer and ale from our brew-house.'

'Hard words, Brother, against your Prior and his governance,' said Danforth. His voice had turned caustic. 'Whether you approve of your Prior or not, he is your Prior nonetheless, and his words ought to be your law. To rebel against them is to be a traitor rebelling against his sovereign. No, Brother James,' he repeated, 'your words are dangerous.'

'Yet they are true,' said Brother James. 'Thought I do not much like them, and it pleases me not at all to speak them. It is no sedition to speak the truth, nor is it slander. I am sorry if what you have heard disappoints you, sir. This place is my mother and my father, now, and good parents discipline their children, as my true parents did before God called them. Right good discipline, not slackness and liberty. Yet you will meet with me beyond the walls?'

'You have some knowledge of the murdered girl?' asked Martin. In response, the monk gave them only a brief nod and another glance from his expressive eyes, before biting down on his bottom lip. 'Are the bruits true, and some brother here had immoral traffic with her?'

'Tonight, please, sir, away from here. For the nonce, I shall say only this: though the Prior now tells the world that there are only fifteen amongst the company of the order here, there was another. Where he is, I cannot say, but may suspect. I will open my heart to you tonight.' He backed away from them, replacing his hood against the rain and hurrying back towards the infirmary, a little raven in flight.

9

Danforth let Martin to return to the inn whilst he took himself to the barber's. It was a gloomy little bolt-hole on the St Mirin Wynd. As he approached it, the now familiar sound of carousing echoed from a lodging deeper down the wynd. The shop was empty, the ancient barber delighted at the prospect of custom. Small stools stood around the room beside a table littered with water lavers and brushes. A polished steel mirror reflected candlelight dully.

'In out o' the rain, sir? Wise indeed.' The barber was a tiny man, his white hair and beard oiled. His fingers were laced with scars, proof of his long experience if not his efficiency. 'What brings you? You're not hurt, are you, wounded? Hair needing cropped? Nails needing trimmed?'

'I should like a shave,' said Danforth, pulling his eyes away from the calloused hands.

'Very good, sir. You would like, perhaps, the king's fashion? It's very well liked at Court, sir, is the king's fashion. You've too narrow a face for the square cut favoured by the English king, though that's very much beloved by young gentlemen. Suits a fat face, mind you, and a broader neck. O' course the fashion is growing for straggling beards.'

'Certainly not.' Danforth put his knuckles to the thin, fair stubble on his cheek. 'I wish to be rid of it all.' He did not like beards. They struck him as fripperies – either the trifling ornaments of courtiers or the unkempt thatches of the unwashed poor. They had no business on a serious man.

'Very good,' repeated the barber, a note of disappointment in his voice. 'Please sit.' He did, as the old man prepared his water and razor. 'You'd be a rich man, then, sir?' Danforth sighed. One had to pay a barber for any information received with information given. He wondered what information Martin had been induced to impart.

'Not so very. I am in the employ of his Grace the Lord Cardinal Beaton.'

'Is that so? I said it when you walked in here, sir – "carries himself rich, this fellow", I said.' He looked around the empty shop as though inviting disagreement. 'You'll be the fellow the other spoke o', the young man with the black beard, then? Aye, a jolly young man, that. Said he was travelling with a companion, another Cardinal's man, though a wee thing older and not so given to conversation. Said you flew from King Henry – he o' the square beards and the army on our doorstep. *That* young man took an *excellent* cut.' There was the answer to Danforth's question. 'And you're investigating some naughty words against his Grace, is it?' Danforth gave a brief nod, hoping his frown would discourage the drift of discussion. 'Well, I see yon fellow spoke the truth.' He draped a towel around Danforth's shoulders and set about mixing a bowl of sour, tangy soap.

The barber began to shave, humming discordantly as he worked. Danforth despised the act. He always had a strange feeling that the blade would slip, by accident or design, blood spurting. Were it not for his dislike of beards he would reject the whole exercise happily. Yet he had come for another reason. 'Master Barber, you seem to know a great deal of me. I wonder if I might ask you about some of the burgh's business? Unless, of course, you are not privy to it ...'

'Now that might depend on the business,' said the barber, careful not to be drawn too easily. Danforth cursed inwardly. He had been hoping for a stupider man. 'Now o' private matters I say nothing.'

'I was thinking on matters now public. What know you of this young lass who has been murdered?'

'Old Brody's daughter? Oh, that's a sorry tale.'

'Do you think her father her killer?'

'Do you not, sir?' The old eyes glittered. Danforth merely tilted his head back to let the man at his throat. 'Och, it may be so. Though in truth that girl had many men after her. The pretty ones always do.'

'Men of what nature?'

'Men o' every nature. Some even o' the better sort. Or as like to the better sort as we have in a wee town.'

'Oh?'

'Yes indeed, sir. Are you sure I cannot leave a little beard on your neck?'

'No. Which men have you in mind?'

'Well,' he said, a conspiratorial look on his face. 'I shan't name names nor point no fingers, but there's a fellow who isn't too far from the keys in a certain office in the burgh, sir. A fellow with a red beard, in here for a trim often enough. Never kept his mouth closed about the looks of young Kate Brody, that one. Though I shan't say nothing about that, save she was too young and too fair to look at that great lump.'

Logan, thought Danforth: the repellent burgh gaoler who had spoken of Kate Brody as nothing but a body. Somehow there was little to be surprised about in the man being a lecherous bawd. 'I think I know the fellow,' he said, realising he must play the game and abide by its rules. 'He is not a married man, I think?'

'No, though not for lack o' trying. He'd try and force the affections o' any maiden, and think them his due because of his station.'

'This man forces himself upon women?' Danforth's voice had turned sharp; he had not meant it.

'Now I didn't say that, sir. I say only that he thinks highly of himself – he reckons himself a fine catch to any lassie, rich or poor, fair or uncomely. You know what some men are like when they fancy they have some authority and wealth. It addles him the more that no lass has ever shown herself inclined to him. He must feel himself a grand baker with a tray o' freshly made pies, yet every hungry customer turns up their nose and strolls past him.' He licked his mottled lips. Danforth could see Logan, puffed up, believing himself deserving of women and entitled to press his suit. It was not pleasant. Disappointed men could be desperate men. Savageness could be the result of their bitterness.

'I do. Was there any talk of the girl having a lover in the burgh? Some gentlemen or lad with whom she might have taken up?'

'You think a lover may have tired o' her, sir?' Danforth bit his tongue. He was tiring of the man answering his questions with questions. It was irritating.

'I cannot say. I am no baillie.'

'Yet your mind runs on the matter?'

'It is natural.'

'That's so, sir. There. What do you think?' He had finished shaving. Danforth, for the first time, looked in to the mirror. He was surprised. How long had it been, he wondered, since he had looked at himself? For weeks, or perhaps longer, he had been content to button and lace himself without benefit of a looking glass, confident that experience would turn him out presentably. His only glimpses of his reflection had been the fleeting, distorted images allowed by water and the occasional spoon. It was a shock to see a man older than his twenty-nine years looking back, even without the beard growth. His cheeks had hollowed and his fair hair had grown thick. He looked sad and solemn. He nodded at himself. 'That is well done of you, Master Barber. Your work pleases me.' He looked quickly down and fumbled for coins. 'What is the reputation of the monks in the burgh?' he asked, trying to sound as nonchalant as possible.

'It is very good, sir.' An edge had come into the old fellow's voice. 'There are none in the town will say aught against the Church or its men.' He took back his towel. 'They produce the best beer and ale. We need no taverns in the burgh with the monks here; why, every man's home is a tavern if he buys from the Abbey. Did you mark the noise outside? And if some men grumble at the prices, if some men say that the brothers get rich off the backs o' the poor, well, some men have busy tongues. I should not lend an ear to those that say yon Abbey is a very vegetable lamb.'

'A what?'

'A vegetable lamb, sir, o' Tartary. Have you not heard tell o' them from the sailors?' His eyes lit up at Danforth's hesitance. 'They say that in the land of the Tartars there is a living creature that resembles a lamb, white and fleecy and all innocence. It grows from a seed, as a plant might, and is attached all its poor life to the ground from which it sprang by a strong root – like a mother's birthing cord fixed to her bairn. Wolves come for the lamb, and he cannot run because o' that root. But even if the wolves do not come, the pretty wee thing can go nowhere, and instead must consume all that is within his reach. When there is no more pasture left around him he starves, even without the wolves to trouble him.'

'An extraordinary tale, Master Barber, though I think there is less meat to it than there is to this unnatural lamb itself. And people say the Abbey is such a creature, assailed by wolves and devouring the land around it until it withers?'

'Oh,' he shrugged. 'Some men lean towards such fancies.'

'I am glad, then, that you are not such a man.'

Danforth nodded his thanks silently and then stepped back into the rain, turning up the wynd and back up the sloping High Street towards the Oakshawside. Music, laughter, and the image of Logan the gaoler harassing a dead girl chased him.

10

They awaited their appointment in Danforth's room. Martin made free with the mattress, whilst Danforth sat at the desk, poring over the Cardinal's letter. Between the neat lines of script he sensed anxiety. This was an unpopular war, and the Cardinal was blamed for encouraging it. If England should be victorious …. He turned his mind from the possibility. He had been a youth himself when King Henry had turned England on its head. Fleeing a land where no man trusted the next had been a relief. Now Scotland was his home. There would be nowhere else to run.

'Your mattress is no more comfortable than mine.' Martin's voice drifted over, querulous.

'I suppose not. It is little wonder our hostess cannot make a success of this place, offering such meagre hospitality. I wonder she makes her rents, in her husband's name. It would be better for her if the old devil had died and let her succeed to it as a widow, an old relict.'

'Perhaps. Do you think,' he ventured, 'that this missing monk, whom the Prior would make a ghost, that he might've been the one who took the virtue of the Brody girl and left her name mud?'

'It is possible. I cannot say. At present, all is conjecture.'

'And our friend the barber gave you nothing new?'

'No.' He had decided against telling Martin that the barber had insinuated that Logan had had some interest in the girl. He had started to dislike the boy's fascination with the dead girl. In fact, he had begun to wonder about its nature. It had suddenly occurred to him that he had no idea if Martin had a young lady of his own in mind to marry. He had made it a point never to pry, even in his own mind, into the private lives of his colleagues. He would never have dreamed of doing so. Yet now he wondered if the boy had lost some sweetheart – if perhaps that might account for his interest in another dead young woman. 'And I should thank you in the future not to speak so freely of me or our employment to strangers.'

'What strangers? We're guests here and seek friends. If people know who we are and grow accustomed to us, they'll be more inclined to speak to us. You must learn the value of openness. People, Mr Danforth. You have to treat them like you'd like to be treated. Like friends.'

Danforth made a little moue of distaste at the word. 'Wise men trust no one with even the least information. Yes, even those who seem to be friends,' he said, raising an objecting hand. 'Only fools reveal their knowledge of any suspect matters to a smiling face. My lad, I would not trust *you* in this business had you not been stuck fast to me like a limpet since coming into the west. Ah, it is no matter. The barber said nothing. I am more wary of this spirit monk.'

'But how can it be that a man can disappear, be written out of the history of the place?'

'That is easier to answer. The Prior need not name him in the accounts, nor subscribe his name to the Tack. Burn all papers naming him. He might only be found out if someone speaks of him.'

'Then we're lucky that someone has.'

'Quite.' Danforth sighed. Disappointment seemed to build upon disappointment. If the Prior had been corrupted, the corruption of his order would follow. 'A silent order that has such monks in it. What a world.'

'What troubles you, mon ami?'

'By my truth, I do not like the suspicions that breed in my mind, Martin. I would this matter was resolved, and not to the detriment of that holy place. Yet I cannot now think it otherwise.'

'The truth, as ugly as it might be, must be got at,' said Martin. 'Would you have the girl's father hanged and the matter closed, as the Prior hopes, when you entertain doubts of his guilt?'

'No.'

'Then we must meet this fellow and hear what news he has.'

'That I know. Come, I can find no comfort in sitting here. Let us stretch our legs a little. The hour draws near.'

'Ah, you can't stand too much of my company yet?' Martin smiled, and Danforth rolled his eyes, standing up from the desk and stretching.

Downstairs they found Mistress Caldwell, making a desultory effort to tidy the inn. She rounded on them immediately. 'It's late, sirs; are you leavin'?'

'Only to take the air, mistress.'

'You'll find a lot of water in it.'

'I find it refreshing,' said Martin. 'I like my air with water and food, not dust and hunger.'

'It's late for business,' she persisted, her eyes eager for gossip. 'Is there somethin' in the wind of the army, or of those matters touchin' the Cardinal's honour? Is it true right enough that you're engaged in this business of Brody? You think the man innocent, perhaps? The talk of the burgh is that he claims innocence, though we each know of his treatment of the wean. He did it, you mark me.'

'Mistress, you might tend to your own affairs,' snapped Danforth. His left eyelid was twitching insistently. Too many people had irritated him today. 'And leave off that of others. Your husband may be absent, but that does not give you license to cluck your tongue, nor to turn it to the questioning of men. Cease your prattling, or else we might report it to the Town Council.'

Mistress Caldwell bowed her head and then turned on her heel, stomping back into her private quarters. 'That was hard,' said Martin. 'She's already a sour, melancholic creature.'

'And was she not deserving of it? She is little better than the Clacher crone.' But Danforth already felt guilty. He was growing irascible, he knew. He tried never to speak roughly to women, even when he felt they warranted it. But to abuse a sad creature like Mistress Caldwell was the tactic of a bully, and he did not like it.

'You know what the Cardinal says?'

'What?'

'Women are either all sugar or all shite. I'll give you three guesses which she is.'

'You should know better than to listen to his Grace when he

is in a jesting mood,' said Danforth, biting his tongue.

They left the inn and took the High Street towards the market cross. The rain had ceased. The darkness of the night encroached upon the few lights that peeped out from windows and shutters like solitary beacons warning of a hopeless battle. For the first time Danforth understood the notion of darkness falling: it seemed it was pressing down on the earth, and carried in it a glittering, crystalline frost. Still there persisted the roar of the swollen gutters and the river itself, risen high on its banks. Brother James was waiting for them, staring out over the bridge at the Cart, a black figure against the black of the night. The lanterns that stood covered on either side of the Bridge Port cast a slight glow upon him. His youthful face wore a pensive, pinched look. When he saw them coming he stepped back, and drew them with a gesture into the deeper darkness on the inside of the Bridge Port, where its rough, undressed columns blocked the lanterns.

'The river is high,' said James. 'The rocks lethal. It is quite frightening to look over. A fall would be death.'

'I do not doubt it.'

'Well, Brother, what news draws us here?' said Martin. 'What of this missing monk?'

'First, bless you, bless you for coming, sirs. I feel I might trust you. You have honest faces, Godly faces.'

'Thank you, Brother. But this monk?' prodded Danforth.

'He was a friend of mine, sirs.' James kept his voice just loud enough to be heard over the crashing of the water against the bridge supports. 'He was not much younger than I, though only recently out of the novitiate. Brother Hector was his name, and before that Hector Watson, an orphan of lesser burgesses. He attended the school. An orphan, like me…'

'And what was the nature of this youth?' asked Danforth.

'He was a devout lad, sir, strong and athletic. He was, I think, not made for learning and the order, yet he had a sharp mind that shaped him for learning. Or so the Prior thought. He was … not satisfied with the novitiate, required always to remain in the kitchens watching the food being prepared, then left alone in his private room to study. He was lost, sir.

Myself, I accepted a new mother in the Church, a new father in the Abbey. He could not.'

'Did he have converse with Kate Brody?' said Martin, his eyes hungry. Brother James nodded his eyes downcast.

'They fancied themselves to be in love, and wished to run away together. Until the girl's body was found, I suspected that they had succeeded, and there an end to it: they escaped to begin some hard life afresh. I prayed for them, that they might be forgiven.'

'They just walked out of the gates of the Abbey?' asked Danforth.

'No, sir. The girl returned home after her day's labour. Brother Hector was in our company, his manner quiet … in the morning he was gone. We rise early, sir, for matins. He was gone by then.'

'Gone? But the gates are locked at night. The Prior said so.'

'So they are. But he was gone all the same. He did not get out that way.'

'And do you think,' pressed Martin, 'that the father, that Brody might have discovered them as they made their flight, and killed the girl?'

'Brody?' asked Brother James. 'The man is a weakling, a nothing. He beat Mistress Brody mercilessly, until she could take no more. I think it would have been more likely that Brother Hector – that Hector – would have knocked *him* on the pate if he tried to stop their escape.'

'Then, in your opinion, Brother,' said Danforth, 'what is the solution?'

'I know not. I know only that if the girl is slain and her body spat up by the river, it is as like that Hector suffered the same fate, yet was less fortunate in having his body returned for proper Christian burial.'

Danforth's mind worked quickly. 'What you suggest, Brother, is that someone did not want this amoral pair escaping, and perhaps bringing censure on the Abbey if their crime was uncovered. What you suggest is that someone of the order might have stopped the pair with violence.' James only looked at them levelly. 'I cannot credit this. No scandal could be so great that any man of the Church would bury it in blood.'

'I cannot say, sir. I have heard nothing. Yet the Prior will not speak of Brother Hector, and conducts himself as though the lad never existed. We each live in fear of breathing his name. And since the discovery, there is greater terror amongst us that one of our own has some knowledge of the crime, and the Prior content to let a man hang who is too stupid, witless and poor to make any case for himself. You gentlemen, it is said, have some authority, yet not over our house. Still you might bring this matter to the Cardinal, to the king.'

'Have you anything further that might aid us,' asked Martin. 'Anything, no matter how little you attach to it?'

'I cannot think, sir. Only that there might yet be answers in the river, if the rains have not swollen it so that it has carried them beyond your discovery. I would have justice, sir, for my friend as well as for the girl. I would have the light of truth shone.'

'As would we all, Brother,' said Martin. 'What happened, though, to your hand?' The monk looked down in confusion.

'I cut it.'

'An unfortunate mishap.'

'I am prone to them,' he shrugged. 'I cannot fight back. I must return to the monastery.'

'Thank you for your help, Brother James.'

'Peace be with you,' said James, inclining his head. He took a few steps backwards before turning and heading back towards the Abbey's gates.

Danforth threw back his own head, inhaling the cold night air. At every turn things seemed to get further tangled, everyone holding their own secrets and protecting their own interests. What unity could there be in such a world? The unpleasant memory of London came to him, the fear and suspicion, the divisions and attacks, the abuses accused and the abuses carried out in the name of correcting them. Smoky streets, men whispering in alleys, midnight raids. The thought of his adoptive land following the same crooked path made him shiver.

'There's no question of our dredging the river,' said Martin. The pensive look Brother James had worn had transferred to his face as he stared moodily over the Cart. Below, the water tumbled and frothed. Two swans, flashes of purer white against the white foam, stood out amongst the reeds, semi-distinct in the darkness. 'And should we find a second body, it will be one more crime levelled against that miserable creature in the Tolbooth.'

'And can we be sure of a second body, of the corpse of a fugitive monk slain alongside his quean?' asked Danforth. Martin turned to him, full of curiosity. 'I do not think we can. Did you hear that young Brother's claim – this Hector was a strong and athletic youth, as like to knock a man's pate as otherwise.'

'I did. What does it signify to you?' Martin's gaze had turned sharp.

'Only this: we have a murdered woman and a father likely incapable of the act, who in any case pleads innocence. We have also a strong youth, with the means and brawn to do the deed, who has himself vanished. It might be that this Hector was of a violent nature, and lured the girl to her death for his own pleasure, with no intention of marriage in some foreign clime. It may be that he regretted breaking his vow, or being shackled to the poor wench, or both, and slew her himself, running afterwards.'

'There is that possibility,' conceded Martin. 'But somehow the tale becomes more tragic if the girl was killed by her lover, by the man she hoped would give her release from a hard life, you know? Yet it's also possible that someone connected with the Abbey slew them both, as this young fellow suspects, so that their transgressions would be buried and their names erased with their lives. To be honest, I thought it strange that Brother James should speak against his Prior so.'

'Did you, Mr Martin? Might not any man speak against his master?'

'I've never heard you speak against the Cardinal. And you can't say you're pleased hearing him speak like that. Yet maybe our friend there had a liking for young Kate himself. A young man's a young man, whether he puts on a black cowl or not.'

'What a track your mind drives upon. He may be only a young man full of principles and worry. And by my truth I do not like either. Bringing the Abbey and its brothers into the matter adds complication, and none of it to the good of the Church. With Kate Brody dead, either we have a runaway monk with blood on his hands, or a dead monk and his killer connected with the Abbey. I see no good in either. We must be grateful to young Brother James, at least, for being a friend, for not sealing his lips to us as others do.' He crossed his arms and again threw back his head. 'It is as you said, sir. The truth must be got at, no matter how ugly.'

Martin stared for a moment, and then smiled. 'Let's get at it then.' Without another word, be inclined his head in the direction of the Abbey, and then began sauntering towards it.

'What are you doing? Martin, come back here!' Martin did not break his stride. In frustration, Danforth balled his fists and pressed them against his neck. But he followed.

The Abbey gates were still open, though James had disappeared. Martin strode through, as though he did not care whether he was seen. A short distance behind him, Danforth tried to blend into the dark, pressing himself against the open gate and sliding into the precinct. Martin, to his relief, avoided the open path and squelched across the grass towards the collection of buildings beyond the church. He paused, as though judging where to go, and then slipped between two of the smaller ones – the bake-house and a shorter, ancient stone pile with an old-fashioned oaken door. The rotten smell drifted from it.

'What is this madness? You cannot think to spy on the monks?' whispered Danforth.

'You want to know if this Hector escaped the Abbey, don't you?' said Martin. 'Or if he's being sheltered here, or something. I had an idea about another route out.'

'I … I do not care. Come, let us get out of here before they lock us in for the night.'

'What did that odd little monk say? "He did not get out that way."' Did his tone strike you as odd?' Danforth thought back, cursing. Brother James had said that, but he had not taken note of his tone. Even when it was possible to remember what someone said, it was rarely easy to recall exactly how they had said it. Perhaps Martin had caught something he had missed.

'So?'

'So there's another way in and out of this place, and I think I can guess what it is.'

'Well?'

'This,' he said, pointing at the squat building. 'Near to the bake-house, right? What is always near to any kitchen?' Taking Danforth's blank stare as encouragement, he went on. 'The drain. To get rid of waste. The source of the bad smell.'

'Martin, what do you hope to learn, exactly?' Danforth shook his head slowly. It was apparent to him that Martin had embarked on a useless mission, intent on proving some private theory. It was almost as though he wanted to discover a great conspiracy.

'I want to see how Hector got out. If he got out.' With that, he stepped towards the outhouse and pressed on the door. It scraped open. Danforth turned around, looking into the gloom for any sign of life. No lights. No sounds. No movements. He slid into the doorway after Martin.

Immediately Danforth raised a hand to his face, nudging the door shut with one foot. The smell was at its height, centuries of rotting food, human waste and mould. It was pitch black. 'Martin, I cannot see you. Where are you?' Fear tightened his throat. The repeated striking of a tinderbox answered him, as Martin brought a little candle to life.

'Never without one,' he smiled.

The light from the tiny flame did not do much, but it was enough to reveal that they were in a small, windowless room. Its only feature was a shallow flight of stone steps leading downwards. 'Must be ancient,' said Martin. 'It goes underground, this drain. Like a secret tunnel.'

'I am not going down there. A drain is a drain. Wade through monks' … leavings … yourself, sir.'

'Fine,' snapped Martin, a hard edge to his voice. 'Walk out

through the gate. I'll see you back at the inn.' Bending forward, he descended the steps.

Danforth stood for a few moments, the dark enveloping him, and then felt for the door. Grasping an iron ring, he pushed it open and stepped back into the night. He would not be coerced into some madcap scheme. He began to creep away from the entrance when a sudden noise reached him. Heavy footsteps were marching across the path, accompanied by cheerful whistling. He stood rooted to the spot until they died away, to be overtaken by the sound of the gates clanging shut. He was being locked in.

11

Panic seized him. He fought for control, willing his heart to slow. Wild thoughts raced through his mind: banging on the gate; rousing the Prior and announcing that he had been surveying the grounds and got locked in as he stopped for a piss; perhaps he could invent some urgent message and say he had come to convey it. Nothing seemed plausible. He ran a hand through his hair and bent low. He lurched to the drain house, threw himself in and kicked the door shut.

'Martin,' he cried, as loud as he dared. 'Martin, where are you?' He dropped to his knees and groped for the dip of the first step. By touch, he began to inch his way to the bottom of the worn stairs. As his feet splashed into black water, he cried out again, his voice echoing in both directions. 'Martin, come back here, damn you!'

After a few seconds came a rhythmic splashing and a bouncing light. Martin reached him, and in the glow of his candle were revealed the walls of a stone tunnel, tapering up to a vaulted, sandstone-ribbed ceiling. 'We are locked in, by God. How do we explain that to the Prior, sir? You have led us on a fool's errand, and we will look foolish if not criminal in being caught at it. The Cardinal, Martin! What will the Cardinal say, should he discover that his servants were trapped in an Abbey, creeping around when on his business?'

'Are you done?'

'Done? We shall both be undone by this!'

'Calm down, Mr Danforth. Look, this water goes on for a bit, and then falls into a channel with stone paths on either side. It leads back the way we came above ground. Towards the river. The old builders knew what they were about.'

Danforth squinted in the direction Martin had come from. The tunnel was like something out of a grand romance from centuries past, all grey stone and arches. All it lacked, unfortunately, was a procession of torches. They had come into it midway along – it ran ahead of and behind them, the water flowing surprisingly slowly the way they were going. 'We could be trapped down here. We have no idea where it leads,' said Danforth.

'We can find out then.' Martin clapped him on the shoulder and began to splash off again. Already Danforth could feel the hem of his robes beginning to soak through, the weight of them pulling down on his neck. 'Shit, and slide in it,' he hissed. It was one of the Cardinal's curses.

Martin had been right. After walking further than it felt they had walked above ground since entering the gates, the tunnel widened. The channel of water remained the same width, but instead of bleeding slimy greens and browns up into the stone walls, it fell between two flag-stoned paths. Danforth allowed the lither Martin to help him step out of the running water and onto the walkway on the right. As he did so, fear gripped him. Though not afraid of the dark, he was certainly afraid of the breathless and blind unknown, as the curving walls seeming to press down and in. The air was cold, the smell even fouler. The place seemed to have been given no attention, the stones half buried by dirt and piles of rat droppings.

'No one has set foot here for years, I should think,' said Danforth.

'No one with a broom, no. But it has to go somewhere.'

'The river, of course. But it will be blocked.'

'We'll see.'

They made slow progress in the dark, but Martin's candle held out. If anything, it seemed to glow brighter into the drain, as though the noxious airs gave it life. With no points of reference their direction was uncertain. Eventually Martin stopped, and Danforth bumped into him, before peering ahead.

'Ha! You see? A grate.' In front of them, thin iron bars descended from the ceiling.

'A broken grate. Look.'

Danforth leant forward and scowled. Martin was right. The rusted iron bars had been smashed away on the left walkway, allowing passage. They stepped lightly through the sewer water, around the collection of unidentifiable floating objects which bobbed forlornly against the grate, and up onto the other side. Bits of snapped iron jabbed down at them. 'Mind yourself,' said Martin. 'Catch your hand on one of those, and the cut will turn rotten and kill you before a physician can.'

'Just hurry,' said Danforth, his teeth beginning to chatter.

Through the grate, the stone pathways came to an abrupt end, and were replaced by sludgy silt, as though the drain itself had turned into a minor stream. Nearest the walls, the dirt was dry, and they pressed themselves against it.

'How far have we come?' asked Danforth. There was a change in the air. He sniffed at it. 'It is less odorous here.'

'Don't know. I think we must – here, wait. There's something. Danforth, I stepped on something. Merde!'

'We are in a drain, sir,' sniffed Danforth. Before he could say any more, the light wobbled and Martin gasped.

'Jesus Christ. Oh, hell, Danforth, I think I stepped on someone.'

Danforth drew his breath and resisted the urge to cross himself. 'Mr Martin, the light please.' He got no response. 'Martin, give me the light.' With trembling fingers, Martin passed it to him, and he bent down on one knee, holding it close.

On the ground at their feet, laid out along the wall of the drain, was something covered in a black sheet. Near the top sat a crucifix. Danforth picked it up. It was new, of polished wood. He set it aside and looked up at Martin. 'Shall I lift this?' Martin, his face shrouded in darkness, nodded, and Danforth swept up the black cloth. The movement caught the flame. It faltered but held.

It was a body.

'Christ Jesus, is it Hector? Is it a young man?'

Danforth said nothing, pouting as he let his eyes run over the corpse. It was desiccated, almost a mummy, the preserved flesh that was left turned to parchment. It was clothed, but much of what it was wearing had been eaten away. What was left was old-fashioned, the crude tunic and hood of the previous century. 'Is it him?' Martin persisted. He was not looking at the corpse.

'If it is, he has decayed himself unnaturally quickly. No, Mr

Martin, this poor fellow has been here since before I was a boy.' He waited for the jest, but it didn't come. 'The clothes, you see, the apparel. Always pay attention to the apparel of the dead. It tells us just as much about folk after death as it tells us when they live. Ho, what is this?' Around the body was scattered a random assortment of objects. Purses. Danforth picked one up and turned it upside down. Some coins fell. He retrieved one and held it to the light. 'Old. From the reign of the third King James.' He put it back by the corpse. 'There is a stone here too.' Next to the body was a broad chunk. Danforth held the light to it and traced a finger along the carvings. 'Music. Ancient music. A valuable thing.'

'What does it mean?' asked Martin, sounding agitated. 'I stepped on him, Jesus.'

'I think we have stumbled upon the den of a long-dead thief. Look at his head, Mr Martin.'

'Must I?'

'We are all come to it, sir. You have nothing to fear. Look.'

Martin briefly glanced down at the mummified corpse and then looked away again. 'So?'

'Unless the rats have had remarkable care in their nibbling, this creature has had his ears cropped. A thief. I should imagine that, in his day, he used this tunnel as a lair. A hole from which he could take from the Abbey or the town, hidden between both. No, I am not so interested in him.'

'Let's go, then. Let's get out of here.'

'You wished to find answers here, sir. I have no interest in the body, but what covered it.' If he expected some excitement, he was disappointed. 'This crucifix,' he went on, 'was freshly placed. And the black sheet. Did you mark it?'

'Yes.'

'A monk's cowl.' He picked it up and waved it again, this time triumphantly.

'Brother Hector's, you think?'

'It is possible. Likely, even. Our young Brother Hector made his escape through these tunnels; like us, he chanced upon this corpse, and, being a monk – to some degree – he covered it with the vestment he wished to be rid of and placed a crucifix.

I ask you, Mr Martin, does that sound like the action of a man on his way to butcher his lover?'

'No, indeed not. It sounds like what a good man would do.'

'A good man would not have a mistress, nor seek to depart his duty.'

'Can we go?'

'By all means.' Danforth picked up one of the coins and dropped it into the black hole of the body's mouth. 'You have crossed your Styx, sir,' he muttered, before replacing the black cowl. 'Lead on. Here.' He passed Martin the candle, and they continued through the subterranean tunnel, neither speaking. With alarm, they realised that tunnel ceiling began to lower, but, as it did, the sound of rushing water increased, and the air grew fresher still. Martin had to cover the candle flame with his hand as a breeze met them, carrying with it the wild smell of woodland. The tunnel, much tighter than it had been, ended in a forest of brush and scrub.

They emerged into a thicket by the Cart, where the drain's water rushed forward to join forces with its bigger brother. Both gulped in deep lungfuls of fresh air, uncaring of the brambles and twigs which plucked and nipped at their skin and clothing.

'So, where are we? Outside the Abbey's walls?' asked Martin.

'We must be. It would do little good to funnel their waste only a few yards away, within their same walls.'

'Thank God. But I was right, you have to admit.'

'About this Hector escaping the Abbey through the drain? Perhaps. Yes, I rather think you were. But what does that tell us?'

'That he escaped, he got away.'

'Away, into the woods by the river. The river where his lover was found slain, and he gone.'

'But you said he didn't do it.'

'I said no such thing. I presume nothing. If anything, we now have a channel from the Abbey to the river, where Kate Brody was washed up. I do not like it, but there it is. Anyone might have carried her along that tunnel.'

121

Martin kicked at a stone half-buried in the ground. Danforth realised that the younger man was nervous, his exhilaration at sneaking into the Abbey deflated. Probably he would expect him to be annoyed by the reckless adventure; probably he expected recriminations. Danforth stood quietly, shaking his cloak, unwilling to give the satisfaction of a predictable reaction. 'Should we report that body down there? The ancient thief?'

'Indeed we shall not. How might we account for finding it? "Father, we were clambering around like knaves in the bowels of your Abbey, because we suspect you and yours of murder, and we came upon a mouldering corpse. Kindly bury it." We should never live it down. No, Mr Martin, that poor creature has his grave. His dusty bones would only be thrown in the river, or some unconsecrated ground. He has the luck to be lie beneath one of Scotland's holy shrines. Let him lie.'

'The river is over there,' said Martin. 'We have to cross it to get back to the inn.'

'Then let us, before any of the Town Council discover us skulking about in the woods. I am freezing. Jesu, but how to explain to our hostess that we carry on us the stench of a sewer.'

'That's the good thing about city living, Mr Danforth,' said Martin, attempting a smile. 'You can smell like shit and no one notices any difference.'

Together they trooped through the undergrowth and back to town, shivering and stinking.

Later, Danforth wrote in his Book of Hours, 'Wise people think before they act. God forgive me. The Holy Place has secrets. God forgive them.'

Friday morning dawned bright and rosy, the clouds edged with cheerful pink hues. But the rains had left the streets and buildings washed out, like a painting faded and blurred with wear. Before Danforth and Martin could leave for church, a glowering Mistress Caldwell informed them that their new shirts had arrived. They returned to their rooms to change, and brought down the soiled bundles, Danforth asking their hostess if she might have them cleaned. Attempting conciliation, Martin informed her that there was no need to rush. 'I'll have Archie tend to them. Though his feet are more leaden than winged,' she said, giving Martin a smile before turning an acidulous look to Danforth. Evidently, he had not been forgiven for dealing with her roughly.

Freshly shod, they gave their customary morning glance to the horses. 'How do you fare, Woebegone,' asked Danforth, 'trapped and stabled with this Cur?'

'Eh?' screeched a petulant voice. It was Archie, lingering in his little shack at the back of the stables by the water trough. 'Ye call me a cur?'

'No, Archie,' said Danforth, 'I was speaking of Mr Martin's mount.'

'Oh.' His face brightened at horse talk.

'You are doing a passable job. You shall be rewarded for it.' The hint of a reward got Archie to his feet, and he began a little display of labour in tending the horses. Danforth and Martin turned away from the stable gate, chuckling.

'He's a good one, I think,' said Martin.

'Aye, perhaps. How are you, sir, after last night?'

'Fine,' said Martin. His eyes betrayed him. They were hollow, the black patches under them deep.

'It was not a pretty sight. I know that. Let us hope you have to look upon no more.'

'Have you thought on what we saw, sir? Come up with any … any solutions?'

'None that please me. Say a prayer for the poor soul this morning. You will feel better for it.'

'It's just … the thought of that Abbey, lying in splendour above the bones of a poor, dead nobody.'

'Do not think on it. Mr Martin, if you stopped to think of the bodies that lie beneath the earth, and have done since time immemorial, you would never again step – set – foot outside of your house.' Danforth had no wish to coddle. It had only been a dusty old corpse. 'Come.'

They made their way towards the market cross, intending to

climb the wynd to St Nicholas, and were stopped by a little crowd of hooting, jeering people. They spotted Mistress Clacher, her voice raised above the others; young Jardine, his eyes wide; Pattison the baillie, pushing and grabbing. Martin elbowed his way through them, Danforth following. Soon they found the source of the mirth. Scattered about the street, being picked up and passed around, were little scraps of paper. Martin snatched one from a woman's uncomprehending grasp and read it.

'The Cardinall ys ane whooremongere.' Danforth's face whitened. 'Sweet Jesus,' said Martin. 'But our libellers have lost their wit.' Burgesses – those who were not laughing and reciting the line – were trying to restore order. Regaining his composure, Danforth began collecting up some of the scraps, and then turned on the burgess who had a sheaf of the ragged papers in his hand.

'What is this, sir,' he said, his voice hoarse. 'We are servants of his Grace the Cardinal, and we will have the truth of it.' The burgess shot him a look half-apologetic, half-fearful, and then held out the pile of papers for him.

'These were thrown about the street, sir, during the night. None will claim knowledge of them. What are we to do? We have enough trouble here trying to keep the drinking and the fighting down.'

'You are to do nothing and to say nothing. This is our affair now.' A look of relief crossed the man's narrow features.

'Bless you, sir. Please explain, please tell the Cardinal that nothing of the like has taken place here before. We harbour no Lutherans in these holy lands. We are good Christian people, true in the faith and loyal. Some devil from abroad has passed through in the night to slander both his Grace and our burgh, sir.' His eyes were open and pleading. Danforth sensed the fear in him. He should welcome it. Fear, he supposed, ensured that men would stay true. But again, that was the thinking of an Englishman. It was the thinking of King Henry's spies and informers. No man should love God out of fear of reprisals.

'Silence. Disperse these people to their devotions and tell them that if any word of this is breathed abroad, they shall suffer for it. Bid them pray that they are forgiven for giving eyes and ears to the defamation of a man of the Church.'

Danforth turned his back on the nodding burgess, just as the man raised his voice to scream at the people to be about their business. The laughing and raillery gave way to low grumbles and mutters. Storming back up the High Street, Danforth held the cheap, soiled papers out in front of himself. Martin kept pace with him. 'Shall we neglect Mass this morning?' he asked.

'Yes. I have no desire to be in the company of such a people as these.'

They took the papers up to Danforth's room and spread them out on the desk next to one of the verses from Glasgow. Each newer page bore the same message, in the same ugly hand. Martin cast a critical eye over them. 'These are not the work of the Lutherans, or the university japesters, or whoever made merry with the Cardinal's name in Glasgow,' he said. 'The handwriting is different, so's the spelling. And here's no verse, but the crudest of slanders. No sir, I'd say that these words are the first blast this author has composed. There's nothing subtle in them.'

'I agree,' said Danforth. 'All writings carry in them something of the essence of their author, intended or otherwise.' For a second, the words from his Book of Hours echoed in his mind: 'Rember your love in yr gud prayers'. He blinked them away. 'Here,' he said, 'I perceive a base and bloody-minded creature: a person with no other desire than mischief. These bills were not made to hurt his Grace, but to attack us. Someone is playing a game with us, sir. Someone does not like our interest, and would divert us. Mr Martin, what does a man who writes do?'

'Think?' offered Martin.

'Often. Not always. What he always does is observe. Someone has been observing us, sir, and now hopes to confuse us. And in doing so, he has made a grave mistake.'

12

The afternoon saw clouds regather to block the sun, and Danforth and Martin again within the precincts of the Abbey demanding an audience with the Prior. The light in the room was poor, the fire causing tiny moths to chase wildly about the painted and tapestried walls. With pursed lips Walker leant over his desk, mouthing the words of the papers Danforth had thrust before him. He then turned a blank gaze upwards.

'I don't know what you would have me say.'

'Is that so? These vile things were found strewn across the streets of the lands belonging to this Abbey, Father. I would hope you shall quickly think of something.'

'I might ask the Town Council to start privations, raids.' His voice was noncommittal. 'The news out of the south is that men wax weary of this war, and blame the Cardinal for it. Perhaps some grow lusty.'

'Father, I think you do not grasp the serious nature of this offence. Such papers have been found in Glasgow, and might now have spread here. An attack on the Cardinal is an attack on the Church, and an attack on the Church is an attack on the Abbey.' At this a flicker of realisation crossed the Prior's lined face.

'The Abbey threatened?'

'Naturally. An attack on the Church's good order is an attack on us all: on the faith. Are you not assiduous in protecting the Mother Church?'

'I am as true in allegiance as any man living,' said the Prior. 'I will do anything to defend this house from without.'

Martin and Danforth exchanged glances, and then the former took a breath. 'Would that extend to harbouring and protecting a murderer, Father?'

The Prior's eyes popped and he gripped at the edges of his desk, the veins in his fingers purpling. 'I .. I ...' he stammered. Danforth almost pitied him. Then he remembered the body of the dead girl, and he took up Martin's questioning.

'You must be frank with us, Father. These notes, these vulgar scribbles, are not of the nature of those posted by the Lutheran heretics in Glasgow. Plainly these latest affronts were designed to distract me and Mr Martin from investigating the death of Kate Brody, and her connection to this house.'

'But I told you only yesterday, sir, I have no knowledge of that matter. It was her father killed her and rightly he shall hang for it. I cannot think why you persist in making mischief, if not to bring this Abbey into contempt.' His eyes flew between Martin and Danforth's, wary and sharp. Outsight the light changed, and the room took on a warmer red glow.

'And I suppose,' said Martin, 'you shall claim no knowledge of one Brother Hector Watson.' The name hung in the air between them for a long moment. The Prior then closed his eyes and hunched over his desk, his head in his hands. His lips moved rapidly in prayer, as Martin and Danforth exchanged glances again. They had been unsure what reaction they would receive, but neither had imagined this.

At length, the Prior raised his face to them and tears gleamed in the corners of his eyes, ready to flood the nearby furrows. 'To whom have you been speaking?' he asked in a low, strangulated voice.

'That is of no consequence, Father. When we said we wish to make no trouble we spoke in earnest.'

'What … what are you going to do?'

'As I said,' said Danforth, 'nothing prejudicial to your estate nor that of the Church.'

'We seek,' said Martin, 'only the truth, whatever that might be.'

The Prior rose from his seat and crossed the room, gazing into the fire. 'Brother Hector,' he said. 'Young Brother Hector. I had such hopes of him. I watched him grow as a scholar, gentlemen, from the time he was the bairn of burgesses, before the Lord took them, and before that they bid me and the order have charge of him. When they died, I took him in as a novice. Like a son to me, a child. That was my error. He was not meant for the order, though I could not see it. Lord, that child loved to talk. That alone might have warned me he was not suited for a silent order. And the spirit in him! The joie de vivre, Mr Martin.' He turned and smiled weakly at Martin, then looked back towards the fire, its glow colouring his face. 'It could not last of course, a bright young creature like him in a cage such as this. The Abbot, had he been here, might have seen that, but I have been so eager to make decisions.' Slowly he shook his head.

'What of the girl, Father? What of Kate Brody?'

'That daft little chit. It was always a mistake to have her here. We are temperate men, those of us who are born to this life, but we are of frail flesh and blood yet. Brother Hector was unrefined, a child himself. I turned my eyes from it, though I knew they grew close. I came upon them in the cloister some weeks back, his arms around her and his lips on her cheek. I sent her out. I slapped him, and was frightened at the anger and hatred in his eyes. I prayed that he would find the strength to overcome her wanton temptations.'

'Yet,' said Martin, 'it is apparent that he did not.'

'No.' The Prior turned away from the fire. He wiped away tears with a knuckle and then smoothed a loose hair. He took his seat before them again. 'No, they made their plans and they fled, and, God forgive me, I did all I could to clear the sordid tale from the Abbey. By my faith, I hoped never to hear of them again, that they had got clean away and would never be connected to this place by thought or deed.'

'But now the girl lies buried, murdered most brutally, and this Hector missing.'

'Yes.'

'You can see, Father,' said Danforth, 'that there is perforce some suspicion that Brother Hector may have killed his lover, whether in some terrible crisis of faith or in some other panic to rid himself of her company?' To their surprise the Prior smiled.

'Your thoughts run as sordid as the affair itself,' he said. 'No, gentlemen, you shoot at the wrong mark. I tell you I have known this boy since he was but a green sapling. He grew to be a lusty youth, it is true, but he could no more have taken that wench's life than I.'

'Then we are at an impasse, I think,' said Martin.

'I do not see how that is so, sirs. The girl's father stands accused, and I see no other who might be indicted. By my faith, my only worry is that he has struck down our young Hector, and his body is lying yet unmourned. I must ask you again, gentlemen, are you minded to carry your knowledge of this matter abroad, though it should hurt this Abbey and all who worship here?'

'No, Father,' said Danforth. 'We spoke in earnest. If it is true that you have done nothing but look through your fingers at the disgrace of two young people, and buried evidence that one of your order dallied with the murdered girl – and if it be true that you have no other knowledge pertaining to that crime – then you have nothing to fear. I would only that you had spoken freely to us earlier, that you might have been spared this. It is secrecy between the brethren of the faith that gives our enemies leave to attack us, and ammunition.'

The Prior bowed his head. 'Shall you take these wicked papers away from me?' Martin leant over the desk, gathering them up and depositing them in his pocket. 'Those are nothing to do with any man here,' he added with feeling. 'And I apologise to you, sirs. I understand that you wished to come to this place on pilgrimage, and am sorry that you have found only disorder and disharmony. When the murderer be himself hanged, things will be as before.'

'If,' said Danforth, 'the murderer be found.'

As they made their way back to the burgh, a thoughtful Martin turned to Danforth. 'I thought the man spoke true.'

'As did I. And yet he has lied to us before, and therefore may be practiced in the art. Though these wretched bills seem not to be the work of such a man as he.'

'Not by their appearance, no,' agreed Martin. 'They appear rather as the work of one unlearned, unskilled. Lacking knowledge of this practice of defaming the great in verse. Yet that might be their art. Some man of knowledge might wish to disguise his guilt by inducing us to suspect an ignorant dolt. Their crudity might be a trick. Ah, I find I cannot but see evil in this rainy place.'

'The thought did occur to me,' said Danforth. His head was beginning to ache. 'And it troubles me. When men begin to doubt and suspect others there is no end to it. The suspicion divides and then falls upon so many that no man is true any longer. One might hear tales and imagine the ways of a killer – his nature and means, his fashion and attire – and then force that crooked suit of clothes upon any man one does not take to, however ill it befits him. In faith, I find myself bone-weary of this whole matter. I do not know who to believe, for rather it strikes me that the Prior speaks true and yet Brody speaks true also. That leaves us with an innocent man imprisoned and no suspects respectful enough to cast doubt on his guilt. Whilst someone wishes to distract us with scurrilous bills. And still a man is missing who might hold the key to the whole. Are you to come with me back to the inn?' They stood where the market cross met the High Street, the familiar sound of musical revelry floating through the rain from several dark and secretive vennels.

'No, sir. If you don't mind, I shall go for a proper wash at the barber's and have a bite afterwards. I suggest you do likewise. I do not like to turn nurse, but you have not been eating as you should.' Danforth looked at him, amused, and Martin decided to venture further. 'May I speak freely with you, Mr Danforth?'

'Pray do.'

'I do not wish to make a window into your soul, sir. But I know that you had a wife and child, now lost, in England. I know also that some strange imbalance of the humours has resided within you since you lost them, sir, since the plague carried them off. But you were spared. I feel certain they wouldn't want you to live a life of strictures and self-punishment, wrapped in a hair-shirt of your own devising. You do not choose to tell me what it is that leads you to punish yourself, and I don't choose to press you. I ask only that you let it go, sir. Eat, drink and live. Listen to that music. It is a wonderful gift.' When he had finished, he stood back, as though expecting a storm.

'You are an odd fellow, Mr Martin. Though I think a kindly one, despite your tiresome ways. May I trouble you with a question?'

'One question begs another.'

'Were you ever to be married, sir?' Danforth felt himself begin to redden, and suddenly hated himself for thinking to ask so personal a question. But the words had been spoken. He might as well satisfy his curiosity. 'Have you lost a love?' Thankfully the younger man did not laugh at him.

'In faith, sir, I did once hope to be married, but it did not happen.'

'I am sorry. Did you lose the young lady?'

'I did. Yet not in the same manner as you lost your wife. No, the girl I hoped to marry did not have the like desire. Marion; she was a sharp little kitty, but very lovely. She married some other, or so I believe.' A faraway look had come into Martin's eyes. 'Yet I take comfort that it was not to be, and there might yet be another. There are a great many turtledoves in the sky. Were I a clever man I might turn the melancholy memories to poesy. Alas, I am not. What compels you to ask, my friend?'

'Nothing. It is nothing. Perhaps I do not ask enough questions. Or at least not enough of the right ones. It is good of you to indulge me. Thank you for your care. And enjoy your meal.'

Danforth continued up the High Street towards the Oakshawside, ignoring the music that drifted towards him.

Grateful to find no sign of Mistress Caldwell, Danforth climbed the stairs to his bedroom. He removed his robes, doublet and boots and sat down in his shirtsleeves. A new entry went into his book:

Remember to beware of false prophets, who come to you in sheep's clothing but inwardly are ravenous wolves. You will recognize them by their fruits. Are grapes gathered from thornbushes, or figs from thistles?

After 'thistles', he wrote, in a more childish hand, 'Scotland, where I do live'. In a nod to comfort, he got up and found his pack, which he placed at the head of the mattress as a makeshift pillow. He closed his eyes and settled down to doze, his cloak pulled over himself. He could feel his heartbeat in his temples, and felt it slow as the sharp headache began to fade. The sensation of each beat washing the pain out was pleasant. He felt himself drift, felt the business of the libels and the mystery of the missing monk become as nothing. His doze had already developed into a long, satisfying nap when an almighty bellow found its way up the stairs.

He jerked up and stepped into his boots, not bothering to pull on his doublet and robes, threw open his door and flew down the stairs. Martin, freshly shaven and cheeks gleaming, was not far behind him. When they reached the bottom, they found the extraordinary tableau of Mistress Caldwell with her thick arms wrapped around a scrawny, bearded figure that had fallen to its knees.

'What ails you, mistress,' cried Danforth, 'are you robbed? Does this vagabond do you mischief?' Martin held a dirk in his hand. Caldwell paid neither of them heed. Her eyes were searching the pitiful creature's face, gazing into rolling bloodshot orbs.

'What has that hoor done to you, Tam? What miseries has she inflicted upon you? Oh, but it is yourself, it is yourself. Oh, sweet, merciful Jesus and all the blessed saints.' Finally, she seemed to become aware of the presence of her lodgers. She turned to them, the ribbons in her hair – laced up in gaudy bows – bouncing. A smile spread across her face as she announced, 'It is Tam, sirs; it is my own Thomas Kennedy, escaped from the tortures of his vicious, thievin' hoor and come back to me.' For a heartbeat Danforth was reminded of the carved saints along the wall of the Abbey, their serene expressions now carved onto the doughy, grey face of his hostess.

13

'Regard, gentlemen, what she's has done to him,' cried Mistress Caldwell. 'He has nothin'. He stands even in the clothes he left in two years since, and no' a penny to bless himself.'

Tam Kennedy was certainly a sorry sight. His eyes were wild, his hair and beard unkempt. What must once have been a handsome, tall man had grown desiccated and shrunken. His ill-fitting suit of clothes was all that marked him as a well-to-do burgess, the rich velvets unmarked save for some discolouring around the chest, where his filthy, matted beard had left faded but indelible stains. 'The war,' was all he could bark, his voice rusty and hoarse.

'Pray do somethin' for him, sirs,' said Mistress Caldwell. 'He's ravin', I can't get sense of him, nor will he tell me what's been done to him or how he came to return.'

Before Danforth could cross to him, Archie made an appearance from the back of the house. He rubbed his eyes in disbelief, and then shouted, 'the master's come hame. Whit's it a' aboot?'

'He's no time for you, you wretch,' yelled Mistress Caldwell, and the boy, pouting, turned and left. 'Please, sir, get sense from him. Have him tell me where he's been, what he's done wi' our money.'

Danforth bent before Kennedy, recoiling from the sour breath. 'Mr Kennedy, can you hear me?' The only response was a groan, and a thin trickle of spittle running from the corner of purplish lips. His breath rattled out, his chest racking with it. He might have been trying to say 'Tam,' but could get no further than 'Tah'. Danforth held a hand before his face and moved it around, but the eyes did not register anything.

'What is it, what ails him?' asked Mistress Caldwell.

'I know not, mistress. I am no physician. This looks to be the result of hard living, of the kind usually suffered by the poor. What time is it?'

'Past seven o'clock.'

'Is it possible? I must have slept longer than I expected. Mistress, know you of any physician in the burgh?'

'There's none, sir.'

'Are all medicinal needs tended by the Abbey, all sicknesses remitted to the infirmary there?'

'Only by special permission – and of course if you plead poverty and desperation, like a lowly beggar desirous of Christian charity, then they'll take you for a space. I shouldn't like to drag my husband down to the Abbey, show him as he is before the burgh like a jester in a mockin' play. He's no beggar, but a free man and a burgess. They're no' a hospital, sir; they give charity, not physic.' Defiance had raised her voice, her bearing turned proud.

'I can understand that, knowing this burgh as I have come to.' Silently Danforth wondered if it was she who would play the jester in any such performance. 'Tomorrow we might fetch an apothecary who can give aid. There is one, I think, off the market cross.'

'Apothecaries, fie. They're no better than the physicians, and they're goddamned fools,' said Martin.

'Yes, sir,' she said, ignoring him. 'A new man, come here in the summer. Though I've no knowledge of his skill, for I'm ever in rude health. But can you do nothin' for him tonight?'

'We might put him to bed,' said Martin, sheathing the dirk still clutched in his hand. 'There's a flock bed in your rooms, I think?'

'Aye,' she said. 'Come, Tam.' She pulled him up with a grunt, and Danforth and Martin were surprised at the height of him. In healthier days, he must have been a rare giant, and even in his shrunken state he was a tall man. The three of them managed to manoeuvre the delirious, ranting Kennedy through the small passage and throw him down on the bed, his wife patting and fussing and making soothing noises. The big man closed his eyes and began snoring instantly, his untamed beard quivering.

'Thank you, gentlemen,' said Caldwell, in her element. Danforth smiled at her. He felt sorry for handling her so roughly the previous day. There was something pathetic in seeing the unkempt ogress suddenly transformed into the picture of wifely devotion by the reappearance of a man who had humiliated and demeaned her. 'I'm sorry that your evenin' has been disturbed.'

'It's no disturbance, mistress, when Odysseus returns to Penelope,' said Danforth, drawing confused looks from Martin and Mistress Caldwell. 'But I should like to sleep properly; I find my strength peculiarly sapped of late.' He gave her a little bow and turned towards the stairs, joined by Martin, who whispered, 'she's a damned fool to accept that wreckage back. Better to live alone than with such a man as that.'

'She has little choice in the matter,' said Danforth when they reached the top. 'She married the brute, and has the fault of it. Though I doubt he will prove a help to her, nor a support, even if his presence is a comfort. That creature is not like to live long. He has come hither to die; I heard it in his chest. And did you note the colouring of him? His skin turns to wax; it is almost luminous. I have seen that before. It presages death, as though the skin dies first, knowing what it protects has no chance of life.'

'Mon dieu. You are right, then, to let the damned apothecary find the will to tell her. It shall serve the bugger right. They're too smooth of tongue, that breed, like the devil himself. At any rate, I shouldn't fancy the job of it. Not for wealth or a pretty girl, even. Goodnight, sir.'

'Goodnight, Martin.'

The Book of Hours was open again. He read through the parable of the lost son, but found nothing in it. He flipped backwards. November was proving a busy month for entries. 'Men alter', he wrote, 'very greatly in their travels, whether by vice or virtue. Pray God that I am not like he.'

He returned to his mattress, hoping to regain his dreamless, interrupted sleep. He pulled out his rosary, but only got to six before his mind wandered and he had to put it down. In being forced to think again about death, something had begun to trouble him. The word 'war' played on his mind.

14

He rose before the sun, and padded around his bare room, thinking, before Martin woke. He lit a small nub of candle that had lain buried in his pack, and looked again over the papers that had been dropped around the High Street. Something about them was vaguely familiar, but whenever it drifted close enough into his mind's eye that he might grasp it, it danced away again, laughing, before he could reach out.

As he sat looking, his stomach growling, he was startled by a loud bang at the front door of the inn. The window in his room was too small and mean to allow him to see anything, so he went downstairs. Mistress Caldwell was blocking the front door. 'On no account,' she was saying 'this is no fault of mine nor any of my folk. That place is intended for the security of the burgh, and this is no' the first time that a creature has–'

'Trouble, Mistress Caldwell?' asked Danforth. She turned to him, looking irritable, her eyes ringed with black. She must have lain awake through the night tending her ruined husband, although at some point she had changed into a gayer dress, more befitting a merry goodwife. She attempted to give him a smile, with ghastly results.

'Mr Danforth. You're a man of authority, and lately engaged in the business of that foolish Brody girl. Please, come, you won't believe this. They've let the man go!'

Danforth crossed to the door, his heart thumping. Baillie Pattison stood there, his face even more drawn than usual. The matter, he realised, must be important to have got a town baillie out on a cold morning. In his hand, he carried an unlit lantern, its shutters closed. He could not even muster up scorn for Danforth. Instead he said quietly, 'Brody is gone. In the night. He has flown the Tolbooth.'

Danforth was momentarily lost. 'How can this be? He was kept close.'

'That fat fool Logan, our gaoler. He opened the cell to make sport of the man in the night, and claims Brody leapt at him, struck him down. He will face punishment for it, be assured, and none of his badly written reports protesting innocence will plead for him. It is not the first time he has allowed a prisoner escape the Tolbooth. It's not as secure as it ought to be. Might as well have given him a key. Perhaps if we had hanged the beast immediately...' he added, the scorn finally making an appearance.

'Then you might have been brought to task rather than Logan. Have you any idea where the man has flown?'

'None. Although he railed against the monks. Semple is informing the Prior. They are quite safe from the rabid fool though, behind those walls. It would take an army to bring them down.' A red blush crept into his sallow, gaunt cheeks at the ill-chosen words, and he hurried on. 'My guess is he has fled the burgh, but we are searching the town lest he has crept into some hole hereabouts. In fact, we're minded to search each house, as we have searched along the High Street, the Causeyside to the Espedair, and into the Oakshawside and Prior's Croft. If Mistress Caldwell would allow us entry, we could finish here and turn to the Well Meadow and Under the Wood.'

'My husband,' announced Mistress Caldwell, her voice turned haughty, 'has returned.'

'Kennedy is back in the burgh?' asked Pattison, raising an eyebrow. 'When?'

'Yesterday evening, about seven o'clock,' said Danforth. 'Mistress Caldwell, I shall show the baillie through the house and garden, if you wish to attend upon your husband.'

'Very well,' she shrugged. 'Keep your voices low. I don't wish Kennedy disturbed, no' in his condition.' She retreated through the passageway to her husband who, by the sound of it, still snored.

Danforth led Pattison upstairs and showed him into his room. The baillie eyed the libellous bills curiously, but when he spoke it was not about them. 'So Kennedy is returned.'

'It would seem so.'

'And fit to return as a burgess and make this place profitable, I trust. God, but look at it – a fine home turned into a pit. If he's not to be hauled before the courts ecclesiastical for his spiritual crimes, of course.'

'I doubt that Mr Kennedy will answer to anyone save God,' said Danforth, crossing himself.

'He's in a poor state, then?'

'Look upon him yourself when we venture down. He is not like to live long, by my reckoning, though I shall summon the apothecary to attend on him.'

'His whore must have ravished him to death. I can believe that,' said Pattison. 'A forward bitch if ever there was one. Married a man near seventy when she was sixteen, and then all the time taking old Kennedy in sin.' Pattison smiled at the reheated gossip of yesteryear. 'Still,' he said with a wink, 'if Kennedy is suffering now for it, I reckon those two years will have been worth it to the old dog, with such a wife as her downstairs. I wouldn't mind going that way myself one day.'

Danforth said nothing, already tired of the man. They woke Martin who, rubbing sleep from his eyes and throwing on his clothes, absorbed the news of Brody's escape from the Tolbooth with avid interest. 'Well it's not exactly the Bastille, is it?' was his assessment.

'Pah,' snapped Danforth. 'Frenchman are so backward they wouldn't walk out of an unlocked prison without the express command of their masters.' Martin only laughed. Danforth felt a strange stab of jealousy; Martin could only be six or seven years younger than himself and yet he seemed able to snap from sleep to alertness in a click of the fingers. Danforth himself usually required a quarter of an hour's burrowing and rolling in his bed before his mind adjusted to temporal concerns. The trio then stumped downstairs and into the Kennedy living quarters. Pattison's eyes ran over the master, and it was his turn to cross himself, drawing a frown from their hostess. Danforth averted his eyes from the wasted form, turning his attention instead to the meagre possessions with which Kennedy had left his wife, and to which he had returned: her chipped washbowl and chairs, her tattered account rolls and sagging, bare walls. The only valuable thing left had been the immoveable bed that he was once again infecting. They passed out of the backdoor and into the garden.

Not much had changed, save the rain turning much of the space into a marsh. They skirted the puddles and inspected the back fence, which formed a makeshift town boundary. Mistress Caldwell's brambles and nettles were still serving as defences. Some dew and lingering rainfall had left little pearls of water between the twigs and branches, and the strong smell of wet greenery wafted from them, an antidote to the foul airs that Kennedy had brought home as a souvenir. The branches beyond rose like a cluster of arthritic, badly burned hands. They swayed, creaked and crackled in a light breeze, disturbing some birds.

Satisfied that Brody had not broken the fence, they crossed back towards the house, detouring right to the low wall that formed the back of Archie's squalid little wooden hut. Pattison rapped and eventually Archie appeared, bundles of wet straw in his arms. 'Ho, wretch – did you see anyone abroad in the night?' Archie shook his head. 'Speak, boy, or I'll rip your tongue from your head.'

'Och' said Martin, 'there is no need to be so hard on the boy. Archie, did anyone rouse you last night?'

'No, sir,' he said, trembling under the baillie's stare.

'And how fare our horses?'

'Well, sir,' he said, looking up and smiling. 'Very well. Ah had a care whit ye said and gied them extra care, an' Ah don't 'hink an ostler anywhere'd dae better. No, sir, no' even the king's.'

'That's very good, Archie. Thank you.' The boy beamed, gave them a bow and returned to the horses.

'Well, gentlemen, the accursed fellow has not passed through here, nor any other house in the Oakshawside or Prior's Croft. I doubted it, in truth. If he has even a little wit to him, he will have run quickly, and like as not he will fall as a beggar or die on the road. The hue and cry is out; if he's found, he'll hang for escaping and if he's not, then the matter is likewise at an end. His daughter murdered and he, the accused, flown. It is not the end I would like to have made to it, but it need concern us – and you, and the Cardinal – no longer. Good morning to you, gentlemen.' He gave them a stiff bow and walked back towards the house, his lantern tucked under an arm.

Danforth and Martin waited for him to depart before they re-entered the house. 'What news?' asked Mistress Caldwell.

'The devil has not molested your garden,' said Danforth. 'And Pattison thinks the matter may now lie. Brody will be dead on the road from a journey he cannot hope to make, else found and brought back to swing.' His voice was emotionless. 'But we have other business, and we have neglected it too long. I came here as a pilgrim, not a coroner, and yet I have let my former trade catch me and bend me to it, as Zeus condemned Sisyphus to continually roll his boulder uphill. But first we pledged you an apothecary.'

Before they left the inn, Danforth returned to his room and, finding the rejected apple Martin had brought him – still serviceable – the two went outside. Further down the street huddles of people were gossiping on their way to Mass. Danforth turned his back on them and went to the gate of the stable. Finding the latch hanging loose, he went in and split the apple, giving half to Woebegone. The Cur would not take anything from him, so he passed his half to Martin, who split it into quarters and gave one apiece to Mistress Caldwell's palfrey and Coureur. The black horse gobbled, its tail swishing. Archie appeared from the garden, stepping over the low wall. A sheepish look stole over his face. 'Ah've fed the horses,' he volunteered.

'I don't doubt it,' said Martin.

'But you have let them stamp at the lock.' Archie peered around Danforth, to where the gate was lying open, its bolt shaken loose. 'The runaway could have taken any one of these if he'd come this way.'

'Oh,' said Archie.

'Have it fixed.'

'And do not,' said Martin, reaching into his robes for coins, 'let your mistress know of the expense or the oversight.'

They left the boy hiding his meagre placks, exited the stable

140

– shutting it lightly so that it would not swing open – and strode down the High Street. The clouds hung low above them. The weather had turned mild. Although it was not falling, the prospect of more rain loomed. 'They are quiet now, but the Hyades beckon,' said Danforth as they passed the poorer tenements.

'The whom?' sighed Martin wearily.

'The rainy ones. The daughters of Atlas who open the clouds and let the water pour.'

'I do wish they'd find some other occupation.' Danforth chuckled. They attended St Nicholas first, where the churchyard had turned into a pond overnight, and then went in search of the apothecary, Martin grumbling all the way that he would have no traffic with the man. The shop lay down one of the narrow vennels off the market cross: one of the dark alleys which turned into a place of festivity and carousal whenever night fell. The haphazard buildings on either side hung over it like crooked judges.

The inside of the shop was the usual jumble of items designed to cure the sick and hoodwink the gullible. Along the shelves were bottles of varicoloured syrups and potions, magnets and lodestones, herbs and delicate little animal bones. The whole place smelled strange, sweet and spicy. That was, thought Danforth, part of its allure. Always that which was unknown – the cause of a knotted stomach or a pain in the joints – must be countered with something equally unknown, foreign and exotic. Martin was reaching for a bottle of some black substance, when a nervous voice caused him to jump.

'The remains of an Egyptian prince from Africa, ground into a tincture most meet to staunch bleeding under skin.' Danforth and Martin turned in unison to the shadows in the rear of the shop, where a nervous young bespectacled man stood watching them. His gingery hair stood up in tufts around a patch that was prematurely thin. Before him was a counter sagging under the weight of scales, pestles and mortars. 'I do not mean to cause affright, gentlemen,' he said, looking at their robes. His eyes fixed on Danforth, and hope mingled with clinical interest, both magnified by the glasses, rose in them. 'You are ill, sir,' he divined. 'No flux of the stomach, I think, but it is lack of sleep from an ache in the head that ails you. Rhubarb, mace and wormwood–'

'I am not ill,' said Danforth, his voice tight and his tone short.

'Then you, sir? You look closely at me. If it is your eyes which ail you, I have had some success with slugs–'

'As full of vigour and spirit as a young bull.' Martin flashed him a nasty smile. 'My eyes are sharp and my teeth are complete and unmarred. You'll get no bloody business by me.'

The apothecary's tone changed, something business-like taking charge. 'I am very busy, gentlemen, mixing some herbs for customers. What brings you?'

'We have a grievous sick man in our lodging,' explained Danforth, 'For myself I cannot see that he will live. But we have given our pledge to the hostess that we should bring her one skilled in physic to examine him. What is your name, Master Apothecary?'

The apothecary gave them a long, measuring look, full of doubt. He then cast a glance around the shop. 'Zachary, sir. I am engaged in labour here, delicate work.' He waved his hand towards the scales, on which was piled a little pyramid of sparkling powder. 'And I cannot leave this place unattended; these items are of great value. There is a burgess in town – I shan't name him – who finds hair on his mattress each morning, and would have me mix the grease of a fox with crushed beetles, to form a paste that I know prevents baldness. I am expecting a lady who wishes to pay the credit she owes for my salving her belly worms – most expensive stuffs, she took. I regret I have no apprentice; I'm new to the burgh. I would not have my name and credit slandered by visiting private homes as though I were a physician. I supply medicines only – that is my trade.'

'Yet I have no doubt you will do it for coins, as any of your profession will,' asked Martin, and Danforth gave him a sharp, silencing look.

'We are not come hither to examine your ethics. There is no physician in this burgh to whom we can turn. Master

Apothecary, I am certain you do not work, sleep and live in this place upon each hour. You might lock it for a spell and accompany us. You will,' he added, sighing, 'be paid for your labour and the loss of your earning.'

The apothecary needed no further encouragement. With a grin, he disappeared under the counter, rummaging for a cloak and his key. Martin gave Danforth a quizzical look. 'You're generous, Mr Danforth.'

'Not so very,' he returned, smiling. 'I shall deduct the sum from our payment to Mistress – or, I suppose, to Mr Kennedy. The Cluniacs are unparalleled tutors indeed.'

15

The apothecary trailed in their wake as they took a brisk walk back to the Oakshawside. He eyed the drab exterior with distaste, and his lip curved further downwards when he entered. Danforth led him through the back to where the patient was taking laboured, ragged breaths. His eyes were now open, but glazed and sightless. After a moment's revulsion, the apothecary turned professional. Mistress Caldwell stood back from the bed. 'Please, save him. His breath grows weak.'

Martin and Danforth stood back, irresolute, unsure of either the necessity or the propriety of their presence. Martin wore a hard, distrustful look, not taking his eyes from the apothecary. It was almost, thought Danforth, as though he expected the man to produce a dirk and put an end to the fellow himself. The apothecary instead put an ear to the rattling chest, then sniffed at the sour breath, pulling back as he did so. He touched the man's eyelids, mumbling under his breath, then examined dirty hands and broken nails. After his examination he stood, turning to Danforth and Martin with a shake of the head. 'I believe I can ease his chest, sirs, but it is no sure thing. This man will die.'

Mistress Caldwell let out a little croak. 'A very thorough examination, Zachary,' said Martin, the sarcasm heavy, 'and it's glad we are that we've brought you here to upset the lady and tell us what we might suspect for ourselves. Even an apothecary might learn to sometimes be gentle. This is the fellow's wife.'

'Oh,' said Zachary, a blush rising in his cheeks. 'I apologise, mistress.'

'Do somethin' for him, won't you? He will no' speak, he will no' tell me where he's been, nor of … well, of our money.' She gripped and released her faded skirts over and over. 'Do *somethin'* for him.'

'I can spread a poultice on his chest,' said the apothecary, removing his spectacles and wiping them on his robe, 'if you will allow me to return with it. It may ease the phlegm and restore his speech, but I can go no further than that it may.'

Mistress Caldwell turned pleading eyes on them. Rolling his eyes, Danforth said, 'go to, sir. We shall find payment for your labours.' The apothecary nodded and, tightening his cloak around his neck, hurried out.

'That man is no' a physician, sirs,' said Mistress Caldwell. 'He might have physic will aid my husband, and yet be in error about his death.' Martin cast his eyes to the ground.

'I fear he spoke true,' said Danforth, with as much gentleness as he could manage. 'You husband is not like to live, I fear. Yet take comfort that he has returned to you. Better he died at peace by his wife, as a man should, than ...'

'Yes,' she said, tears prickling. 'Better that. I thank you both, gentlemen, for fetchin' the apothecary. It's a rare kindness, I'd no' have expected it. If he can smooth my husband's passage that'll be a comfort. And I shall take the price of his physic and his time from your bill.'

'There is no need, mistress,' said Danforth, earning a surprised and respectful look from Martin. 'You have done us service by allowing us to lodge here without settling our bill in advance. Consider it our gratuity.' She smiled– the first real smile they had seen on her unhappy, ageing face, and they left her.

They retreated to Danforth's room. The ceiling had begun to leak, thin droplets of dirty water falling onto the floor by the desk. When heavy rain fell during the night – as most nights it did – it became a frustrating stream, leeching into and between the loose floorboards. The room had become a cell – a meagre and mean prison no better than the one from which Brody had made his escape. It had even taken on an unwholesome smell of its own, of dampness and mossy thatch. As though reading his mind, Martin spoke.

'Jesus, what a dank place, better fit for a prison than a gentleman's lodging.'

'In truth, I was thinking the same, Mr Martin. I am beginning to feel as though we have been forced into exile in this burgh, or rather cast adrift here, the rain forming an unforgiving sea around us, as Scylla and Charybdis stopped sailors passing out of the Straits of Messina.'

'Now that one I know, sir. The sailors could not avoid one danger without coming close to another, to be either smashed to pieces or sucked below the raging waters. What an uncanny tale.'

Danforth nodded, a little put out that Martin had understood his reference and gone beyond it. Since he had begun softening – a little – to the younger man, he had preferred to see their relationship as one of master and student, of the wise elder in comfortable superiority over the ignorant and callow youth. All relationships must follow some model, and that one pleased him best. It would not do at all if Martin started matching him in wit. He would have to reach more deeply into his store of classics.

'I do wonder what's happening in the world, the real world' continued Martin. 'We have heard nothing of the Cardinal – or perhaps it is that Prior Walker has sent us nothing of him.'

'He is a man of the Church. He would not keep knowledge from us.'

'You needn't pretend you have any greater liking for him than I. Indeed, I think you like dislike him even more, to be honest. You just forbear to show it.'

'As a man I find him sleekit and cowardly, I shall admit. But the office is greater than the man, and it is the office which I commend.'

'Very good, sir, yet very English. In England they teach you a love of institutions, no matter who provides their face. In Scotland we are loyal to men for their natures and deeds.'

'Hold your peace. I am loyal to the Cardinal and King James. When the King of England became corrupted he lost my loyalty, and so did his crown and kingdom. How does that for your notion?' Martin shrugged. 'There, you see?' he continued, glad that he had scored a point. 'We are not all so easily understood. There are neither Scotsmen nor Englishmen any longer, but only heretics and those knit together in the true faith.'

'The faith is important to you, sir.'

'As it should be to all good men,' said Danforth, unsure if it was a question. His faith, he had come to believe, had provided him with a new family, a new father, in a foreign land.

'That is so. And do you find that Scotsmen agree with you? About there being neither English nor Scots, I mean.'

'Yes. Although I confess that English birth can weigh heavily when that madman Henry waxes bellicose. Still, those who see the real troubles that infect this island see as I do.'

'Yet you might on occasion remove the scales from your eyes, and see that not everything's unity and kinship, not even in a realm that acknowledges the authority of the Pope. Even within the Roman Church there are wicked souls, sheltering behind vestments and cowls. There are priests who make free with harlots, monks who turn their gaze on boys, and nuns who live openly with the brothers of their orders too.'

'And God sees and judges these misdemeanours, and lets his judgements be known through the Holy Father. Pope Paul is a wise man, as stout in his hatred of corruption as in his curbing of the Lutherans. Any more of your blasphemy and I shall think you favour the Reformist creatures and their complaints.'

'No, sir. Not I. I understand the world well enough.'

'Is that so, young Martin?'

'Yes. It is like this. Suppose that a man has a grievance and wishes redress from the king. Or suppose,' he said, cocking a thin, black eyebrow, 'that he craves a pardon for some imagined transgression. Does he march into his Grace's inner chamber and receive an immediate audience? No, sir. Learned and noble men who have earned the privilege of the king's ear must intercede for him. So it is in matters spiritual. We may offer prayers to God and pay Him homage, but He answers our pleas and our petitions through His appointed and anointed. Such men must exist, yet I am not so blind to think that they are all without blemish nor even that they all incline to virtue.'

'Enough of this, Mr Martin. I am too weary for theology. You make free with my bed, sir.'

Martin had settled himself on the flat mattress, leaving

Danforth to perch on the desk. He stretched out, luxuriating. 'I find my mind turns more quickly when I'm at rest.'

'I am relieved to find it turns at all. On what wheel does it spin?'

'I'm thinking of the other matter, if you must know. God might have driven us here and left us wrecked to bring justice to that poor, dead lassie.'

'Why,' asked Danforth, interested, 'do you tilt towards her so?'

'To be honest, sir, the case of a lost young girl touches me near. I wasn't in Scotland when my sister died – Christian, I told you about her. Only eighteen she was, when she was taken from my mother. From all of us.' His brow wrinkled.

'How did she die, sir?' Martin only threw back his head. 'Forgive me, Mr Martin. It is not my business.'

'Some malady, some illness, ou quelque chose comme ça ... I wasn't present. A damned physician has her blood on his hands, or so I heard tell. Bastard butcher.'

'Let it lie. I should not have asked. You have never pressed me on my history, and it were wrong of me to pry into yours. But this Brody girl – something troubles me about it all. I would have answers. But we do not know this burgh. We can only wait on Brody being captured alive. There is one matter on which I would press him. But I suspect that we will not have it from him.'

Before Martin could speak, he and Danforth were interrupted by the bang of the front door. In the private quarters they found the apothecary, returned with his tools. He rolled up his sleeves, gently unbuttoned the oblivious Kennedy's fine, stained doublet and shirt, and began to rub a brown, gritty ointment into the coarse black hair. Instantly a sour, acidic smell filled the room. After a few seconds the prone figure began thrashing, and Danforth crossed himself. 'Mistress, have you any ropes to bind him to the bed?' asked Zachary.

'Aye – those that keep the roof in place.'

'There is little wind. The roof shall survive. I shall wind the sheet around his chest.' She shuffled off to loosen the ropes from the stones in the front room, whilst the apothecary began to tighten the sheet around the unfortunate Kennedy's body.

'You've no more savage means, then?' asked Martin, a caustic edge to his voice. The apothecary ignored him and continued heaving and handling his patient.

'There,' he said finally, rocking back on his heels to admire his handiwork. 'His breathing shall soon ease, I hope. Though I would bleed him to be sure.'

'Bleeding will kill him,' said Martin, whilst Danforth simply screwed his eyes closed. The thought of bleeding sickened him. Even the memories of his own regular spring bleedings made his head light. The smell of the lotion had invaded the back of his throat, catching and making him want to cough and wretch. His head began to swim, the room momentarily tilting. 'He has not the strength for it,' said Martin. The apothecary turned a shrewd, affronted eye on him.

'Very well, sir. I did not think you a physician, but rather a lord's man or the king's.'

'We are the Cardinal's men, as I thought the whole burgh would be aware.'

'Is that so? The fellow shall not be bled, then. Though I shall not answer for it if he expires the quicker,' he said. 'Now, gentlemen, I must turn to the matter of my payment.'

Martin dug in his purse for coins and threw the apothecary's money to the floor, hissing, 'there, the cost of a man's breath.' Zachary seemed not to mind, bending over and gently scooping up his pay.

'Very good, sir – I thank you, as I'm sure will this lady.' Caldwell was standing by the bed, a rope in her hands and eyes fixed on her husband, humming. Danforth noted the neglected ribbons she had recently worn were lying on the room's trestle. Sad little things, he thought, designed to bring a little show and gaiety, now forgotten.

'We shall see you out,' he said to the apothecary. He was eager to be away from the foul smells of what had become a sickroom, made more putrid still by the strange medicine.

They watched the apothecary scurry down the High Street, and for a few moments Danforth and Martin stood irresolute in the doorway. Returning into the house of sickness was deplorable, and there was no reason to visit the Abbey. It might be time, thought Danforth, to seek news of the roads and return to Glasgow, where they might be closer to war news and certainly close to news of the Archbishop's investigation. 'I begin to suspect this matter may prove an Achilleid, Mr Martin, no sure conclusion to it.'

He was starting to enjoy the questioning look on Martin's face when he heard a commotion further down the High Street. A chorus of shouting voices carried through a light rain. 'What is it? What news?' called Martin to no one in particular.

They stepped out of the doorway and into the street. A woman and child in plaid shawls were skidding along through the muck a little way down. 'You, woman, what is the to-do?' shouted Danforth.

'The battle, sir! The battle's fought and lost, we're all lost, we are beaten! The war's over. We lost! King Henry's men are coming to put us all to sword and flame!'

16

The market cross had become a warzone. Men and women jostled, screaming and shouting, the women with their arms around each other's waists and heads resting on shoulders. Danforth's heart fluttered. Perhaps the woman had been mistaken – perhaps the furore was some smaller matter. He and Martin elbowed their way into the crowd.

'The king's deid!' was one old man's opinion. 'Deid an' they're no tellin' us. That's the news we're no' gettin'. A' for glory, these daft wars, and hurt for us.' Martin asked him where he had heard this news, but the old man only shrugged. They moved on. Another group was cheering that the Scots had been victorious. How did they know? No one knew. Still another woman pronounced that the battle had yet to begin, and the rest were fools to listen to rumour. Where had she divined this? It was, she said, simply common sense. Danforth spied Grissell Clacher and Wilza Darroch conspiring, drawn back together by something bigger than their recent sparring.

It was not long before Danforth and Martin realised that there was no real news to be found in the market cross. Every item, every scrap or bruit purporting to know what was happening was untraceable. As in all crowds, a whispered word grew wings and flew about, being grabbed from the air, mangled, and then thrown onwards. Martin shook his head, inviting Danforth to abandon the search. It was worse to have mock news than to know nothing. Instantly the heart would soar and then sink. If only, thought Danforth, he could lie down somewhere and sleep, and then awaken and have it clear and correct. But he knew that no sleep would come.

They had already turned away from the market cross's great central pillar when the door of the Tolbooth opened. The gruff Baillie Semple led the way, followed by Pattison. Logan the gaoler was nowhere to be seen. Semple marched towards the cross, his silence silencing the crowd. When he reached the pillar, he held something up. It was, Danforth realised, the burgh wakestaff – the obnoxious little stick used to beat on the doors of slugabeds. He struck the pillar with it three times, and the silence of the crowd deepened.

'Citizens of Paisley,' he called out. 'This day word has come upon the Abbey, and thus come upon us all, that a great battle against the English heretics has yesterday been fought and lost in the border country to the south.' There was a collective intake of breath, followed by some anguished groans. 'Fear not, I command you. Our sovereign lord's army has been defeated upon the field, yet his Grace is unharmed. The English have retreated southwards into their own lands with sundry captives, and plan no invasion. There is no danger to any man, woman or bairn. Any found reporting false rumour shall be punished most severely. The Prior bids us all offer our thanks to God for delivering his Grace the king from his enemies, and to pray that in defeat we shall prosper. Pray for the coming of our new princeling. Go about your business. There is no more.'

Danforth, his throat a desert, turned to Martin. The younger man's eyes were closed, his lips moving in silent prayer. 'We must get away from this place, find the Cardinal, find better news,' croaked Danforth.

'Leave Paisley? To what end, sir?'

'To what end? We have been sitting musing upon the moon here whilst this thing has happened. I cannot … I … we must find his Grace.'

'By now the Cardinal will have received notice of our presence here. If he writes, it'll be to here. What good to turn out upon the road in a frenzy, not knowing where he might be or at what labour? We must await our summons arriving at the Abbey, not miss it upon the highway.'

Danforth looked around, despising Paisley, feeling trapped. His gaze fixed upon the Tolbooth, just as the door closed on the baillies. 'Come.' Martin followed him towards it.

Semple stood twirling the wakestaff in his hand. He looked up at the intruders. Pattison, seated, leaned forward, squinting, his squashed-fruit face bored. 'Good morning, gentlemen,' began Danforth. 'This foul news, I can scarcely believe it. Yet the king is well?'

'You needn't think we owe you more than we have given our people,' said Semple.

'Peace, Mr Semple,' said Pattison. 'There are Cardinal's men, mind. Men of esteem and credit. Or they were.'

'We're his Grace's servants still,' said Martin.

'You misunderstand me. Though it's being kept yet from the ears of the general rabble, word from the south is that the king is greatly troubled in his mind by the defeat. Down on the border, they fought, marsh country near the Levin. Not an Englishman was harmed, as is said, but good Scots were drowned in the marsh. Many men of good blood were captured. It tends towards our realm's humiliation. They say the king blames your master as the chief man responsible for this bootless war. It was to be a raid! Just a raid, and then this!'

Danforth and Martin looked at one another. Danforth felt his anger rise. It was a good antidote to shock. 'You might have a care, sir. Your own house is in disorder. A man you call a murderer escaped from your Tolbooth, and now somewhere abroad? You might have a care indeed. You might be murdered in your bed next, English invasion or no.' He turned on his heel and left.

People were still milling about. Some were weeping, though most seemed unconcerned. They were safe from invasion. There were even some nervous giggles. 'What,' said Martin, shall we do now?'

'I do not greatly care,' said Danforth. There had come upon him the strange feeling that accompanies disasters – the desire not to think at all about it, but to talk endlessly about it.

'Shall we see if the Prior knows more than those little rats?'

Danforth turned and looked over the Bridge Port, his heart still racing. 'You go to the Abbey, Mr Martin, and then meet me at the inn. Make purchase at their fine brew-house. Get cups. I would have a drink, Martin, if you would join me. I would have several drinks.'

'Do you know what Eubulus said about strong drink, Mr

Martin?' Good alcohol always lent an impassioned intensity to his voice. He was in full flow.

'I don't. But then, I don't know who You-bulla is? You-buss!' Martin hunched over, laughing. 'What a wee tit I am! Je suis un imbécile.'

'Eubulus said, and I quote, the first three cups of wine are meet for the temperate: one to health; the second to love and pleasure; the third to sleep. After these, wise men go home. But we cannot go home, sir.' They were each on their fifth cup.

Martin had been to the Abbey brew-house. He had found Brother James there and purchased a jug of wine and two cups. James knew no more about the battle of Solway Moss than the baillies did, but he did know that no letter had come into the Abbey from the Cardinal. Thus, Martin had returned to the inn, ignoring the curious gaze of the distracted Mistress Caldwell, and brought the bounty up to Danforth's room. Together they had discussed the imagined battle, the unfortunate necessity of remaining in town, and the Cardinal's fortunes. Martin had even teased out Danforth's opinion on the Cardinal's other servants – 'scoundrels!', and his mistress – 'shameless!'.

'Here,' said Martin, 'what is the fourth and fifth cup?'

'Fourth … to violence.'

'There's been enough of that in this realm, enough in this burgh, even. The fifth?'

'To uproar.'

'God preserve us from that. And the next?'

'To …' Danforth screwed up his face. 'I … I can't recall. I *know*, but it won't come. One cup goes to hurling furniture, though. This wine's strong. Those monks know what they're about.' Martin barked laughter. 'Peace, peace, you'll disturb the hostess and the delicate host.'

'I'm surprised,' said Martin, 'that the host hasn't come up here to beg some from us. Looks fond of it.'

'Aye, that's true, right enough.' A little silence fell as they drank. 'I feel bad, Mr Martin.'

'Arnaud, please. And little wonder, drinking like this. Don't feel too steady myself, to be honest.'

'No, it is … it is a strange thing. I would not speak of it otherwise.'

'If you weren't enjoying the Abbey's fruit, you mean. What's on your mind, mon ami?'

'I can't escape this thought: that somehow this news, this great fright, the Cardinal's woes … that it's my fault.'

'That's madness.'

'Well, perhaps I don't mean my fault. I … but rather that I could have helped it to a better end.'

'How so?'

'You know, if I'd behaved in a different manner.'

'Sir –'

'Simon.'

'You speak in riddles. You weren't part of the battle. We've not seen his Grace in weeks.'

'Aye, yet … listen to this: I try to always count my beads before I sleep, to offer a fair number of prayers to the Virgin. Seven. Last night I neglected my duty, and so invited this ill fortune. Six, I got to. I hate six, unholy number. Tempting providence.'

'Simon, last night the battle had been fought and lost already.'

'Yet,' Danforth persisted, 'I didn't do it, and today comes this news. I also haven't yet made my pilgrimage to the Abbey church. And today comes this news. I haven't found the murderer of this Brody lass, after the task has been given into my hands, and–'

'And today comes this news, aye, I see your theme.' Martin shook his head in wonder. 'How can it be that so sharp and rational a man can live by such superstition?'

'If you think to mock me,' said Danforth, swaying to his feet. 'I shall leave, sir.'

'This is your room, Simon. And I don't mean to mock you, so calm it. But, if I might allow, this is borne of some desire to see a greater measure of … like, well, of control, in greater things than anyone can control. You neglecting your rosary for one night no more caused bad news to come than …' His eloquence failed him. 'Than anything else trifling. It's a conceit to think it so, a strange fruit of the mind. Pray do me one thing, mon ami?'

'What?'

'Stop that kind of thinking.' Danforth said nothing, but sipped moodily at his cup. 'And as we bide in this damned burgh, we shall unmask the devil who walks amongst us. We need your mind clear, Simon, to find him. Not clouded by doubts.'

'My mind's always clear, clear as crystal. Here,' he announced, abruptly shifting the subject. 'Remind me some day to tell you about my little idea. On the ordering of the world.'

'Only a little one?'

'Little, aye, but on a great matter. The biggest.'

'It's not that thing about the world being a sick man, and God a physician, is it?'

'No,' said Danforth, jutting out his bottom lip. 'Forget it. I'll turn it into a little book one day, mark you. Layman's book of course, mere scribbling. For the Cardinal alone to read, at his pleasure.'

'Is that it?' Martin pointed at the Book of Hours.

'No. Don't touch that.'

'I'm nowhere near it, Jesus. What is it, a French book of filth?'

'Don't be a fool. It is nothing to do with you. My book is yet to be written. I'll do it someday.'

'You do that, Simon,' yawned Martin. 'Great matters aren't for me.'

Though they did not throw furniture, their next cups saw Martin falling back into his own room, and Danforth sleeping folded on the floor of the garderobe, his arms around the vomit-flecked chamber pot.

They did not speak the next morning, Danforth feeling too pale in the face to chance long discussion and debate, and worried still more about the state he had allowed himself to get into. He wrote, 'DO NOT DRINK OF HARD WATER' in his

Book of Hours, and made ready to go to Mass. It was a Sunday, after all. Embarrassment flooded him. He had told Martin about his superstitious beliefs. He knew they were irrational, but he could not give them up. Even giving them up might invite misfortune. Fate would not take it well, having a thumb bitten at her.

They met downstairs. To Danforth's chagrin, Martin looked hale. Even in his youth, Danforth had never mastered the art of drinking late and appearing refreshed the next morning. Always his head swam and tilted. 'Good morning, Simon.' Martin's voice was light and chirpy.

'Morning. Mass?'

'Aye.'

Appearing from the private rooms, Mistress Caldwell gave them both an amused look. 'You slept well, I trust, gentlemen?'

'Passing well,' said Martin. 'How does your husband?'

'No change.'

'Then we're sorry for it. Perhaps it will be that his condition improves. This realm and our people are due some fair fortune.'

'Thank you, sir. I pray it be so. Though it's good news we're not to be invaded, though all my buildin' up the fence for nothin'.'

'Better to be safe than sorry.'

'Good day to you,' said Danforth, tired of the conversation and already disgusted by the smell of the invalid. He stepped out into the morning light, and felt its shafts pierce. A sudden urge came upon him to walk down to the Cart and dive in, drinking deeply. Then the girl's body came into his mind and his stomach twisted. Another pang of pain shot through his head as he heard raised voices, not from the direction of the market cross, but the other end of the High Street, where it met the Well Meadow. He looked right, as the activity came into focus.

The owners of the voices appeared. Baillie Semple was marching down the street like a Roman emperor, his protruding gut leading the way with pride. Beside him were chattering burgesses, undoubtedly men of the Town Council. Behind them were two servants carrying a makeshift litter, its lumpy content draped with a sodden blanket. Danforth's mind returned immediately to that other sheet he had seen recently. His stomach lurched.

At once the noxious smell from the inn caught him again, his throat constricting. A wave of nausea seemed to sweep over him, and the burgesses leading their gruesome train tilted. They resolved themselves for a second, and then tilted in the other direction. He took a step back towards the lintel, needing strength, needing solidity. As the world seemed to waver and fade in clarity and sense, he heard Martin's voice calling, 'Sir – Mr Danforth – Simon!', but it seemed to be getting further away, whilst the ground, rain-splattered and muddy, grew closer and closer. He wondered briefly if he was dying and willed himself to reach for his medal of St Adelaide, but he was no longer in control of his limbs.

17

All was blissful blackness and peace. But sometimes the deep bells of the Abbey and the shriller chiming of the Tolbooth echoed. Then he saw Prior Walker standing in his office, pushing a young monk into the great fire and laughing. The flames danced higher in excitement. But suddenly they turned black, flared and went out. Danforth instead found himself staring into Tolbooth gaol cell, and there seemed nothing odd in the transition. The young monk had changed too – he had become Brody, shrivelled and curled up on cold coals. Danforth reached out to him, but he melted away, taking the cell with him. Nothing. Blackness, for an unaccountable time. Then shapes resolved themselves, and there was Alice, lying on a table, dead. 'Alice Spivey, I am your husband. You have told me before you are not dead – rise up, prove it!' he cried. On her wooden slab, her neck swivelled, and she turned a battered face to him.

He jolted awake, and was conscious of being on a lumpy mattress, and that wasn't fair. He had been in touching distance of his lost wife only seconds before and wished to be again. Arnaud Martin – damned fool – would press food and water on him, and the stuff would go halting down his throat, burning its way and hurting his stomach. If he was to die, then he wished that it would happen quickly, not leave him hanging on to the threads of life. Then he would sleep again.

When he awoke properly he had no conception of the time or day – his room hung in a twilit netherworld. Then a thousand memories came flooding back, and with them a thousand more questions. The battle had been fought and lost. Had the Cardinal written him with a summons? Had the king made peace with his Cardinal? Had any more defamatory verses sprung up? Whose body lay covered on that litter?

He sat up and let his eyes grow accustomed to the dim light. He felt well enough, if still exhausted. He sat there awhile, content to think, to ensure that no great matter had escaped him during whatever ailment had overcome him. He let his mind make a list, and when he could see it, he began to read through it, checking off the items that troubled him. He was interrupted by the door sliding open.

'You're awake, sir,' said Mistress Caldwell. She stood in the doorway, her stout body a great grey wall against the dankness of the passage beyond. With her came the smell of medicine and sickness. 'Thank God; I had thought perhaps some illness of my husband's had infected you. Thank God it's no' so.'

'Your husband, mistress – how does he?' His voice was hoarse. She frowned, casting her eyes down.

'There is no change. Still he doesn't speak, and still he can't tell me where he's been. Rather he's grown worse. He's seldom awake. I fear he has no' long left in this world.'

'Then I am sorry for it.'

She was carrying a bowl of broth – the first food he could recall ever having been offered by her. She brought it to him and he took the wooden spoon. He dipped it into the grey liquid and touched it to his lips. It was tasteless, like overboiled gruel. 'This is good,' he said. 'Thank you for your kindness.' She brightened.

'Have you any news? What time is it?'

'Near noon, sir. It's Wednesday. The rain has ceased. You slept and were abed all Sunday, and Monday and Tuesday. We feared for your life.'

'Wednesday! How can this be? What happened to me?'

'I cannot say, sir. You fell by the doorway on Sunday morning. Mr Martin and I carried you up here. A fine young man, he is, and so fair.' She blushed. 'I entreated him to fetch that apothecary, but he'd have none of it. I think he dislikes the man, for all he eased Kennedy's sufferin'. All day yesterday he tended to you. He put food in your mouth and attended to your toilet,' she said without embarrassment. 'It's exhausted him.' Danforth settled back on the mattress, ignoring the rest of the broth. So he had passed out and lain for days, being attended like a child by his younger colleague. He closed his eyes, shamefaced, whilst she prattled on. 'I think Mr Martin is a good friend to you. Few people have such friends. I know I have none.'

'What news is there, mistress?'

'We've heard nothin' new. The common bruit holds that the king's retired to somewhere in the east. Possibly to see the queen. No one knows anythin' of her Grace and her comin' wean, although that itself is good news of a sort, isn't it? But England and its forces, they've gone south, takin' … I don't know, sir, some great lords and barons as prisoners. Some are sayin' it's the end of the world, or at least the end of Scotland, but nothin' has changed round here.'

'And there have been no more foul papers cast abroad in the streets? No words of infamy touching the Cardinal's honour?'

'None, sir.'

'That is good. So, three nights I have lain insensible, and in the brain of your fine lodging rather than within the belly of a whale. Mistress Caldwell, what has become of that body? I saw Baillie Semple leading it from the Well Meadow. Did it belong to a monk?' She wrinkled her face, confusion and interest wrestling for control of her brow. She must, thought Danforth, think him mad.

'A monk, sir? Why a monk? No monks are said to be missin'. A scandal of that complexion would have quite flown through the burgh. The only mention of monks in these dark days has been that Brody accused them of takin' his daughter in sin.'

'Forgive me, I must still be soft in my mind, and thinking of nothing but Church matters. Who was found?'

'That vile old wretch Brody.' She looked almost happy, a wicked grin splitting her face.

'How – slain?'

'No, sir. Your mind does run crooked today. The drunken sot tried to escape the burgh after the Tolbooth, but found the river no' so obligin' as Mr Logan. He must have slipped and fallen, and was washed up by Snawdon, no' far from the Nether Common where he threw his daughter. They brought him back through Under the Wood and down the High Street.'

Danforth bit his lip, thinking. There might indeed lie an end to the unpleasant business. Certainly it would please the Prior, the baillies and the Town Council, who could now draw a line under the affair. A girl had been murdered, her father accused, escaped – proof enough of his guilt – and then drowned himself in the attempt. Such things happened. If Brody was innocent; if Brody had suspicions about the monastery and its brothers ... well, dead men could not tell tales. A minor embarrassment for the burgh officials might be swept away by greater news. A scandal touching the Abbey would not be so yielding.

'And there is an end to that,' said Mistress Caldwell. 'Yet I think the scandal of it might keep the people of the burgh exercised for some time. Do you not, sir?'

'I do, knowing this burgh and its people.'

'I have a question, Mr Danforth,' she said, looking at him intently. 'Though I know I've no business, you bein' so kind in fetchin' that apothecary and all. If it's a trouble, please say, and I'll leave you to your broth.'

'No, mistress, it is no trouble,' he said, his eyes sliding down to the offensive bowl. 'What have you to say?'

'It's in regard to my husband.'

'Mr Kennedy.'

'Tam, sir. I know he'll soon be dead. No, pray don't look sad on my account. He was a rotten husband and a weak, intemperate man, though a fair gallant when I wed him. Too gallant. I've been more the man of this house than he, these past years. Yet I confess it's a comfort to me that he's returned to die under his own roof and no' ... no' abroad I don't know where.' A surprising sparkle of youth crossed her hard face. 'I told a lie, may God forgive me, when I said that he was abroad on business. He fled the burgh near two years since, when he knew he would get no sons by me, takin' every penny pertainin' to this house and more besides. Wi' a widow of the burgh,' she spat, 'who must have brought him to his present condition. In his absence I've lived as worse than a widow. My husband has remained my master, yet he has no' discharged his duties. I have been under his coverture and he no' here to see that this inn flourishes. Those who owe us money laugh at me, deignin' only to deal wi' my husband, and knowin' that he's no' here.'

'Is this so, mistress? I did not know.' She drew back, eyebrows raised in disbelief. 'I am sorry to hear of your troubles, but what would you have me do?'

'I've written a will, sir. And I have put the pen in Kennedy's hand, and his hand to it.'

'That is wicked, mistress. It is no better than forgery.' She looked downcast. 'You say you have no children. This will, it bestows upon you the rightful half of your husband's estate owed to a childless widow?'

'It does, sir. No more than my due. I've kept up his estate as best I could whilst he, I can only think, made his own life elsewhere. I don't know what he might have earned in the last two years, nor where it might be, for he will no' speak. I had thought if we could regain his speech, I might discover it. But if that is no' to be, then I would have only what the law says I might have.'

'Then I am sure that if Kennedy predeceases you, he would wish you to be provided for as far as the law allows.' She smiled at him. 'And free, I suspect, to be your own mistress once again, to recover the debts owed to your estate and marry again, if you list.'

'I believe so, sir. My life these two years past has been one of miseries, every day hearin' gossips in the burgh make merry with my name. I've thought myself beyond all hope, and prayed God might just take me.'

'Now, none of that kind of talk. You should pay no heed to tongues better suited to bridles than to prayer.'

'Still I would put an end to it and begin anew.' He felt a stab of pity for her. How many people, he wondered, suffered in misery, scratching their way through life, constantly under the attack of malicious tongues? 'Mr Danforth, you're a well trusted and important gentleman: a great man of state. Would you bear witness to this will, and assert that it's all right and proper? Your word will carry weight. Mine will no', no' to any notary livin' in this burgh where I'm a figure of raillery.'

'I am no lawyer, mistress,' he protested. 'Not even a scrivener.'

'I want no lawyer. I have neither time nor money for men at law.'

He looked at her for a moment, at the sad, eager face, and then he gave a brief nod. 'I will do what I can do within the confines of the law.' Her smile broadened and for one terrible moment Danforth thought that she might kiss him. Instead, she gave him a strange little curtsey before making for the door, turning briefly to say, 'I forgot; your shirts are cleaned and dried. Forgive me, but I attended to them the other night and then Tam ... well ... There's still a wee bit of blood on your cuff, pink now, though. Nearly away. Be sure and eat your broth, sir.'

A short time later Martin knocked on the door and entered. He looked tired, but his smile was full of genuine pleasure when he saw Danforth had woken. He sat himself down on the desk, knocking the stumpy nub of candle on its side. They both watched as it rolled along the desk and fell to the floor with a muted thud. Martin held up the palms of his hands in a sham of innocence.

'Must you wreak havoc wherever you tread?' asked Danforth.

'I fear so. My maman tells me that as a child I was a little whirlwind of destruction. At that age you, mon ami, were likely reading Livy the Roman and being a terror of another kind. What's this?' He nudged the bowl of cold broth with a foot.

'Broth. With the compliments of our hostess.'

Martin whistled. 'As like to broth, I think, as Mistress Clacher is to Queen Marie. I thought for a moment there that you had taken to pissing in a bowl. With such offerings I do not wonder at your present condition. You're recovered?' The frivolity drained from his face at the question, to be replaced with concern. Danforth was touched, despite his irritation.

'I am. Though I know not from what I have recovered.' Martin gave him a measuring look, his head cocked to one side like a curious sparrow.

'It was a mystery to me. At first I suspected poison, sir. I thought that our murderer had tired of your prying and turned to some covert means of hushing you. There are, I hear, poisons that can be spread around doorways, sickening the first person who passes through them. But of course that's a whole lot of foolishness. A poison must be eaten, or drunk. I know it was not what you drank, for I had more of it. And there I landed on your illness, sir. For you so seldom eat. And therein lies the cause of your case. You have been starving yourself, Mr Danforth, and for some time. You see, I've learned a little of your trade – I watched and I thought.'

'Do not be a fool,' said Danforth, but a blush was creeping into his cheeks. He had not intentionally starved himself; he had neither taken to asceticism nor tried to show God his penitence by refusing meals. But still he had only picked at food since coming to Paisley. Perhaps he had done so for a lot longer, and been unconscious of it.

'Ah, I see that you know it to be true, sir. I'll take you in hand henceforth.'

'Yet,' chanced Danforth, his mind turning, 'there must be some meaning in it. Yes – God in His wisdom must have brought me to this pass for a reason; there must be something He wished me to think upon in my weakness.'

'Now, Mr Danforth, you speak like a foolish old cunning woman, like the kind who said Queen Marie's sons would live and reign forever, after looking at entrails. There's no great mystery here, if you ask me. You're weakened only by not giving your body nourishment. There is no need to search further. Not every event, not everything, has the hand of God in it: follow Master Erasmus, not Luther, sir.'

'And you say you have no learning.' Danforth smiled.

'I say I have none of your classics. Yet I've got ears to listen, and the Cardinal has a tongue that seldom rests. God leaves us free to make our choices as we wish – and I would that you should choose to eat. Already I've been plying you with food, though I can attest to its low quality.' He lowered his voice and gave a wink. 'Old Caldwell's become your partisan, sir. Her husband's dying – even now he is tied to that bed like a hog, poor old whoreson, hissing and puking like a madman. I fancy she might like you for a husband. Though I think,' he said, 'you might do better elsewhere.'

'Thank you,' said Danforth. 'Not for your saucy jests – I can do without those – but for your care. I confess I have been an idiot. So concerned have I been with worldly matters and … and those of my own making, that I have not had a care for myself.'

'My pleasure, sir. You might thank me also for keeping that bloody apothecary from you. Mistress Caldwell would have had him up here, wrapping you in a winding sheet. I would have none of him or his medicines.'

'And it seems you were right. I am quite well, my strength restored. His Grace has not yet summoned us?'

'There's no word.'

'You have spoken to the Prior then?'

'No, but enquired at the Abbey. Usual bruits. The king is here, there, and everywhere. The Cardinal is said to be chasing him. How true, who can say?'

'Hmm. You spoke of our murderer. Mistress Caldwell says the body is Brody's. Is it so?'

'I fear so, though I've not seen it. Didn't fancy it. It is what is said about the burgh, though.'

'Have they buried it?'

'No, sir,' said Martin, smiling again. 'I know you a thing too well. After I and that great ox had carried you up here and saw you abed, I took myself to the Tolbooth. Friend Semple was eager that Brody be taken quickly to some spot and buried, but I had a mind that you would wish to look upon the corpse. What is it you said? It might "tell us something". And so I told him to keep it where Kate Brody had lain. He wasn't happy.'

'I can imagine. However did you convince the fellow?'

'Oh, French charm, such as I exercised on the Archbishop's secretary in Glasgow. Pattison joined him and he also tasted it, and now neither of them shall soon forget us or our master. The cold weather also pleaded for me. Whatever's left of Brody should have remained somewhat … fresh.'

'Then thankful I am for it.'

'When do you wish to see the body?'

'At once – as soon as possible. It has lain there for over

some days now, and the cold can only do so much. If I leave it too long there might be little it can tell us.'

Martin drew an aggrieved breath, clutching at his coat. 'Toil, sir? I should think you would wish to rest now until the *next* Sabbath, so far gone are you in sloth. I think your illness and weakness of mind might linger.' Danforth frowned as deeply as he could manage.

'My good humour and gratitude can only be pushed so far, you young rakehell. Have you any other news?'

'Of the monks, only the usual: their prices are too high, or so it's complained.' He yawned. 'Otherwise the people of the burgh enjoyed their market day on Monday all the more, knowing that the battle against England is lost. You'd have thought they perceived the Apocalypse the way they filled the market cross. Oh,' he said, as though suddenly remembering. 'As I returned from St Nicholas one morning ...' His forehead wrinkled. 'What is this? Wednesday. Sunday morning. I ran into that Mistress Darroch. You recall we saw her clucking with Clacher when the news of the battle with England came?'

'Aye?'

'Well, this will shock you.' Danforth leaned forward. 'The woman is back to hating the old termagant – she reckons her to be a proud thing, and spiteful with it.'

'She is not wrong,' sighed Danforth. He had hoped for something useful. Martin's sarcasm was astute – when gossipy people made uneasy alliances, they were the more likely to despise and distrust one another.

'There's more besides. You know Mistress Darroch's son that went up to the university at Glasgow? Well, she now fears talk against the Church. She thought it wise to turn informer.' Danforth winced at the word. Informers were the minions of the world's Cromwells. Martin was still talking. '... to impress upon me as a Cardinal's man that none of her ilk would involve themselves in what the firebrands say or do. The universities are all turning into gardens for raising up Lutherans, to hear yon woman talk, but her Jamie, of course, is no part of it. He's to be Saint Jamie of Paisley, to hear her speak.'

'A mother wolf protecting her cub. Little strange in that. Unless she fears he has raided the chickens. Did she mention the Cardinal, or any speeches or writings against him at the university?'

'No, but I didn't want to stop her tongue by trying to guide it. What are your thoughts, sir? The ramblings of a worried maman or something more?'

'I cannot say for the moment, Martin, but when we return to Glasgow we shall know more, I hope. Go and attire yourself. You shall come with me to the Tolbooth, and this time you will not duck the unpleasant task.' This subdued Martin a little, and he nodded silently before returning to his own room. Danforth put his head in his hands as he waited for him. It would now be easy to turn his back on the Brody slattern and her useless father, to let them lie in whatever dubious peace they might have found. But he knew he could not. His conscience would not allow it.

The pain and the fear are too much for me, and I know that I want strength.

I commend myself to you, Jesus, that you will hear my prayer

went into his book. Under it, he added 'This month of November, 1542, I was saved from death by ~~a friend~~ by God. This month the Church was attacked. Pray hear us, and save us, O Lord.'

He braced himself for the sight and smell of another corpse, for another image that would burn itself into his mind and come at him frequently, no matter how much he tried to focus his thoughts elsewhere. Every body he had ever seen lodged somewhere within him, none content to remain locked in their coffins or wrapped in their shrouds. Sometimes he wished there might be some markers for the common dead, some stout tombs that held them all. Casting them into unmarked graves until they rotted, and then moving the bones to charnel houses when the churchyard became full, seemed almost to leave them unsatisfied, vengeful. It came to him in his fonder moments that these were the real ghosts. There was no need to see spirits walking the earth, intruding upon the living with mournful wails, demanding redress. No, the true ghosts were simply the memories of those that the living could neither release nor expunge. Man created his own spirits and invited them to haunt him.

When Martin returned, he was still in a grave humour, and Danforth almost laughed at the pun as it formed in his mind. Instead he clapped him on the arm and in silence they left the inn, ignoring the guttural wails of Kennedy, and set off down the High Street to the Tolbooth, where the third corpse in a week waited for them with a cold, necrotic welcome.

18

To Danforth and Martin's surprise, Logan the gaoler was back keeping office in the Tolbooth's grimy, open courtroom. He was not, however, full of the same fire and insolence. Danforth wondered how many errors the man had made, how many men had escaped his custody, and how futile would be the baillies' condemnation of him. It was an ugly, thankless job. He retained it, likely, for that reason alone. Martin could not resist a smile at the man's evident unhappiness.

'The Cardinal's men,' he said when they entered. His voice was flat.

'The same,' said Danforth.

'I understand ye've been unwell, sir. I trust ye're recovered.'

'I would not be here otherwise.' He could not muster a smile for the man, even for the sake of cordiality. Rather he felt his skin crawling. Logan reminded him of a side of bacon, his cheeks perpetually rosy and his eyes mean and narrow.

'To be sure, sir, to be sure. What news o' the world? Has the Cardinal made his peace wi' the king? Or the queen had her wean yet?'

'We have brought no news of that. We are here to see the corpse.'

Something of Logan's former insolence returned, the ruddy features under their ginger whiskers changing. 'Ye'll find him a thing quieter than last he wiz,' he leered. 'An' even fouler smelling, if it be possible. Even the curious, the vulgar, have stopped comin' hence to gaze on the face o' a murderer. Well, it's his own fault for runnin'. Dross like him have an animal cunnin'. It returned when he sobered, but little good it did him. The baillies are no' happy, sir, neither of them. Yer man there gave them a stack o' abuse, I hear.' Martin beamed.

'Mr Martin is not "my man". He is the Cardinal's man, and thus an officer of the Lord Keeper of the Privy Seal.'

Abashed, Logan threw up his hands. 'I meant no offence, gentlemen. It's the baillies as say they're no' happy, and would have ye out o' the burgh. It's proud they are o' their authority, and jealous o' it. They dinnae want the corpse o' a murderer bringin' disease and infection here. I think,' he added, a doleful expression taking over, 'that's why they have me here again – that I might be closer to the foul wreckage as punishment for not beatin' the bastard until he feared liberty worse than his comin' punishment. Though it's no ma fault – I've told them till I'm blue in the face that this place is no fast prison. Written out report after report beggin' them to make it secure. They're needin' a new one built. Well, you know where he lies.' Already Logan was opening the door to the courtyard. The noise of the cross's ever-present crowd filtered over the fence. Just over the fence men and women were going about the daily business of living, death the furthest thing from their minds. 'Ye'll no' find him as hard to look at as yon other yin,' Logan winked.

Danforth and Martin took the familiar path to the old barn, both ignoring the gallows, slick and wet. Some geese were waddling around the yard, uninterested in them. When they reached the door, Danforth said, 'I would have you come in here, Arnaud. It is not as the baillies do to that brute Logan, not to punish you, but to educate you. This body will look … somewhat different from the poor wretch in the great drain.'

'I understand, sir. To be honest, I'd rather look upon the corpse than spend any time in the company of that fat guts in the Tolbooth.' He attempted a smile, but could not manage it.

'Life is full of strange novelties, Mr Martin, strange sights, most of them unpleasant. Expect nothing, and you will be surprised by nothing.'

The sun's rays broke through a quilt of clouds as Danforth opened the doors, and they stepped into the room.

Brody had not been done the service of being covered with a sheet. That dignity was lost to him, although no baaing sheep intruded on his sleep. Instead he lay facing upwards, his eyes open and staring in terror, frost glistening on his beard. Danforth crossed the room and looked downwards, Martin following. He was surprised at how whole the man looked. No violence had been visited on him. If he had been murdered, it had been done without the crazed hatred that had ended his daughter's life.

'Look here, Martin,' said Danforth, speaking slowly and taking only the shallowest breaths, 'he is not beaten. No rocks have torn him.' Martin, ashen-faced, nodded. His hands were over his mouth and nose. Catching the shifting colour on his colleague's face, Danforth asked, gently, 'if you cannot stand it you can open the door for a breath of air.' Martin only shook his head.

Danforth turned the man's head on its side. A little water poured out from between the blue lips. He pressed hard on the chest, and it became a spurt. His eyes then narrowed at the sight of blotchy marks on the back and sides of his neck and shoulders. The marks of his trip through the river and the Common were upon him: twigs and sticks of straw were stuck about his upper half, but no open wounds. Danforth turned to the hands, opening them up. Thankfully Brody had been dead long enough that they gave easily, entreating him to find out what had happened. The nails were broken, but they might always have been. Some dried blood stood out under them. Other scratches criss-crossed the palms. Brody, it seemed, had struggled as he drowned.

Danforth continued his examination, occasionally gesturing for Martin to lean in closer. There was little else to be divined. Brody's boots were surprisingly clean and unscathed, his hose only as ragged as they had been when he was arrested. When finished, Danforth nodded to Martin and gestured towards the door.

Back outside, they sucked in lungfuls of cold air, appreciating even the faint smell of animal waste. The sun, having promised much, had retreated, and a stiff wind was picking up. 'Mon dieu,' whistled Martin, 'but it is strange to see a man lying dead, and he accused of being a murderer himself.'

'It is never pleasant.'

'Did it speak to you, sir? Did it tell you something of the man's end?'

'I believe it did. Did you note the marks upon his neck?'

Martin nodded grimly. 'The poor wretch was held under the water. He did not fall upon it, and did not strike rocks. And as he was drowning, I fancy he struggled and fought with his hands, likely to remove himself.' Again, Martin whistled a sigh. 'And so I think we still have a murderer. But the question now is who might profit from his death. Who might find benefit in the matter being closed?'

'The Abbey. The Prior. The Town Council. There's more who wish to see the matter closed, and neatly, than otherwise.'

'This is true. Or that it might be the fellow was killed in revenge, by one who believed him responsible for killing the girl.'

'Her lover, this Brother Hector?' Martin arched an eyebrow. 'You think he might remain somewhere in the burgh, waiting for his chance? I can't see it, even if he was led to believe that Brody killed Kate.'

'In truth, I do not know; I must think on it. If Brody is innocent and yet was killed by one who believed him guilty, then we have two unknown murderers at work. And that I cannot fathom. Not in a small burgh.'

'Then we return to the same person killing both daughter and father, in the hopes that their silence would put an end to something not wished known.'

'It is possible, but I can go no further. Come – it is so cold. That wink of sunlight was as mocking as Dolos, and of the substance of Zeus visiting Danaë.' He paused to observe the effect. His father had had great learning, a vast wealth of classical knowledge. He liked to feel that he matched it; or, if not, that others at least would think it of him. Satisfied with Martin's confusion, he started across the courtyard. Already the day was giving way to night, though the Abbey and Tolbooth were only beginning to chime three o'clock.

They left Logan with instructions that Brody could be buried whenever and wherever the baillies saw fit. He received them with neither gratitude nor interest; he had returned to cracking his knuckles in a groaning wooden chair. Out on the packed market cross Danforth looked up at the sky. That strange, autumnal smell was again heavy in the air: bonfires, frost, dead leaves and wet ground. It was comforting. Even the hubbub of folk at business and trade was regular and soothing.

'Ho!' said Martin, breaking Danforth's thoughts, 'our young friend Jardine has lost his place. He stands outside the draper's playing the apprentice.'

'Then his father is returned,' said Danforth. His mind turned. 'Yes, I wish to speak to this travelling merchant. I have awaited his arrival.'

'On what matter, sir? Your shirt's not falling apart already?' He looked down at his own cuffs, and then struck a pose, one hand splayed on his breeches.

'Only on the matter of some business in which Mistress Caldwell has engaged me,' he said laconically.

'Ooh, the lovely Mistress Caldwell, ooh,' said Martin. He smacked his lips, making kissing sounds. 'Seriously, you pity that old crone.'

'I … well … you pity her little slave.'

'Archie? Give yourself peace. This is not a tournament.'

They passed the younger Jardine, who in any case had given up on being courteous now that he had been returned to minor duties, and strode into the shop.

Jardine the elder was a massive man, his stomach swollen and his features jolly. Immediately they came through the door he rounded on them, the buttons on his doublet straining. 'What news, gentlemen. And what fine gentlemen.' A little gleam of greed came into his eyes; a good nature could not quite efface the ingrained mercantile outlook. 'But alas, for such fine fellows to be in such poor shirts. It is a crime. It is a scandal. I know you have come here to purchase the best quality, and that is all we have to offer. I am recently come back from the west coast and have fine silks and linens. The finest. Young Tammy Toory Tap here,' he said, pointing at Martin, 'would suit a fine silk.'

'We are not customers, sir. Or rather we were. We purchased the material for these shirts from your son,' said Danforth. Jardine seemed to deflate, his face reddening. 'I would speak with you, Mr Jardine, but it is not of the quality of your wares, which satisfy me.'

'Oh?' Jardine seemed torn between mortification and curiosity. Natural good humour voted in favour of the latter. 'Then pray, my friends, what is your business? Tom Jardine lets no man leave this place without satisfaction.' He swept off his cap, revealing a pink scalp laced across with some dun-coloured stragglers.

'You are recently come, your son informed us, out of the far west.'

'Aye, out of Ayr, Troon, Irvine, up as far as Largs. I do business everywhere, and would have been back sooner if the rain hadn't made such short shrift of the roads. There is not a man on the coast that doesn't know the name of Tom Jardine. There's a fellow down Mauchline way–'

'Peace, Jardine. We are secretaries to his Grace Cardinal Beaton, Lord Privy–'

'A fine man.'

'Quite. Yet we have come to be engaged in another business, helping our hostess regain rights that have too long been lost to her. First though, I must attend to the Cardinal's affairs. Is there any word in Ayr of libellous writing against his Grace's good name? Have any seditious verses been pinned to market crosses anywhere in the west?'

'No, sir,' said Jardine, scratching his head. 'No, all talk is of the war and how it might affect our trade.'

'And no little notes, poor and railing things, have been scattered in the streets, bringing the Cardinal's name into the hatred of the people?'

'No, sir. Most definitely not. There is little appetite for blasphemies or slanders against the Church in the west. The only mention I heard tell of his Grace was some doubt about his love of France, sharply reproved. You know, gentlemen, the usual common gossip and prating about great men. Nothing of substance. Idle sporting talk for the dull witted.'

'Good. This news pleases me, as it will please the Cardinal. Tell me, do you know of a woman, Blackwood, in Ayr?'

Jardine whistled through his teeth. 'You mean the Blackwood lassie that took off with Tam Kennedy?'

'Yes. I believe so.'

'Aye, she dwells outside Ayr now, or so I hear. She has never bought anything from *me*, right enough. Keeps to herself, they say, on some fine lands outside the burgh itself. She wouldn't set foot in Ayr; too feart people might find out about her history. They say she killed her husband to make room for Tam.'

'Yes, yes,' said Danforth, nodding, 'but does she dwell there still?'

'I couldn't say, sir. As I said, she doesn't come to town.'

'And Kennedy, that they say she ran off with – did he dwell with her in Ayr?'

'So it's true he's not for speaking then. Oh aye, I heard he's back in Paisley. It's been the talk of the place. Well, that and the other, the bootless father of that Brody girl dying, since she has made for Ireland.'

'What?' shouted Martin. 'What is this about Kate Brody?'

'Gone off. I saw her myself. Pretty little thing – always was.'

'Where? When did you see her?'

'Oh, it must be over a week ago. I tarried in Ayr – it's a fine burgh – though I'm but a draper, you'll want for no wines or salt as long Tom Jardine pay visits to Ayr. Just don't be telling the deacons. She must have followed in my wake, though I've been out that way a good space. I didn't know she'd fled Paisley when I left. But there she was, as large as life and twice as pretty, with the sorriest mule that ever I've seen. Turned as white as snow when she saw me see her.'

'And so you say that the girl lives,' said Martin. 'Kate Brody lives still.'

'Unless her ship is wrecked, taking her and her young man to the depths.'

'Who was the young man?' asked Danforth. 'Of what nature was he?'

'Oh, a lusty youth, handsome, leading the mule. His head had been shaved. Were I a suspicious man, I might think him a monk. But then,' he smiled, 'I'm a friend to the Church. I shan't say anything. Young Kate Brody fled Scotland alone, as far as Tom Jardine knows.'

'Have you told the baillies of this? Do they know that it is not Kate Brody lies in that grave?'

'I have not, sir. If the girl wishes to be gone, let her be gone.'

'That means letting a murderer run free.'

'How is that, sir? From the bruits, old Brody murdered and confessed. If it was some other wench that was murdered, it's for the lass's kin to claim her.'

'Kate Brody lives,' said Martin, a little reverently. 'I don't know why, never having known her, but the news pleases me. Pleases me a whole hell of a lot.'

'Is that so?'

'I take my victories where I can find them,' shrugged Martin, smiling.

'And yet,' said Danforth, 'a girl is still dead.'

'Who, but? If Kate Brody is alive?'

'Some other lass, obviously. Some lass who has run away, a maidservant or some such, whose flight no one cared enough about to report. You have grown attached to the image you have constructed of one girl, Mr Martin, but this other deserves justice in her place. We shall report this properly, Mr Jardine. We shall deal with it discreetly. You give us your pledge, though, that you shall say nothing of this young monk? Though we owe loyalty to his Grace the Cardinal and not the Abbey, yet we have good Christian respect for the honour and reputation of so holy a place.'

'Which young monk is that, sir? I know of no monks save those who worship in the Abbey. And I've heard no word of one of their company being lost. But as long as we speak of loss, sir, what of he who is found? You made mention of Kennedy.'

'I did. Kennedy is dying, and is like to become another loss. Did he dwell long in Ayr with this Mistress Blackwood? I would know how he came to be in his current condition before I commit myself to giving aid to his wife.'

'I'm sorry, gentlemen. I never heard tell of him dwelling with the jade. Actually,' he said, his brow furrowing, 'I think there was some talk a year or two back that Blackwood bought a house for two, and kept horses for two. Bought clothes for two, too, though as I say she never did business with me. But beyond that I cannot help you, I'm afraid.'

'It is no matter, Mr Jardine. You have been a help.'

Jardine smiled at them without guile, his rosy face gleaming. 'Then the truth it is that no man leaves Tom Jardine unsatisfied. Come again when you require new clothing. Though you shan't be in need of shirts for a long space. Those,' he said with a grin, 'are of the best quality.'

They left the draper's, Martin giving young Jardine a tip of his cap. In return, he received only a blank stare. When they had walked away, Martin asked, 'what was that, sir? Why do you take on the business of old Caldwell? I might start to think you really do lean towards the old dragon. And she has turned soft towards you since you paid for her blood-letter.'

'Why do you, sir, frame your mind so closely to the Brody wench?' Martin only offered a sour look in return. Then his elated expression returned. News of the girl's survival, the news that she had run away with her fellow to begin her new life, seemed to have made him buoyant. Danforth felt a little pity for him. Had he not known better, he would have suspected young Martin had fallen a little in love with this girl of reputedly great beauty and a tragic life. The boy seemed to have a softness for tragic maidens.

'Well, keep your own counsel, if you will. For my own part, I cannot say why this girl has affected me. It is not simply some feeble memory of my lost sister, who was a good girl, virtuous and chaste – though I confess that drew me at the start. Some tales, some crimes, simply capture the imagination and refuse its release. Some months back I could not sleep for thinking about King Henry executing his pretty young Howard queen. But by all means, sir, keep your own mind close.'

'That is generous of you, Martin. For myself I am minded to put an end to something.' Martin's eyes lit up.

'Then we are to go to the Abbey, sir? It appears we yet have a murderer running free.'

'I fear we must. But a little later. It might yet wait until tomorrow. I should like to sleep on it. Unless you have had some revelation of your own?'

Martin did not have time to answer. Tottering up the street as quickly as his bandy legs could carry him was the chaplain of Our Lady. He was heading towards the Oakshawside, his head bent against the wind. Dancing around, bidding him to hurry, was Archie. Nodding at each other, Martin and Danforth took off in pursuit.

On entering the upper High Street, the chaplain was waylaid by Grissell Clacher, a black shawl wrapped around her scrawny shoulders. 'What news, Father?' she cried into the wind. The priest made as though he did not hear her and kept his pace. When Danforth and Martin passed, she pressed upon them. 'You, gentlemen, what news? Is it the war? Has there been another death? You live with Kennedy; has he given up the ghost? Has he repented his sins? What news?'

'Perhaps, mistress, you might return to your house before that tiresome, prating tongue of yours turns black and gives up the ghost itself,' said Martin, smiling. Mistress Clacher, her mouth hanging open, stood her ground as she watched them continue towards the last house at the end of the Oakshawside.

19

Death was leading Tam Kennedy a merry dance. He had lain bound to his bed for days, reeking of his own waste and the medicines designed to stave off his end. When Martin and Danforth arrived, they found a weeping Mistress Caldwell attended by the doddery old chaplain. Both stood by the flock bed in the inn's private room. Kennedy had been unloosed, his breathing the barest whisper. The priest, half blind, was dithering over the last rites, splashing the body and making the sign of the cross on various parts of it.

'Per istam sanctam unctionem,' he trilled, 'et suam piissimam misericordiam, indulgeat tibi Dominus quidquid per visum, audtiotum, odorátum, gustum et locutiónem, tactum, gressum deliquisti.' He stepped back, almost catching on his robes. 'He may die in God's mercy and love.'

As though to be difficult, Kennedy continued to breath for a quarter of an hour, his wife, the priest, Martin and Danforth waiting in silence. Archie had returned to his lair. Eventually the chest stopped rising, and each person in the room felt that they could again breathe normally. It was strange, felt Danforth, that they had almost stood in solidarity with the dying man, holding their own breaths as he fought for his last. It was Martin who stood forward and wrenched the sheet from the dead man, drawing it over him.

Mistress Caldwell began wailing, the priest giving her admonitory glances as he tried to comfort her. Danforth set about hunting the room for something to offer him. He stepped into the garden, where he inhaled some more fresh, living air. He looked around for Archie, and over the low wall at the horses. Woebegone was defecating; the Cur was slurping from the trough; the grey palfrey was watching both without much interest. He returned to the house. All he could find was a bottle of wine. He opened it, found some cups, and passed it round, the priest taking a long draught.

'Aye,' he said. 'Come back a shadow of himself, it looks.

But he has been forgiven.'

'His burial,' said Mistress Caldwell, her wails having died to a sniffle. 'He must be buried in consecrated ground.'

'That he will be, have no fear. I will alert the burgh. He might be buried tomorrow, if you don't wish him to be visited upon. Do you, mistress?'

'No,' she said, 'Tam has been gone so long. We have no kin. No one will wish to say a farewell to him. What a bootless marriage we made, eh? Ah, but our parents were living, and would join the Caldwells to Kennedy, and now no kin I know of remain. Have him put to rest with speed.'

'At once, my child.' The old priest took one last look at the body, made one last sign of the cross, nodded at Danforth and Martin, and attempted a stately exit. Danforth waited until he had gone and then took Mistress Caldwell by the arm. 'There is nothing more you can do, mistress. All is at an end. I will write a notice of your widowhood and my witnessing of your husband's will tonight, and have it ready for you in the morning.' She looked at him with hope in her eyes, and he felt his heart wrench. He released her, unable to meet her eyes.

'Thank you, sir. I'll rest here for the night, in the chair by him where I slept in his last days.'

Danforth and Martin climbed the stairs in silence. 'I'll join you for a spell, if it doesn't trouble you, sir. But first I'll fetch something.' Danforth nodded, grateful for the company. Unpleasant thoughts were swirling in his head, as they always did when he looked upon death. His dreams would again be crowded. There would be no peace. Already an idea had formed in his mind, too strange to be believed. He would have to ponder it, make sure it fit.

Martin joined him with a treasure trove of salted beef, smoked bacon and a dusty bottle of wine. 'You see, I mean what I say. You must eat.' Danforth was not sure that the food would sit well on his stomach, but he did as he was bid, and for a while the two sat working their way through it. They spoke little, and only of light things. What a fool fat Jardine had been, not to recognise his own wares; the garderobe at the end of the hall outside had finally seen a change of water. If

Mistress Darroch was not a friend to Mistress Clacher, then it was apparent that the irritating old neb had none, and would make an end chattering her maidservants to death; Brother David was a good old soul. Martin's observations even managed to draw some reluctant laughter.

When they had finished, Martin looked up at him. 'You've softened a little, sir.'

'How is that?'

'Your handling of Caldwell. She's nothing – an old trout. Yet you show her kindness. You are not so hard a man as you think.'

'Or perhaps it is you that have misjudged me.'

'Still, I think that our coming to this place has been good for you. Though it would be better still if we resolved matters. My mind's waxing strange. The only new man to this town, save for ourselves, sir, is an old man: Kennedy. Two people are dead and this man returns. And the Prior eager to bury all talk of the missing lovers. It's a mystery. We must have some answer to it.'

'We might yet. But not tonight. I still must think. We shall go to the Abbey tomorrow, if I am right. News of Cardinal might come in, and we shall know how he fares in the king's favour. He might convince him to resist the Antichrist once more.'

'Do you really believe that? That King Henry is the Antichrist?'

'You doubt it?'

'Don't avoid the question.'

'I know only that the man is a glutton and worse. The office of his Holiness in Rome is ancient and full of God's mysteries. The King of England wants such an office for himself. It is madness as well as sacrilege for a temporal sovereign to claim he has God's whispered advice over men's souls. He was born to be a king over their secular governance. His usurpation of papal rule should no more be heeded than a raving lunatic claiming God speaks through him, and who would believe that? No, my fear is that in time King Henry's fantastic claims will be taken seriously. He pulled down the Roman Church because of his greed. Because of his lust for money, his lust for infamy, for the Boleyn woman. And now he lusts after Scotland.'

'And yet he won the day and Solway Moss, and his forces didn't march up to conquer us.'

'Not yet. But King Henry is a man of evil appetites. Our king is not a glutton. He does not seek to add England to his crown as Henry does to Scotland. You know, the old Henry, the present king's father, said that if Scotland should ever be joined to England, even under a Scots king, it would not be the addition of England to Scotland, but rather Scotland to England, as the greater part of the whole island. Such is the feeling in England. If the line of Henry and his wee bairn fails, and our queen is delivered of a good Christian prince, he might one day inherit England – yet England will then inherit Scotland. And should a girl be born and claimed as bride by an English sovereign ... well, in Scotland your ladies marry to join kin to kin, clan to clan, family to family. In England the bold man absorbs the lady, and what was hers becomes his. And so the seventh Henry would again be right. Any marriage between England and Scotland would be the pouring of a smaller vessel into a larger.'

'Henry VII ... that old pinchpenny.' Danforth couldn't help but smile. The old King Henry was long in his grave, but the reputation he had earned in life endured. It had become common knowledge even to those who had never breathed the same air as him.

'That was before my time, but the feeling remains.' Martin's head rocked back and forth slowly.

'It's a strange thing, an Englishman in Scotland and so desirous of Scotland's freedom from England's rule.' Danforth had been expecting such a question.

'You might well wonder why I am so wedded to Scotland, as an Englishman – I agree we are a rare breed. It is because this kingdom retains my religion and my beliefs, and my former kingdom revels in their destruction. I would not have Scotland added to England, lest that destruction be wrought here. Nor would I have those inclined to English policy and

England's wicked heresies sway our king and government. Such men are no less than traitors to Scotland.' He caught the question that briefly made a crease of Martin's brow, though the man had tried quickly to smooth it away. 'No Catholic, sir, can be a traitor to England simply for refusing to be subject to a tyrant.'

'Yet there are men of the faith in England still. The Duke of Norfolk's said to favour the true religion. Wee Catherine Howard was a daughter of the Catholic faith too, or so they say.'

'Bah! So strong that the one serves King Henry and the other shared his bed. A traitor to the faith and an English Messalina. No true Catholic man or woman could serve an excommunicate – worse than an excommunicate: an avowed enemy of his Holiness' authority.'

'So you do not think the stories about Henry leaning back towards the true faith are to be believed?'

'He is old and ill. He might fancy he can save his damned soul by appearing contrite, the foolish creature. No, England is lost as long as Henry swallows up the Pope's rights. It is right that the Cardinal stands firm, that he leans towards the French, as a race true in the faith and loyal to Rome. Though I confess,' he added, 'that your breed inspires in me no great love.'

'Mais vous avez tort, mon ami. My father's land was the very seat and cradle of love. Not even in Scotland do poets speak so fair. Think on Queen Marie's son: a prince of the realm half Scottish and half French. Could any princeling be more blessed?'

'Away you go,' smiled Danforth. 'But I am bone-weary and bedward. I must bid you goodnight, sir. Tomorrow, I worry, shall be a terrible day.'

'You've not forgotten some regular activity, nor taken an odd number of steps to make it so, surely?'

'No. Goodnight, Mr Martin.' Already Danforth was tucking himself under his cloak. Martin went to the door. Before he could go through it, Danforth muttered from the mattress, 'I am glad your young friend lives, for all she was a slattern who has seduced a holy man and turned him into naught but an apostate.'

Sleep came with difficulty. Danforth's mind turned with possibilities. He felt that the truth was before him, and yet he shied away from it. Something within him, however, told him that it must be confronted, and that only by facing it could he finally come to enjoy peace. Everything that had happened since coming to Paisley, he felt, had been a trial, set for him by God. He was right to doubt that a pilgrimage could be as little as a few short hours' ride across a neat, unfaltering road. It required pain; it required some epiphany. He was being tested, his will and strength put on trial. He must let the ghosts of the unknown dead girl and the man who was not her father, and unlikely to be her killer, have their justice. Only then might he be freed of his own terrors and his own sin.

The Book of Hours lay open by his bed, turned to Matthew:

Ye have heard that it was said by them of old time, Thou shalt not kill; and whosoever shall kill shall be in danger of judgment ... But I tell you that anyone who is angry with a brother or sister will be subject to judgment.

He slept, dreaming fitfully.
The next day he would confront the killer.

In the morning, he rose early and got down on his knees to pray. He begged God to give him strength. He prayed for a good outcome, for an end to the madness that had infected this community. If he was to be God's instrument in the safe delivery of the burgh from a great and terrible evil, he would require support.

He woke Martin with a knock, and the pair attended Mass. He took Communion gratefully. It gave him strength. Afterwards, Martin began marching purposefully down the steep wynd, along Moss Street and, as they reached the market cross, he turned left towards the Bridge Port. Danforth stopped him with a hand on the shoulder. Martin turned to him, confusion on a face shining with wetness from the returning sparkle of ticklish, powdery rain.

'You said, sir, that we are to put an end to this. Has your mind changed course? Don't you wish to speak with the Prior?' His breath rose in the air like a dragon's. It was strange to see the mist of breath fight against the mist of rain.

'Not yet,' said Danforth. 'We might speak with him this afternoon, after his dinner. Besides, we must get our things from the inn.' Privately he doubted if they would have time to confront the Prior that day.

Muttering, Martin joined him and they walked back up the High Street. As they passed through the lower part, where the tenements lay like a set of carelessly made false teeth, the sound of a cheap bladder pipe and tabor burst out across the street. 'Ugh,' said Danforth. 'Does this town do aught but play music and enjoy song?'

'Pray do not tell me you dislike music and entertainment, sir.'

'I do not, Martin. I …' Danforth's voice lowered, turning a little petulant. 'They have their place.'

They passed into the upper High Street. Mistress Clacher was standing in front of her house on the Prior's Croft side, her head bowed in conversation with Mistress Darroch. Friends again. She moved to wave, her mouth opening. When she caught sight of Martin, her face shrivelled into a hideous frown and she turned her head ostentatiously from them. That was one more thing, thought Danforth, to thank Martin for. It seemed lately that he was becoming increasingly thankful for the man. Though he would not call him a friend, he had accepted him as an ally, as one who could be counted on. It was a pleasant feeling. From it, friendship might grow. And since coming into Scotland, he had made no friends, only colleagues, and the Cardinal who, though a kind, generous man, was a master to be deferred to. He thought of Cicero, of friendship, as he watched Martin swagger alongside him.

Mistress Caldwell was humming to herself as she tidied the public room. It seemed that finally achieving widowhood – that strange position in which a woman might live an independent life – had brought a new kind of frivolity to her.

She had arranged the chairs around the fire, and was even in the process of bringing through her old washbowl, that her guests might have a public laver. Water slopped over the edges and fell to the floor. Martin smiled, the smile faltering when he looked at Danforth. 'You have turned daughter of Danaus, I see' he said, his face impassive.

'Good morrow, gentlemen. Mr Danforth, have you written your letter? I'd like matters to move apace.' Her tone, though sunny, was businesslike.

'Perhaps later, mistress.'

'I don't mean to push you,' she frowned, 'but you did say that this mornin'–'

'Where is your husband buried?' Martin was taken aback by the harsh, stentorious tone of Danforth's voice.

'Sir? My husband yet lies in his bed. He shall be buried anon.'

'No, madam. This twisted jest is over. That poor wretch, that pitiful, nameless creature that you induced into your bed is not your husband.'

20

'You … sir, the man's run mad,' said Mistress Caldwell, turning pleading, fearful eyes on Martin. The peat fire in the room issued thin black smoke. It curled up around her. Martin turned to Danforth, trusting.

'I tell you, mistress, I will have no more. That man is no more your husband than I am a bunch of radishes.' Danforth felt suddenly old, and very tired. He watched Mistress Caldwell closely, reading her reaction. In that he might find the proof of his theory. For several beats she froze, not even breathing. Only the pupils of her eyes seemed to change in size, contracting and expanding in the guttering light.

'But how can you think this,' she said at length. 'Sir, you've no' met my husband. He's altered in his appearance, but that's only the ravage of years spent in sin.' There was something more than demurral in her voice. There was a reluctant, angry curiosity that feigned indignation could not mask.

'If you prefer, Mistress Caldwell, I shall have every burgess and their wife in this burgh pass through this house and gaze upon him. The corpse shall be shaved and they might avow themselves that this man is a stranger to them, for all his height and clothing.' He sighed, shaking his head. 'It were better that you confess freely. Your soul might feel the benefit hereafter.'

She crumpled at the word 'soul', fresh tears – real tears – beginning to run down her face. Then hatred contorted her features. Danforth shrank back under it. It was never pleasant to feel hated. 'How, how can you know this? How can you?'

'You overplayed your hand. If you will forgive me, it was a womanish lapse. Is it possible that any man could return in the state of that fellow you call Kennedy, in the suit of clothes he departed, his body ruined and yet his doublet untouched and fresh? I would say clean, mistress, but for the stains around the collar, stains which corresponded remarkably with those from blows to the face and head. You did a poor job of removing the blood. I shall ask once more. Where is your husband buried?'

'I say nothin', I cannot plead,' she said in confused desperation. 'I have nothin' to say to you. Liar! Mr Martin!' Her posture had changed to that of the aggrieved housewife, one hand on her hip, the other balled in a fist. Once again, Martin looked away from her.

Danforth sighed. 'As you wish, Mistress Caldwell. We might begin by digging up your garden. Or by digging the floor of this house. Unless you threw him in the river and it kept him – but a deep dig shall tell us if that be the case.' Silence fell between them, the only sound her little moans. Eventually she rallied. Her strong hands began to pluck at her white dress.

'But ... but ... how?'

'I am no fool, woman. I thought the clothes curious, but I might not have given them a second thought, had we not learned that the Brody lass lives. And who should be missing but another young woman, and the harlot of your husband at that. The husband who mysteriously reappears, much altered in appearance from his long absence. And right before the eyes of a man whom it suited your turn to witness die. Me, to whom you turned friend. Now where is the true Kennedy?'

'Christ Jesus! Friend! I'm no friend to any man. I ... you ... You'll find Kennedy in the garden, Christ damn him. His vile body is doin' me greater service feeding the chickens than ever the fool did in his miserable life.'

'Then that man,' began Martin.

'A vagrant,' finished Danforth. 'We have seen the poor things, sir: they congregate around the walls of the Abbey; they clog the road leading to the town. I daresay Mistress Caldwell lured the poor fellow with money before fashioning him as her husband, in the clothes she took from her husband's body. It was a weary mockery. A sham.'

'I bid him come here after dark. Took a while to make him understand. He came on the promise of food, no' money,' said Mistress Caldwell, as though appalled at the suggestion. 'Those clothes were too fine for Tam. But the blood never would come clean out of them. He was always a bloody nuisance. It was easy enough to put them on that filthy fellow before rousin' you men from your idleness.'

'A nuisance? Is this why you killed him?' asked Martin.

'No,' she protested. 'I didn't think of killin' him. I planned nothin'. The brute said he would leave me. Take our money, leave me nothin'. He laughed in my face when I wept, when I stormed, when I begged for him to treat me as a wife should be treated. He was packin' his things to leave wi' that … that hoor Blackwood. Black is right, and foul! Still he was laughin' at me as he turned and bent to fill his pack wi' our – wi' *my* things. And so … And so I split his head wi' a hatchet. I don't know what came over me. I was mad wi' fury. It was her fault.'

'And so you killed her,' said Danforth. 'We know that, mistress. We know that Kate Brody lives. She was espied in Ayr. Soon none will believe that her body lies in the churchyard of St Nicholas, hastily buried and forgotten as you'd hoped. But why now? That is what kept me awake last night, what has turned in my mind since we learned Kate Brody still lived. How did it come to pass that this Blackwood creature was in Paisley, and you eager to kill her?'

Mistress Caldwell wiped her eyes and then lowered herself into a seat by the fire. Her face had drained of emotion. She looked, to Danforth, to be carved of grey stone. Her colourless pallor glinted in the firelight. She might almost have been the corpse. 'For two years that monstrous bitch has tormented me. She came upon this house the night I … the night Kennedy died. She saw the blood, even as I tried to clean it from the floor, from the walls. I even had to tear down my good panellin' and burn it, so much blood poured from his empty head. She had come for her lover. But did she weep for him, findin' him slain? No, she didn't. Instead she demanded money. All the money Kennedy had planned for them to run away wi'. I gave her it. It bought her silence.

'For a space at least. She took off wi' our horses and our money – what by rights was mine. And still she came back. She took every horse. Every few months she would return, demandin' still more, more, more to keep her in her fashion. By night she would come, like the harlot she was.'

'The quean on the horse,' murmured Danforth. 'The jade that Mistress Darroch spoke of, that haunted the burgh by night. And so it was no strumpet come hence to feed the lust of the monks.' To his surprise he found a measure of comfort in that – but only a measure.

'That fits her: a jade and a strumpet. I told her to keep to the woods, by the Castle Head and Laigh Common. I told her to wear a disguise. Sometimes she came dressed as a man, the unnatural creature – it were better, she said, to ride safely. Ha! Thinkin' on her safety. Stupid sow.'

'You're a fine one to accuse any woman of being unnatural,' said Martin, 'when your own crimes are made doubly monstrous by your sex. A man in his cups might be known to commit such atrocities, but not even the most evil-minded writer of scandalous pamphlets could imagine a woman doing what you've done. And to a young woman.'

'Enough, Martin. Pray continue, mistress.' She shot Martin a spiteful look before she did. He reflected it.

'She came after news of the Brody girl's flight became known. They were the same height. They had the same colourin'. Men – weak men – lusted after that Brody girl as they once lusted after Agnes Blackwood. I knew that it might be the only chance to be rid of her and her greed. And so when she sent biddin' me to meet her in the Moss, I brought her money. As the greedy creature counted it, I struck her too. I gave the sow,' she said with relish, 'no time even to squeal.'

'And from what Danforth tells me, you enjoyed the doing of it,' said Martin in anger. He could not understand Danforth's detachment. It was clear to him that the woman was a monster, and a monster who had beguiled them into staying under her rotten roof.

'I saw,' Danforth confirmed, 'the fury spent on the dead woman's face. To disguise her identity yes, but done with pure malice too. Enjoyment.'

'More than you can imagine, sir. And there should have been the end of it. It would have been, had you fellows no' come to the burgh and stuck your noses in. But I thought havin' you close might be useful. To protect me. As long as you were no' engaged in the affair, and I just your hostess, foolish woman, left all alone. Well, it was true enough.'

'And that is why you cast those mean, slanderous bills about the burgh. I thought I recognised the papers. They were ripped from those account rolls you keep through there.' Danforth indicated the back room and she smiled thinly.

'I had Archie do that. The witless imp can't read. He thought it a game, to give the gents sport.'

'And so you corrupted an innocent, ignorant child. Your cruelty knows no limits, Mistress Caldwell. You're a foul creature,' spat Martin.

'Am I? Then the world and its people have made me so.'

'Though they have not made a poet of you,' Danforth observed. 'But why not let the matter rest? Why bring this poor palliard in. Why cast up the past?'

'Aye,' Martin enjoined. 'It's he who brought Mr Danforth into suspicion of you. It's your own foolishness has undone you.'

'I had to live when you gentlemen returned to your master,' she shrugged. 'I could no' go on as I had. I would have had Kennedy dead and honourably buried, and been a widow. Who,' she asked, 'would have doubted it, when the Lord Cardinal's own men attested that my husband had returned, ill from his wanderin', and left me what was mine? I should have put an end to it. It would have been the close of my troubles.'

'As I said, you overplayed your hand. Had you left Kennedy out of it, I might not have wondered. Did you speed that poor creature's death?'

'I did not, sir, I swear to it. What, do you suspect poisons, the woman killer's oldest friend? I am innocent of that charge at least. It's this rotten and cruel world brought him to such a pass, led him to cough up his life, no' me.'

'No. You sought only to profit by it and bury with him your own misdeeds. It was a desperate act.'

'Too late, too late. And had the girl been thought Mistress Brody and her father the murderer, still I'd have been in dire straits as long as I were thought married to a livin' Kennedy.'

'Brody … did you kill him, mistress? Or did you have Archie do it?'

'What?' asked Martin, angry, 'corrupt the boy even into doing that wicked deed?'

'No. That wee idiot Archie came cryin' like a lamb when Brody tried to break into the stable and steal your horses. The old ruin thought to escape the burgh by ridin' out over the Well Meadow and beyond. I left Archie in the house and caught the shamblin' wastrel in the act.'

'And then you drowned him in the horse trough and dragged him through the woods to dump him. He still had straw from yonder stable about him. You have been a busy hostess.'

'It was a busy night,' she cackled without humour. 'Well, they say there's no rest for the wicked, and I suppose I prove there's some truth to that, eh? I had to lie that creature down on my bed,' she shuddered, 'and then was disturbed by Brody. He's lucky to have had so easy a death. It is easier the after the first time, you know. Once damned, there's no fear of killin' again. It was thankful I was that the hoor had returned on my own palfrey. I tossed him over it and took him through the woods to the river, though it would no' take him.' She shivered. 'Reminded me of the other week. Goin' through the woods wi' the same horse, that time wi' Agnes' body over it. Scared that someone would find us there in the woods, and knowin' if I was caught in the act I'd be killed for it. Locked away by the men of this town and killed for tryin' to make my own justice. The moon was out then too, over the river… You might thank me. I was able to wash your shirts while I was at labour.'

'Yes,' said Martin, realisation dawning. 'That old prune Clacher said that your husband and Mistress Blackwood had taken off with your stable of horses, and yet that fine grey palfrey sits out there. It's the dead woman's horse.'

'The horse was once mine, and is mine again, for whatever time I have left. Well, gentlemen, now you know all. I would that it had been otherwise.' Her eyes bored into Danforth's, and he turned his eyes downwards. 'But what's done is done and can't be undone.'

Martin gazed at her with barely concealed disgust. Danforth, however, looked upon her with pity. The woman was wicked, her crimes monstrous. Three people lay dead at her hands – each of them unpleasant creatures themselves. If her husband had not tried to desert her, he would live still. If his mistress had not blackmailed her, she would live still. If Brody had not treated his daughter so savagely, she might not have fled him, and he might live still. He looked beyond her, over the fire, to the passageway. There was likely no hope for the creature in the back room. He had been selected because he bore a passing resemblance to her husband. If anything, his part in the wild business had probably given him a more comfortable final few days than had been left to roam in the November air. Mistress Caldwell was a crooked, twisted creature. But she need not have been so.

'And so, gentlemen, what's to become of me? The gallows? The fire?' A quiver of real fear came into her voice at the latter. 'There's no help for me. I am no' insane. Or perhaps I was, when Kennedy tried to flee. But no longer. By Christ, I'm glad to be rid of it all. I've thought about quittin' this world many times in the past years. I was a fool to think that I might yet hope for somethin' different.' A strange, glazed look passed over her face. The saintly look she had adopted when feigning her husband's return had gone, replaced with the waxen effigy of a death mask.

'I hope they burn you,' said Martin. 'No matter what that wench did to you, you beat the life from her like a very devil. I've never heard the like of it. I hope they burn you.' Danforth put a hand out to stifle him.

'Peace, Martin. The lady accepts her fate.' Danforth shuddered. It was right, he supposed, that she pay for the lives she had taken with her own. But the reality of it, of knowing that one now living must have their candle snuffed out, never made the knowledge any more pleasant.

'All I've ever done,' said Mistress Caldwell, her voice low, 'is accept my fate. I'll go wi' you, gentlemen, wherever you're pleased to take me. Death by the noose is preferable to life in this burgh, wi' its loose tongues and hateful eyes.'

'We must take you to the Tolbooth,' said Danforth. 'Though I confess that, despite your crimes, it would grieve me to leave anyone in that place, and with such a gaoler.' She barked laughter again, wild and humourless.

'Fear no'. I have no desire to escape. Not now.' She started to ease herself out of the chair. 'May I fetch my things? They are no' many. I would no' go to that place wi'out my beads.' Danforth nodded slowly, watching her. She paused in the doorway and turned 'It's this town has brought me to this. This town and these people. Men's justice, men's rule.'

'It is yourself, madam.'

'And now they'll kill me for it.'

'You have killed yourself.'

'Is that loathsome creature Logan still actin' as gaoler?'

'I believe he shall be your keeper, until the end be near.' He did not like the strange gleam in her eyes. They had sharpened, somehow, brightened. 'Whatever you might be thinking, whatever the Devil is whispering in your ear, I bid you do not entertain it. You might make a good Christian death yet, and be forgiven in time.'

'It's as you say then, sir. I've killed myself. Yet I think this town shall no' forget me. Goddamn them, they'll no' forget me. Nor will you, or that Abbey and its precious men.' She gave him a long, hard look back and then trod heavily into the back room. He reached out again to stop Martin when he made to follow. 'Sir, she might yet try and flee – the woman's an inveterate liar, a madwoman. Beads! She's murdered three people, one of them a young woman.'

'I think she will not flee.'

'Think on, sir. I'm going outside, to the stables. That would be her means of escape.'

'Better you find the baillies. Bring them hither with speed.'

Martin hurried out the front door, leaving Danforth to wait on Mistress Caldwell. He moved over to the fire, which was burning itself out. It was over. The Church would not be damaged; the damned Prior would have his secret buried, no one knowing of the elopement of Kate Brody and Brother

Hector; Brody might be buried in hallowed ground. But it did not feel like an ending. Still the Church might be damaged by the Lutherans, unless they could be unmasked. He held up his hands. They were cold, but the mournful, failing, peat-fuelled flames did little. Danforth was surprised to feel a tear running down one cheek.

Left alone with the corpse, it seemed to lose a little of its power. Often he had seen death and borne witness to its aftermath, but knowing something of the motives that led to it robbed it of its awesome terror. Death had not cut a swathe through this burgh – humans had fought and lost their own petty battles, like animals baited in a ring.

Martin returned with Pattison and Semple, and graciously told them the whole story, and their part in it. Pattison marched an unprotesting Mistress Caldwell off to the Tolbooth; she refused to speak in defence or confession, but retained an odd smile. The long day spun out like a web, turning into a gossamer night. Semple listened, at first disbelieving, and then with avid interest and excitement. He examined vagrant's body closely, agreeing that, despite the resemblance, it was not Tam Kennedy. Some burgh servants, he said, would be sent to unearth the remains of the real Kennedy. He then left to write to his peers in Ayr, asking them to confirm that Agnes Blackwood had abandoned her lodgings, that he might confirm that her body lay in the churchyard of St Nicholas. Martin studiously omitted any reference to a monk leaving with Kate Brody on a ship bound for Ireland, looking directly at Danforth as he stated that Jardine had seen her quite alone. Undoubtedly the baillies would ask Jardine; Martin felt that the big fellow would be true to his word. For some hours Martin repeated himself, was queried on points, and emphasised others. Arrangements were made for the remains of the vagabond to be taken away the next morning: some of the burgesses' servants would do it. Martin did not ask where it was to be taken.

When they had gone, leaving the bodies on the flock bed, Danforth and Martin went outside and woke up a sleeping Archie. 'Wake, Archie, arise, you little cur,' said Martin.

'Whit is it, sir? Shall ye be wantin' the horses?'

'No; peace, Archie. I have news.'

'Is it the war? We invaded after a'?'

'Be quiet, I said, and listen. Your mistress is taken.'

'Whit, taken where?' He looked from one man to the other.

'The Tolbooth. She is likely to die.'

'Whit?' he repeated. 'The mistress dyin' an a'? Ye're at it. She's strong as any'hin.'

'It's her strength that will see her to the hangman,' he said. 'I thought you ought to be told.'

'Thank ye, sir,' said Archie, confused. To Danforth's surprise, tears began to roll down the boy's dirty cheeks.

'Why tears, Archie? asked Martin. 'That woman was a beast to you. She gave you neither peace or love, despite your lodging in her house, near to kin as can be.'

'Ah knowed them both a lang space. Since 'fore Ah kin mind,' he said, sobbing. 'Whit's tae become o' me now?'

'Be still, boy. You might remain here as a servant yet, unless we can find some better position for you. We'll see. Be of better cheer, and trust in your friends.'

'Thank ye, sir, thank ye. And you,' he said to Danforth, who still stood silent. They left the boy weeping on his straw.

Returning to the front room, Martin asked, 'are we to stay here tonight, in this charnel house? I do not know that I can bear it.'

'Worry not, Martin,' said Danforth, kneading his forehead. 'That poor soul cannot hurt us. None of them can. You have some plans in store for that little urchin, now his keepers are gone?'

'I might.'

'I fear it will be the worse for him, living without masters.'

'I have some thoughts on that, sir. But not for tonight. You know, I can scarcely credit all that I have seen. I felt certain that the dead girl was Kate Brody, and that the Prior knew who had slain her. I confess I was beginning to suspect that he might have ordered it himself.'

'You have heard too many vulgar and sordid tales of England's wicked monks, embroidered by their detractors to bring our faith into hatred.'

'It might be so, sir. I might reflect on that later. But what drives a woman to such madness? At one time she was a girl, at another a bride. She was in no fever, she did not starve. I cannot imagine how she could indulge in such horrors.'

'I think,' said Danforth, 'that not all madness is raving and fury. Some of it is cunning, and the more wicked for it.'

'Then you think some devil came into her and lodged there these last years?'

'Perhaps. I cannot say. But I have thought on it.'

'Oh?'

'There must be many devils, Martin, to account for all the evils in the world. I am no theologian, no divine – but I have considered before that the devil might cast himself in pieces, and scatter those pieces about the world of men. Perhaps one fragment was attracted to Mistress Caldwell, poor, abandoned creature that she was, and it took possession of her soul.'

'That's possible, sir. But it's not a goodly thought.'

'Is there anything pleasant to be found in these events?'

'No.' Martin's face was uncharacteristically solemn, his voice low. 'I just … it's just that I can't believe how deceived we were in her. She was like an actor, on a stage, and we fell for her turn.'

'Ach, all people are actors, Arnaud, masquers, players. We are all of us sewn together from the threads of all the people we have known, or loved, or admired. Or hated. No man or woman is truly his own. Each of us learns our nature. If we are lucky, we blend together good natures. Some are corrupted and weaved together from bad ones.'

'How'd you mean?'

'It is just as I see it. I have an idea on how the world is ordered, you see.'

'Aye, I think I remember something about that,' said Martin. 'When we were having a drink the other night. What's the idea?'

'Only this. Picture a great tapestry, that runs on forever. That is the world. God's tapestry, spinning out into eternity. We are each a small part of it, all in ordered rows, kings at the top, and clergy, and then nobility, and down to us, and the animals at the bottom. Some of us are blessed. We can boast bright threads. Others are composed of frayed ones.'

'That's the idea? A great tapestry of folk going on forever?'

'Yes, forever. Eternally. Millions upon millions of tiny people, including us, stitched into it. And devils, demons, can pull on the frayed threads, making those poor folk come unstuck. Like God, they are not in the tapestry, but stand apart from it.'

'If she were possessed by some devil, might she have been saved by a priest?'

'I cannot say. Somehow I do not think so. But the devil would not forbear to make mischief in such a holy land. Let us pray that if such a thing took hold of Mistress Caldwell, it shall be cast back into Hell with her death. I should not speak of this aloud, Martin. We want to bring no greater scandal upon the heads of these folk, for all they are a prideful, revel-loving lot.'

'For now, all I should like is to make an end of this unpleasant day, and I hope to all the strange happenings in this burgh.'

Danforth nodded gratefully. When he finally retired to bed, he cried, though he did not know for what exactly. Sleep, when it came, was welcome. Though he was lodged in the grimy shack of murderess, a house of the dead, no dreams plagued him.

21

The morning dawned, for Danforth, with a new and strange feeling. For the first time since coming to Paisley, there was no feeling of outstanding business. The Paisley libels had been the work of Mistress Caldwell, eager to distract them from her antics, and the murder of the young woman and her father – or, rather, the man people thought was her father – had been discovered and passed into the hands of the authorities. He could return to life as the Cardinal's English secretary, tasked only with closing the business of slanderous bills attacking his Grace. He would have to refashion his mind to it.

He did not rise early to go to Mass. He was eager to avoid the people of the burgh. Even Mistress Clacher, despite the flea Martin had put in her ear, would be unwilling to pass up the opportunity to harass with incessant questions the men who had lodged under the roof of the murderess. Besides, he had other plans for worship. He spent his time instead writing out a full report of everything that had happened, that he had witnessed, and that Mistress Caldwell had told him and Martin before she had been taken. Committing her actions and her words to paper removed her from the real world, somehow, placing her in the land of legal documents: the realm of stories.

Eventually Martin's customary light rap roused him. He poked his head in without waiting for a response. 'Good morning, sir.'

'Good morning, Mr Martin. I trust you slept well?'

'Not so very well, to be honest. You?' Danforth noted that he was fully dressed, like himself.

'Well indeed. I have come to think, you know, that we each create our own dreams and with them our own torments. Have you been out to Mass?'

'No, sir. I've been talking with Archie.' He ignored Danforth's bemused gaze and continued. 'I have bid him keep the house secure until the baillies arrive. For I think we shall not spend another night here.'

'Nor even a day. We shall flit forthwith. Does the little varlet not fear to stay here alone?'

'Not a bit of it. He's a stouter lad than he seems. I think he's rather less fearful than he was when Caldwell ruled him.'

'Very well. Have you packed your things?' Martin opened the door wider, and hunched forward the pack he had slung over his shoulder. 'Marvellous. Come in and read this report. If you are agreed, you might add your signature below mine.' As Martin quoted the text aloud, Danforth began gathering up the last of his own possessions and put them in his pack. 'Now let us be out of here and away. I should like to see the Abbey now that it has been cleansed in my mind. There I might make good my penance.'

They did not look into the back room of the inn, but left through the front door. It was bitingly cold outside, veiny fronds of frost snaking through the mud, turning it hard. Together they turned around the side of the building and looked in on the horses. 'Ho, Woebegone. You shall see some action again, you lazy brute.' At his voice Archie appeared, cleaner than he had looked since Danforth had met him.

'Ye aff, sirs?'

'Yes, Archie.'

'And ye'll be settlin' yer bill then, aye?' Martin laughed.

'Have no fear, Archie. Our bill shall be settled. But you're not the master of this inn – the Abbot owns this land yet.'

'And he might yet install a new master for you,' said Danforth. 'One who might turn this inn to a profit for himself and the Abbot.' Archie nodded, dejected, and saw to the horses. He reached up to give them affectionate pats, and to Danforth's surprise the fussy Woebegone nuzzled the thin hand in return. He then passed the reins to their masters.

'Be of better cheer, wee man,' said Martin, winking. 'Think on what I said to you.'

'Aye, sir,' said Archie, his mournful look turning hopeful. 'Aye, sir, thank you.'

As they walked their mounts towards the market cross, Danforth turned to Martin. 'What did you say to that little idiot?'

'It's of no consequence. He's no idiot, sir, but a lad who's had no life of his own.'

The cross was bustling with more than usual activity, though it was not market day. Word had got out. As they drew closer they could see that the shopfronts stood largely empty of customers, and the balladeer of the previous week – who evidently stood ever ready to appear before a crowd – was whetting his pipes with a mug of ale, unwilling to sing without the prospect of coins in return. Jardine stood outside his shop, looking towards the Tolbooth, his thumbs hooked into his ample belt. When he spotted them, he gave a friendly nod. Outside the Tolbooth a crowd had gathered, demanding news of the Brody affair. A frustrated Logan was hollering for them to disperse, or be arrested for fomenting disorder. He waved his short dirk in the air, as though it was a musket and not a chipped and weathered old blade. The withered old knock-keeper, the gnome who had greeted Danforth on his entry into the burgh, had joined him his entreaties. Mobs were ever the bane of burgh officials. Pushing their way through rabble, Danforth and Martin tied their horses to a hitching post and went inside.

Baillies Semple and Pattison were both present. Danforth noted with spiteful glee that they looked to have had an unsettled night themselves: both were unkempt and sagging. The air in the room was even staler than usual. 'Good morning,' said Martin, full of cheer. 'I trust you fellows have slept well, knowing the burgh's affairs to be in order.' Both glared at him.

'We've brought a report on all that has passed,' said Martin, pulling it from under his cloak. 'It's signed. All is in order. The Brody girl has fled by herself, out of your jurisdiction. Mistress Caldwell was responsible for the deaths of Thomas Kennedy, Agnes Blackwood and Angus Brody.' He passed them the document with a flourish, and Semple snatched it with a meaty hand. 'Is she in there?' Danforth nodded towards the closed door of the cell that had once housed Brody.

'Aye, and still not speaking,' said Pattison, grizzled face

twisting into a frown. 'Mad bitch. Logan will watch her close, see if her fat lips won't open and reveal her crimes. Well, she shall have no trial if she does not speak up for it. We're minded to hang her on market day. That should provide an entertainment, and warn off any thieves or mischief-makers what happens to their ilk.'

'Then it's pleased,' said Martin, 'that we shall not be here to bear witness to such a sorry spectacle.'

'Oh, no nice demands for this one? No Sheriff's Court, nor demands for a feather bed, or that we should give her a holiday until Christmas?'

'No,' said Martin without expression. 'Hang her high. Do you require anything further of us?'

'Nothing. Save that you leave off this matter now. I, by God's own truth, shall be glad to see the back of you.'

'That we shall do with pleasure.'

'And you shall breath nothing of this abroad?' asked Semple, in a small voice at odds with his frame. 'I would not have the burgh under suspicion for the actions of a woman who is already dead in eyes of the law.'

'Keep the peace here and you shall have nothing to fear. Only ... mind your backs around that woman. She is not as she seems, as we can attest.'

With the briefest of nods their only concession to gratitude, Semple and Pattison walked them out of the Tolbooth, and joined Logan in screeching at the people to go their own ways. As Danforth and Martin took hold of their horses, one voice, reedy and full of malevolent glee, rose above the baillies. It was Grissell Clacher. 'Those men!' she screamed. 'Those strangers, that Englishman, they know – they are art and part of what's been troubling this town!' The heads of multitude turned to them, and their own gabble died down.

'Logan, bailies,' shouted Martin, 'you might think about bringing out your stocks, for here is an old wench who cannot govern her vicious tongue.' Laughter erupted in the crowd and followed the pair as they led their horses away, over the Cart and through the Bridge Port. The sky had ceased its fretful tears, the river ceased its roar. The narrow, winding Cart had calmed to a steady, meandering tumble.

When they reached the Abbey they found the gates closed and barred to them. Martin rattled them irritably, whilst a cold anger began to rise in Danforth. 'You, porter,' cried Martin, 'open these gates and give us entry.' The porter appeared from the turreted gatehouse and looked at them through the bars, a snarl on his narrow face.

'You are the Cardinal's men,' he said.

'As well you know. We have come before.'

'The Prior will have no Cardinal's men in his jurisdiction. He is not required to submit to any authority save his Holiness and the Abbot.'

'Open this gate, you churl,' said Danforth, his cadence deadly.

'I shall open the gate gladly, gentlemen, if you sign yourselves in as guests, and no more.'

'That we shall,' offered Martin, 'and never have we claimed to be anything other.'

The porter duly unlocked and swung open the shrieking gates, and they entered. 'Now you must sign the book.' Danforth glowered at him.

'Stable these horses.'

'Sign the book. And surrender any weapons.'

'You're a weapon! Stable these horses at once, or you'll eat the book.' said Martin. The porter backed away, his eyes wide.

'The Prior will hear of it. You shall answer to the Prior.' But he led the horses off, only turning back to glare angrily at the Abbey's guests when he was a safe distance away.

'What was that all about?' asked Martin.

'That accursed Prior, damn the man, for all he is in holy orders. That, my friend, was a display of power, such as is felt necessary by all weak creatures. The Prior would have us see that we are here only by his permission, and warned that we not meddle. Well, I might show him yet. I might yet tell the Cardinal all about the fool's softness for a young novice, about his readiness to let that monk become an apostate by making free with a townsman's daughter, and then to bury evidence of the act. Yes, I might cause that man a scandal yet, such as may make his hoary head spin.' He began stomping angrily along the path to the Abbot's House.

'Hold, Simon,' called Martin. Moodily, Danforth turned. 'Calm yourself. I understand your thirst for vengeance against the Prior. He's a jealous, petty man. He's just a town Provost in a cowl: governance will come before faith and trust. It's the same the world over, and there's no remedy for it save the poison poured by the Reformists, who want to replace what is with something worse, and to their own profit.

'And there's no corruption here, sir, not really. Oh, some slackness, to be sure, and a Prior jealous of his Abbot's jurisdiction and frightened of a scandal, but we don't see monks fornicating in the cloister. We don't see young boys and jades brought in to indulge the order's lusts. No false relics are worshipped, no mechanical statues weep ducks' blood or spring water from concealed pipes. What is here, Simon? One youthful monk with high principles in a fit of worry about his friend, and who wishes for harder measures. I doubt even Thomas Cromwell could have found good reason to condemn such a place.

'You have warned yourself of divisions within the Church, especially at a time when we are threatened from without. A scandal might weaken the faith, for all it might satisfy your dislike – your understandable dislike – of the man.' He looked up at the Abbey church, towering above them to their left. Standing in stark relief against the grey sky, there was something austere, something magisterial about it. 'Would you have a place that might have stood forever, despite its agonies, attacked for the man who governs it?'

Danforth followed Martin's gaze, then returned to him. For a while he said nothing, letting the words linger in the air. 'When,' he asked, 'did you get so much wisdom?' Martin smiled at him and shook his head. 'But pray do not use my own words against me again. It makes me feel the fool that I almost made of myself. Still I would speak to the Prior on other matters.'

'As would I.'

They continued to the Abbot's House, just as the deafening

Abbey bells began tolling the monks' dinner hour. His secretarial monk was not at his post, and so they took the stairs to his chambers without permission. Seated at his usual desk, his eyes closed in contemplation, the Prior did not start when he heard them enter. Nor did he register surprise at their entrance. The door to his bedchamber was again opened, the great bed a confusion of red sheets and curtains, but the room felt a little airier.

'Gentlemen. I have expected you since the news broke this morning. I have had scribbled letters from the town's baillies informing me of the hideous actions of your hostess, and her subsequent arrest.'

'Aye,' said Danforth, swallowing his dislike, 'she is a wretched creature. It were lucky for us that she thought us the best sort before whom to perform her mummery, else she might have got clean away with murdering three people and putting a stranger in her husband's grave.'

A flicker of distaste crossed Walker's face. 'I have little interest in the matter save that it is closed, and nothing to do with this house. Indeed, I can scarcely see what it is you gentlemen have achieved. You lodged under the roof of a murderess, and yet she killed twice more – one of the Abbey's servants, no less. Now another body lies unburied, and one, I believe, to be pulled from its mean and un-Christian habitation. I do not say you brought ill omens to Paisley, gentlemen, but your presence has saved no lives.' He sat back, smiling at Danforth and Martin's rising colour. 'I trust that your standing here is as guests, and that it has been sufficiently impressed upon you? You have no power here to investigate anything that has passed.'

'Yes, Father. We bore witness to your own mummery at the gate.' Danforth's voice had turned sad. Still the man was suspicious and fearful, lest men of his own faith conspire against him. 'Yet I hope you see, Father, that had you been open and frank with us from the beginning, this affair might not have progressed as it did?' Walker only stared impassively back in response. 'Yet,' Danforth went on, 'as we are here as guests, we are minded to be treated as such. We might now be lodged in the guesthouse, for tomorrow we return to Glasgow.'

Walker leaned back, his hands clasped, deliberating. 'The sooner the better, I think. Yes, it might be so.'

'And we shall hear Mass in the Pilgrim's Chapel.'

'All of our order are ordained priests. You might make your pilgrimage and be confessed there. Yet you signed at the gate?' His eyes turned shrewd again. 'You have declared yourselves guests, and admitted no judicial authority here?'

'We signed nothing,' said Martin. 'Father, you will have to have faith.' Walker's bottom lip jutted. 'There is one thing further, that might prove good faith on either side, if you will excuse the pun.' His eyebrows rose in question. 'The Abbot has lost the freeholder of part of his land in the Oakshawside, Tam Kennedy. You must now find him a new tenant to work the inn there and turn it to profit. There is a boy, a young man, Archie, as was a servant to the man now known to be dead. Might he have the inn, to run as his own business?' Danforth turned to look at Martin, his eyes wide. A new respect bloomed. In the past week he had seen the very worst of man and his workings. Now, in some way, he felt he was seeing the best.

'I do not know,' said the Prior, the lines of his prominent brow deepening, 'I shall have to ask the Abbot. If this boy was a bondsman of some kind ...'

'He is an orphan, and a good ostler, familiar with the property. I am sure that the Abbot need not be troubled with such a trifling matter. You have the powers of Claustral Prior, Father, to discharge in the Abbot's name.'

'Has he the price of tenancy?'

Sighing, Martin produced the money from his purse. He nudged Danforth, who did likewise, careful not to give the Prior too much. Together they passed across the cost of their lodgings at the inn, and more besides. 'Also,' said Martin, 'there is a horse attached to the property, that might be sold as you – or the Abbot – think right.'

'The beast is ours by right of herezeld. Yet this ...' said Walker absently. He was gazing at the money, his lips moving silently as he totted it up.

'We are men of credit and esteem,' said Martin. 'If more's required, it may be raised against us. And it would be smoother, Father, that the inn continue as it is, though without its wicked mistress. There shall then be less scandal and no new tenant to ask questions. We,' he said, his voice laden with suggestion, 'should also be very grateful that the matter be closed, and our lips with it.'

Walker drew a deep breath. 'Very well, gentlemen. I can see little alternative. You have played your game well. Have you anything else?'

'Have there been any letters for us?' Walker smiled.

'Yes. I see that temporal business does indeed carry weight with you.' He picked a letter bearing the Cardinal's seal from his desk and passed it to Danforth. It was unbroken. 'It arrived this morning, with great secrecy and urgency, though I cannot say when it was dispatched. Things are in turmoil, with even the best riders struggling on some of the poorer roads. Though the frost may make your passage easier. You may go now. I have much to think upon.'

'And yet you will send word to the baillies that young Archie is the new master of the inn in the High Street's Oakshawside.'

'Yes.' The Prior's voice was tight. 'Though you have not provided enough for him to make a burgess.'

'If the boy wishes to become a burgess, in time, he shall make his own money for the privilege. He has the means to do so and must prove he has the wit.'

'Very well. That may be a matter for the Town Council. You shall find the guest-master in charge of the guesthouse. Brother James.' Danforth and Martin resisted the urge to trade glances, lest they make trouble for the young man. 'If he has finished his dinner. Good morrow to you, gentlemen.'

They left the Abbot's House, and Danforth looked past it, his heart and his mood soaring. The Pilgrim's Chapel lay further down the path: a neat, pretty building where he might make a good confession. Martin caught his gaze and the smile that followed it. 'You looking forward to making good this pilgrimage, sir?'

'I am.'

'One day, I think, you might tell me what it is that weighs so heavily on your soul.'

Danforth gave him a long stare, not unfriendly, and then sighed. 'Mr Martin, it is a thing that I have carried with me for many years. It might be of little import to some men.' Martin said nothing. 'You know, Arnaud, that I was married and had a child in England. That I lost them?'

'Yes, sir.'

'I think I was not an easy man to love, alas.' Martin gave him a lingering, sideways glance. 'But married we were. My wife, Alice, and my daughter Margaret. They were taken by the plague in September '33. I blamed the troubles in England for it. The king had married his strumpet, cast aside Queen Katherine, and shown the world the path down which he wished to lead the realm. All was suspicion; all was hatred; everywhere there were spies. It was the last time the great plague swept the nation. It seemed that God had turned his rage on the kingdom.

'Yet these past years, though I have hated Henry for his heresies, it has sat upon me that it was not the king's sins that bore the guilt of Alice and Margaret dying, but my own. You see, we met in '31, and were married the following year. Yet we could not wait. Well, you are a young man yet, you know the weakness and the temptation. We were … intemperate. No … no … I was intemperate. We married in haste, because Alice was already growing heavy with our child. The poor thing was begotten in sin, and it was me that led Alice to it. Good woman,' he said, wiping away an unbidden tear, 'she would have waited, but I could not, and persuaded her by gentle means to give up her virtue, telling her that it was of no value, that we would marry anyway, that I had money and prospects enough to keep her. And so you see I was no better than King Henry, bedding the Boleyn before their wedding. She lost her head for her sins, and Alice and Margaret lost their lives. I have tried by all means to shrive myself of it, but until now I have felt it impossible. This pilgrimage, this visit to the last of my chosen kingdom's holy places, I feel, will help me let those spirits lie. And now, for the first time, I feel that it may be so.' He looked again towards the Pilgrim's Chapel.

Martin reached out and clasped Danforth's shoulder. 'Simon, you are a good man. Might I confess something?' Danforth nodded, a little unsteadily. 'To be honest, I only came on this trip to delight in causing you mischief, and to make sport of your piety.'

'On that,' replied Danforth, managing a chuckle, 'you have done a creditable job of work.' Martin grinned. It was an amicable grin, full of good humour.

'Yet I think I've come to know you better. As I said, you're a good man. Make your peace tomorrow, and we can leave this place. If you're the lighter for it, then all that's passed might have been worth it. When love and death have broken your heart, it can seem easier to run, to do without it at all. But it doesn't work like that. You'll never go back to England, will you, even if Henry dies? When, I mean. Your home is here, in this realm and this Church?'

'Back to be gutted or burned? No. Like Antaeus, I draw my strength now from this land.'

'Don't spoil my wisdom with classics. It's good wisdom. Shall we find young Brother James?'

'Let us,' said Danforth, turning away from the Chapel. Then, suddenly remembering, he cried, 'but wait. The Cardinal's letter.' He took it from his cloak and broke the seal, letting the red wax fall to the gravel path. He swallowed. It was brief. 'The unicorn is tossed on stormy waves. I fear – O unhappy day – that it shall sink anon. Black clouds gather. And I find no favour, nor shall, until a name restores my credit.'

'Riddles. I hate it when our master speaks in riddles. The Unicorn is the name of the king's ship, isn't it?'

'The unicorn is the king,' said Danforth, thinking. 'Tossed … sink … His Grace says the king is ill. That his enemies, his Grace's enemies, make trouble for him. He must needs have the name of his libeller to restore his credit.'

'Aye,' said Martin. 'Aye, if we can prove that his Grace was slandered before this damned battle, that he was conspired against throughout, it'll take the king's anger from him and place it on others. We give him the names of these libellers, and he puts them before the king. In such a fashion, he might prove that any words touching his reputation that are spoken following this terrible loss are as like to be based on craft alone, from men who have sought his ruin even before the battle was fought. Tomorrow we shall discover the findings of the Archbishop's commission. Tomorrow ...'

The guesthouse of Paisley Abbey, on the western range of the cloister, was more palace than lodging house for weary pilgrims. In its time it had housed royalty and the nobility, and its furnishings, though somewhat careworn, were quality. Brother James, who had made them his confessors the previous week, showed them into the richly-appointed chambers. When he had shut the door behind him, he had looked at them with open, pleading eyes. Martin had told him of his friend Hector's escape.

'He is now thrown upon God's mercy,' said James. 'An apostate, but one lucky that the monastery shall not be eager to hunt him like rabbit.'

'I see your hand is recovered, Brother,' nodded Martin. James looked down, again baffled.

'Oh yes. It was only a graze from a knife. There is a fellow from the burgh comes here to buy ale from us, and he cares not if he unsheathes his dirk in our presence. He thinks it might lower the price, and I brushed past him when he was in arms as well as his cups. By his station in the burgh this man thinks himself only sufficiently honoured by lower prices than the rest of the town pay. It is my sad duty to look after guests whether they are ungracious or of your fine disposition.' He looked up at Martin. 'You did not think it signified something else?'

'I fancy I know the brute of whom you speak, and I do not envy your labour in attending him. My friend Martin has a suspicious nature, Brother,' smiled Danforth. 'And I think a fondness for scandal. He was almost eager for the Abbey to involved in this terrible affair.' Martin turned sheepish, and began scuffing his boots on the ground.

'I confess my mind waxed strange. But it was a hell of a strange affair, to be sure.'

Brother James nodded absently, confused by the jesting. 'I must return to prayer, gentlemen. As honoured guests, all meals will be brought to you.' He bowed and left them to their luxury.

Whilst Martin threw his things down on an enormous bed, Danforth toured the room. It truly was a lodging fit a king, the bed curtained, gold and silver candlesticks on every table, thick, fringed tablecloths, and gilded designs crossing the ceiling. On the walls were hung tapestries. Ranged around the room, they told the stories of the Abbey's favoured saints. Saint James of Compostella was stitched riding into battle against the Moors; Saint Catherine was depicted with one arm leaning on her wheel, her sword held militantly in the other hand; St Columba was shown at the prow of a boat; Saint Nicholas stopped an unjust execution, his hand held up; and St Ninian, the Briton, could be seen leading a group of heathenish, southern Picts, tiny in comparison to their master, towards a shining cross. It must have taken many nuns many hours of sewing, and have cost many fingers painful jabs, to illustrate the stories of God's chosen miracle workers.

The pair settled in the Abbey guesthouse, content at first with their own thoughts. Both prayed silently for their country's victory. If King James should be die then Henry of England would have claimed the life of another Scottish king: the first his brother-in-law and the second his nephew. Such a man must truly be a monster, thought Danforth. The aftermath of such a catastrophe would be unthinkable, the realm torn apart even if a prince was born. Time moved forwards on leaden feet, and both Danforth and Martin were conscious that, as they sat ensconced in palatial opulence, to the south violent and unknown things were happening. For all the non-spiritual help they could give they might as well have been in England.

Brother James returned when the short day was over, with some food to see them through the night: bread rubbed with salt, cheese, all luxury. At intervals they could hear the chanting of the monks as they raised their voices in prayer. It was the only time the whole of the company was encouraged to use their voices. It was a comforting, soporific sound, but after an evening of silent contemplation, neither Danforth nor Martin could bear the silence any longer. Instead they sat in cushioned, comfortable chairs by a roaring fire. It was a strange feeling to be in such regal surroundings – it might almost have been a thrill. Yet neither took real pleasure from it.

'That was a good thing you did for Archie,' said Danforth. 'It fair delighted me.'

'He's a sorry wee soul. It's my nature, sir. I could never bear to see a dog whipped nor a cat drowned. No lad who tends horses well is a bad one.'

'Think you the lad will make good?'

'Who can say?' Martin shrugged. 'He might be thrown from the place in a month.'

'Then why provide for him?'

'He deserves a chance, sir. Everyone does. Yet so few are given one in this world. Whether Archie stands or falls will now be up to his own wits. Let's hope that his laziness was just protest at his treatment. I know I wouldn't have given good service to such a mistress as he endured.'

'It shall be no easy task making such a dark place so full of mishaps succeed.'

'Perhaps. Or it may be that a burgh so full of folk inclined to idling talk will ensure its success.' Danforth did not answer. It was a strange thing that people should so rejoice in the disreputable and shameful misdeeds of others, that they should be so intrigued by the darkness that lurks beneath the thatched roofs and within the sturdy walls of their neighbours' homes and their places of worship. Yet it was a true thing. As long as there were people, there would be the odd, vicarious thrill of indulging in tales of death, destruction and murder. For a while silence again fell between them.

'We will save his Grace's honour yet,' said Danforth, answering an unasked question. 'God will reward us for our work here. He gave it us, and we rose to it.'

'And we might at that,' said Martin. He had a silver cup of wine in his hand, and he held it out, tilting it this way and that to watch the reflection of the firelight play upon it. 'If the king's truly ill …'

'Do not speak like that. It invites fate.'

'Don't be so superstitious, mon ami, you've been warned. If the king's ill, we must trust to the wee prince yet to be born. Who knows who might grasp for power if anything should happen. But it'll go badly for the Cardinal. This great war against England, his Holy War against heresy, is held to be at his direction. It's the fruit of his policy.'

'That is slander,' said Danforth. 'The English king, with no ounce of shame in him for killing the fourth King James, has threatened this kingdom since before I was born.'

'That long?'

'Do not be light. And since he has thumbed his nose at the Holy Father, King Henry has sought to force Scotland to follow his lead. Because he is determined to cut England off from the great powers of Europe, he demands that Scotland do the like. He is a bully and a tyrant, and invents proofs of his suzerainty over this nation that he lets no man see.'

Martin sat forward, took a sip from his cup, and fixed Danforth with a stare. 'And yet my point stands. The Cardinal's honour must be unblemished if the unicorn sinks. Or his men will have the blame of it. You're an Englishman, Simon. No, do not wrinkle your face, I am simply offering you a fact. The English might not be popular if anything happens to the king.'

'In England, it was death to speak of the death of the king.'

'You're not in England. Well,' said Martin, yawning.

'Perhaps. Who can ever say what tomorrow will bring? I would attend Mass and be confessed, and then take the highway to Glasgow. We might have the names of these Lutheran fellows from the Archbishop.' He rose from his chair, stretched, and then settled onto the great bed for an unbroken night's sleep.

In the pearly light of a misty morning, the Pilgrim's church looked like a little haven. Lanterns had been lit outside it, and the flames lapped at the grey stone. They stepped through its door into life in incense and tranquillity. Inside, the welcome sight of golden crucifix, rood screen and statuary stood like constant friends. A brightly-painted stone frieze stood between two statues. On it was depicted the life of St Mirin, the patron of Paisley. Danforth smiled at it fondly. This was precisely the type of thing that the Reformists hated, and he had never understood why. It brought comfort, reminding him of the past.

The monk who presided over the Mass was one neither Martin nor Danforth had seen, but Brother James, as their host, and Brother David, attended. As always the words worked their charm and magic. Danforth took Communion and then confessed to the monk. He told him of his sin, of his youthful lust, and of his desire for absolution. He did not confess that he knew of Brother Hector's flight. That was not his burden. The monk listened with his eyes closed, and then pronounced absolution. As penance he was told to show charity to the poor, and to serve God by serving his master. Danforth had heard the words before, but they now had a special significance. He happily dug into his remaining money to purchase Masses for all those he had lost, and those who might be suffering torments in purgatory for their unforgivable sins.

He had made a great pilgrimage. He had fasted until his body had almost given out. He had unmasked a murderess and, by doing so, prevented slander and scandal falling upon the Abbey. All in all, he felt, he had passed the strange examination that had been set for him. Now, as penance, he would serve his master by putting to an end the ugly matter of the Glasgow libels.

They gathered their horses and were struck out on the path to the Abbey gate when a servant rushed through it, screaming. Other servants moved towards him, including the gatekeeper.

'What is the matter,' shouted Danforth. He and Martin joined the group.

'The witch, the possessed murderess, Caldwell,' the servant was crying, gesticulating wildly. 'She's oot, she's oot!

Escaped! Pray, Brothers, she's kilt Logan! Strangled him wi' a Rosary and smashed his skull! Run, she's comin'!'

Exchanging glances, Danforth and Martin pushed their way past the group and outside the Abbey walls. The road curved towards the Bridge Port on their right and they followed it. Drifting down from the burgh were jeers and screams.

At the sight of Mistress Caldwell, Danforth crossed himself. She was approaching the Bridge Port from the cross, staring resolutely ahead. It was impossible to make out her expression. Behind her trailed stick figures: the people of the town were behind her, screeching curses and throwing things. None appeared to want to get too close to her. Still she marched onwards. As she did, Danforth could see the matted straw stuck in her rusty hair. 'Christ,' said Martin. 'She's run madder. She's coming for the Abbey. Christ, she *is* possessed, right enough.'

As though she had heard him, she paused on the bridge. She turned to the crowd and spat. Then she turned left and stepped towards the edge of the bridge. Clambering heavily onto the low wooden wall which spanned it, she stood briefly, balancing, and then went head-first over it. There was a whirl of dirty white as she hurtled to the water below. She disappeared for a moment, and then her skirts blossomed at the surface, before sinking down again.

'Christ,' repeated Martin. The jeering crowd ran onto the bridge, their fear sunk, and pressed themselves over the edge to watch. Danforth spotting the supposedly dead Logan, blood seeping from a knock on the forehead. 'Shall we return?' asked Martin.

'No. Let us get away from this bedlam. She was right. The town shall not forget her. She gave the baillies their spectacle, Arnaud. But it was on her terms.'

22

They slid through the great doors of Glasgow castle, bypassing the screen before them, following it to the left and climbing the stairs. In the outer office nothing much had changed, save the muddy boot-prints that trailed the ground in both directions. Still the Virgin gazed down from her tapestry; still her eyes were peaceful; still the flowers surrounding her bloomed. The Archbishop's secretary was not at his desk, and on noticing that, they did notice one difference – the unpleasant little mole had put his affairs in order. His inkwells were arranged neatly in a row, his papers in perfect symmetry against the edge of desk. Martin turned to Danforth, and his mouth formed a question when the door opened. The bespectacled secretary held the door open for a stern-faced young man, his clothes askew from riding. The messenger gave them a brisk nod before taking the stairs at a trot.

The secretary saw them and, on recognition, disappeared back into the Archbishop's privy chamber. He emerged momentarily. 'You gentlemen are wasting your time,' he said. 'His Grace has matters of far greater import than you fellows.' Danforth looked at Martin, and he grinned back, needing no further encouragement. He lifted the man under his arms and deposited him in the chair by his desk, letting Danforth skirt them and open the door. Together they went through, pushing it closed behind them.

'The Cardinal's slaves, eh,' said Archbishop Dunbar, without much surprise. 'And as martial as ever.' He rose from the seat behind his desk and offered his ring. They each kissed it before Dunbar took his seat again, leaning forward and making a steeple of his bony fingers. It was the office, Danforth reminded himself, and not the man that commanded deference. It did not make it any easier. Recently it seemed that he was always being brought before men of authority, men who demanded respect without offering anything that would encourage loyalty or love. Such was the price of hierarchy. Martin had said something to him about the importance of his faith and his Church to him. It was strange that good Catholics should do so much to test it even when enemies from without were seeking to destroy it.

'What news, your Grace?' asked Martin.

'To business with haste, I see.' Danforth noted that Dunbar had deep lines etched into his brow and around his mouth, deeper even that those which plagued Prior Walker. He could not remember them being quite so pronounced on their previous visit. His sharp, dark eyes now also sat above little purple purses. 'To the matter of the verses touching his Grace the Cardinal's honour, there is none, save that my ordering a commission appears to have put an end to them. Of course, you fellows left me no proofs, and so I could investigate no man. I have had the market cross watched, and I have had informers visit every tavern and alehouse in the burgh. No man claims knowledge of these bills, and none have been set abroad. Neither, I am told, has any man even tried to approach the market cross save my men. Perhaps,' he said, almost wistfully, 'the weather has stopped them as much as I have. Still, the Lord Cardinal might yet have a care that his name is not brought into contempt, eh?'

'Your Grace,' asked Danforth. His mouth had run dry, and the words rasped out. He did not want an answer. 'What news of the king?'

'You will know by now about the Solway Moss.'

'Aye.'

'The king did not join the battle but remained at Lochmaben with a fever. He now waxes weary of this life. I believe the queen to be at Linlithgow in childbed, so his Grace may there. It is said he cannot stand to be in the same city in which your master dwells. Instead the Cardinal chases him, begs him, offers to return to France for aid in the defence of the realm. Talks wildly even of getting the Danes to join in the fight against England. King James gives his Grace no ear. Your Cardinal,' he spat, sudden venom animating his face, 'is disgraced and undone.'

Danforth was too numb to feel anger. 'Then all is confusion.

How did it happen? We were the greater number. It was our battle to win.'

'That battle,' said Dunbar, looking fixedly at Danforth, 'was a fool's errand. It should not have taken place when it did. It seems that three of your ilk, sir, three banished Englishmen living as exiles in Scotland murdered a herald of the English king. It was done, so it is bruited, with the sufferance of your Cardinal. Yes, sir, your own master inveigled three English Catholic exiles to murder a man who had safe conduct to enter the realm. Yet I suppose his Grace did this without your foreknowledge, eh?' Little flecks of spittle flew from Dunbar's mouth as he spoke, splattering on the desk before him. Danforth's mouth gaped. 'Do not think I have not heard rumours of what has befallen the burgh of Paisley since you fellows went into it. Men who visited the burgh yesterday tell me that a number of corpses now litter the town and all the talk is of murders and madness. Who's to pay the corpse duties for all this burial – reburial, hmm? It shan't be this house. Death, it seems, follows the Cardinal's imps.'

'It cannot be. I know nothing of this,' said Danforth, still contemplating the murder of a herald.

'His Grace may answer to that himself, though naturally he denies it and pleads the Lords of the Council take notice of him. If he is proven to have been setting his rabid pet Englishmen on honest Englishmen with leave to enter our kingdom and safe conduct through it, it will be the worse for him.

'Our army did not know the land. Around Solway it is bog, not fit even for feeding swine. On finding the ground unfriendly to our cause, they attempted to retreat, and it is said Lord Maxwell instigated a panic before defecting to the English. Hmph. More Englishman than Scotsman, that man. And we ought to fear that others will be content to court England in these dark days. King Henry will do all he can to ensure it. Our men's hearts were not in that damned battle, not in that place. Divers of them were drowned as they tried to cross the Esk; still others were set upon by the English who know the land, and by the wild men of Liddesdale, who would rob the shoes off a beggar and return for his teeth. Only twenty or so were granted an honourable death in arms on the field. Yet near a thousand true Scotsmen have been taken captive. Perhaps more. Two earls to be sure have been captured, and hundreds of gentlemen. Every one amongst them is now in the hands of King Henry, to be ravished by his promises and bribes and perchance returned to Scotland as his creatures and spies. This is your Cardinal's fault, gentlemen. The whole realm speaks of it.' Danforth slouched, trying to comprehend the defeat. The deaths at Mistress Caldwell's hands had been horrific, malicious, but this was on a scale too grand and terrible to make sense. Only twenty granted the deaths of heroes, the rest slain as they tried to escape.

'Then such slanders must be stifled,' he said finally. 'Your Grace, King Henry will press our king to overthrow the Church. It is well known that the English king hates our master above all others in Scotland. That must speak for his good faith.'

'I have faith in the king,' said Dunbar. 'Even though he be surrounded by wicked counsellors.' There was to be no support, no unity from Archbishop Dunbar. The man had taken the news in his own way. He blamed the Cardinal. Martin and Danforth looked at one another, the same question unspoken on each pair of lips: was this what the verdict of the kingdom?

'More serious heads than your master's,' continued Dunbar, 'called for a peaceful cessation to hostility, yet he cried out for glory against King Henry's false Church. If the commons now rail against the folly of the enterprise, then who amongst us might blame them, eh?'

'What,' Danforth managed, 'shall we tell his Grace about your commission? Shall we tell him that Glasgow has been plagued by Lutherans whom your Grace has now brought to heel?'

'Glasgow's people are my own affair, and none of the Cardinal's,' said Dunbar. 'You may tell him what you list, but he shall have no authority here, and none of his men shall investigate that which is mine alone to interrogate. You might, however, tell him that he ought to have a greater care for his reputation. I think that some petty verses set upon market crosses shall be the least of his worries. You may go.' He offered them the ring once more. 'Shall you be leaving my lands, leaving Glasgow, at the present?'

'It is likely, sir. We have no further business here. His Grace may have need of us as he … as he labours in the service of the king.'

'Then God be with you, gentlemen. And your master.'

They closed the doors of the Archbishop's privy chamber as they left it, and again met the eavesdropping secretary. As before, he backed away to his seat when he saw them emerging. Through his spectacles his large eyes glinted. 'You see,' he spat, 'what your master has brought to this realm. Defeat. Death. Captivity.'

'Hold your tongue,' said Danforth. His voice was quite even as he strode around the desk, but his body was trembling. Martin fixed the secretary with a threatening glare, but made no move to touch him. Instead, as he walked past the desk, he threw his arm wildly across it, sending its neatly arranged tenants sailing across it and to the floor.

'You idiot!' squealed the mole. 'You cumbrous clod!' Then, 'that was not an accident, sir!'

'Oh, what a weak-minded blockhead am I,' said Martin with a grin. 'It has been my curse since birth.' He bent to pick up the documents, smiling with relish at the ink spilled on the carpet. He scrunched them up, tearing them as he did, and then threw them balled on the desk. 'There, sir. Your former order has been restored. No, there is no need to thank me.' Laughing, he trotted after Danforth leaving the fuming secretary to straighten his affairs.

'Did you get pleasure of that?' asked Danforth when Martin had reached him on the stairs.

'A great deal, mon ami.'

'As did I. Well played, sir.'

'What shall we do now?'

'The Cardinal desires knowledge of who has been defaming him. But let us not speak here.' As they descended the stairs, they found a gaggle of servants cowering behind the screen, listening. Another messenger passed them as they left the castle. They took charge of their horses and rode out, whereupon Danforth called them to a halt.

'Sir?'

'What did you make of this accusation, this claim that his Grace the Cardinal sent some of his English exile friends to murder a herald?'

'I do not credit it.'

'Why is that?'

'Well, Mr Danforth ... if the Cardinal had sought one of his English friends to murder their former countrymen, he need have looked no further than yourself.'

'Witty, sir,' said Danforth. 'But do not be light. By your truth do you not credit it?'

'No, sir. The Cardinal's a man of great policy, but a man of the Church.'

'This is true. Ach, but I cannot bear the thought of a job only half done. Nor can I bear disappointing one who has put their faith in me.'

'In *us*. We don't need to leave Glasgow this moment,' said Martin, a thoughtful look coming over his face. 'Sir, might we lodge one more night at the inn?'

'I think we might.' Danforth's interest was piqued. 'You have devised some method that the Archbishop did not for catching our Cardinal's slanderers? Perhaps a visit to the university to enquire ourselves of its students?'

'Possible. Let us return to the inn and leave our things. Then I pledge to you, Mr Danforth, you shall know all.'

'How is it that I could fail to see this?' groaned Danforth, stung. He had had enough shocks, enough unpleasantness for one day. Little by little an edifice seemed to be crumbling, like the Abbey of Paisley's patched-up choir, or the fading gatehouse at Glasgow's Bishop's Castle. Martin was looking at him with pity as well a measure of concealed excitement.

'You could not see it for the best of reasons, Simon. You do not wish to acknowledge division within the Church. But there it is. This is a scandal. It is worse – it is a shame. The office of Chancellor, I think, shall soon lie vacant.'

They were in Martin's room at the inn of Glasgow's market cross. It was more spacious than the Kennedys' faded lodgings, and well provisioned with candles, desk and comfortable cot. On the desk were spread the Glasgow libels. Martin had begged them from Danforth as soon as they had entered and he had lit the candles. Beside them was a scrap of paper: the beginning of a letter. It read, 'To my honor'd and truly worthy friend'.

'You have played the role of master thief too well,' said Danforth. Martin shuffled his feet and, to Danforth's surprise, blushed. 'It is not so very much, but I think it will serve our turn.' As Danforth had produced and spread out the slanderous bills, Martin had taken from inside his doublet the scrap of letter. He had taken it, he said proudly, from the mess of papers he had knocked from the desk of the Archbishop's secretary. The handwriting was identical, noticeable even from a few scant words, to that which had composed the scurrilous verses. The hand of the Archbishop's mole-like secretary and that behind the defamation of Cardinal Beaton were the same. The 'r's were unmistakeable, the top of the 'd' looping backwards over its little circle. Even the 'n's dropped low on the last stroke. Danforth resisted the urge to pick them all up, one by one, and hold them over the candle's flame. The little scraps seemed to be mocking him. 'You idiot,' they giggled, 'you could not see what lay in front of your eyes.'

'It is weak evidence, but better than no evidence at all. Now we might prove that the Cardinal had enemies – the most powerful enemies – at work against him even before the battle was lost. Hell, before even it was fought.'

'But how did you know, Arnaud? How could you have suspected this?' Danforth was at a loss. It had not occurred to him that a servant of the true Church could turn on another, could write so violently against him. The notion was detestable. Somehow it was even more inconceivable than would have been a monk murdering a young girl and being protected by his Abbey's Prior. Yet here was the proof of it.

Disharmony and personal hatred were at work within the Roman Church.

'I don't see as you do, Simon. You try and see perfection and unity in our faith. Both are wanting. I've perceived from the beginning that these writings would not be investigated by the Archbishop with any ... well, any zeal. You've known him to be an enemy of our master, yet you'd not have credited him capable of coming to blows against him. The Archbishop must have known that few would credit the notion that he might be involved. He was the king's tutor once, was he not? He is Lord Chancellor. He must think himself untouchable. A little king himself, of the Church.'

'It is my fault; I have been blind, tempested in mind.' Danforth bent forward over the desk, screwing his eyes shut. 'It is this faction within the realm, it is such libelling that helped bring the old Rome to ruin.'

'I am sorry, but it should come as no great surprise. You have seen for yourself how quickly neighbour can turn against neighbour, even when feigning friendship. Recall that old Clacher woman and her secret hatred of her friend Darroch, and Darroch's for her. Recall Brother James speaking out against his Prior whilst living under his rule. It is no great error nor even a great shock that the Church should be so riven. Where there are men there is the chance of it. It is better, my friend, that you see this, for all its ugliness. But take heart, sir. With proof we might yet have the matter investigated. The Cardinal might bring this before the king, and the king might force reconciliation and friendship. This is the time for men of faith to stand firm, to stand beside one another and face the greater enemy.'

Danforth said nothing. He was still dazed. He preferred to cling to the feeling rather than let it dissipate, for he knew it would be replaced with one of foolishness. He would have blamed the men of the university, he would have blamed anyone rather than a man of his own religion, and highly-placed in the Church at that. Archbishop Dunbar may as well have struck the Cardinal in public. If the world knew of this division, the Lutherans would rub their hands in glee. It must be handled with sensitivity. 'You are a man of great cunning, Arnaud,' he said. 'You have clearer sight than I.'

'And yet I would have had Prior Walker in chains in Paisley, Simon, so eager was I to see the faults in our Church. Or wee Brother James, even. We each have our strengths, as we each have our weaknesses. It is a good thing. It makes us stronger as friends.' Danforth looked up at him.

Friends. He had had them at university, fellow scholars and debaters. He had had them at his grammar school. Then had followed lust, love, marriage, a succession of deaths, the world turning upside down as he grieved, and his mad flight through England's postern gate. Somewhere along the path of his life he had either been abandoned or chosen to walk alone. Quite simply he had fallen out of the common step of humanity. He was not keen to continue such a solitary march.

'Great cunning, and as I have had cause to say before, newfound wisdom. I have misjudged of you, my young friend. I thought you a light fellow, inconstant and full of mirth. It is not so.'

'Now, sir, I shouldn't like to be empty of mirth. It's my temperament to be as the air, sanguine and full of hope. But to be serious: a little lightness is no crime.'

'No. I think it is not. Thank you, Arnaud. The Cardinal shall be thankful to you too. It is you have brought this thing into the light, and it is you should be rewarded for it.' Martin shrugged.

'I seek no rewards save my due and the right to see a little of the kingdom and the world when his Grace sees fit to show it me.'

'I am afraid all we shall soon see is the road to Edinburgh.'

'It is a good enough sight and a pleasant enough town.' They sat for a while, each lost in their own thoughts. There was worry. What if the king was ill? What if the prince was born dead? But there was also hope. Whatever might happen in Scotland, they had done their duty, and could do no more.

Epilogue

The whole of Scotland seemed to smell like bonfires, those cheerful signifiers of good news. Following his daughter's birth – a princess, Mary – the king had taken to his bed in Falkland Palace, a building that rivalled only Stirling Castle for its beauty and the architectural efforts lavished upon it by two successive Scottish kings. Soaring towers and Corinthian columns stood at intervals along its straight, scrubbed walls and brightly painted heraldry stood above every portcullis and neatly glazed window. It was to this magnificent house that Danforth and Martin rode towards the at the end of December's second week. Autumn had finally departed, taking with it the constant rains that had followed summer. In their place had come a cold, of the type that chills the bones in the morning, seeping in and refusing to let go until the body has been thoroughly racked by shivering. Even in furred riding cloaks, boots and gloves, Danforth felt his toes compressed into icy blocks and could feel, even if he could not see, the purplish-white of his fingers.

The winter blast had frozen the grounds and parks around Falkland, the skinned trees wearing mantles of frost. The king's tennis court had become a sheet of white, like a river frozen in mid flow, and the gardens, devoid of blossoms, had become mud banks dotted here and there with partially frozen pools of rainwater. Only some stout evergreens, imposing exiles from the surrounding woodlands, shook their piny locks saucily in the season's face. Some might have found an austere beauty in nature's approach to Christmas, but Danforth hungered for it to be gone. The festive season, when it came, should be one of warmth and peace, of reflection before the brightness of cheerful fires. For a moment he thought of the last royal residence he had been inside – the guesthouse at the Abbey of Paisley. There was a place that would be suited to Christmas, the Cluniacs' chants filtering into it and the tapestries guarding the interior walls against the cold that assailed them from without.

The Cardinal had proven elusive, darting about Scotland after the king. He had determined to rouse his sovereign from the melancholy that was the talk of the realm, to bid him take heart, recover his spirits, and look forward to the upturn of fortune's ever-spinning wheel.

Yet Danforth and Martin noted, with sinking hearts, that the people of Edinburgh had begun to grumble against their sovereign. It was that, suspected Danforth, that was the true cause of his disillusion. Both secretaries agreed that they ought to entrust their proof to no other man, and so together they had decided to end the matter themselves, placing Dunbar's letter in their master's hands directly. Once accomplished, they might well be allowed freedom to enjoy the Yule period. The Cardinal would once more be in favour, his enemies shamed; and when the Cardinal was in favour, he was invariably magnanimous to his loyal servants.

The pair entered the palace, which lay in a great 'L' shape of eastern and southern ranges, through a great gatehouse on the west of the latter. Housed within the gatehouse were the stables, were Woebegone and Coureur were left to lodge with horses of finer quality and higher rank. Guards stood everywhere, and it was only with some delay that they were shown into the servants' quarters. Everywhere those in service lingered – not only the king's royal guards but men who, by their liveries, served and protected the Earls of Argyll and Rothes. King James, it seemed, was holding a small Council in the palace, and so the Cardinal's men were left to wait until their master might have liberty to grant them an audience. 'These guards are sombre fellows,' remarked Martin. 'No cheer in them. Are his Grace the king's men always so stern? They ought to try governing his correspondence for their bed and board. But what a glorious place,' he added, 'it might have been lifted from the Loire and dropped here.'

'You have been to the Loire?' He struggled to get his tongue around the word.

'I have not,' said Martin. 'But I have heard tell of its chateaux.'

'Hmm.' Danforth was unsure of Falkland. He had nothing against architectural ostentation – grand cathedrals and magnificent abbeys and priories delighted him. But delicate, finely-wrought places such as Falkland Palace lacked the grandeur, the air of ancient solidity. A great, thick chain of wrought gold, he fancied, would ever be preferable to a thin, pearl-studded necklace.

They had only passed one night in Falkland Palace when a different messenger brought them an invitation to an audience with their master.

Beaton sat behind a small desk – the room itself was an antechamber with a carved cot, its interior the polished wood that seemed to be the panelling of choice in Falkland. When Danforth and Martin were admitted he rose, a smile adding only a little warmth to a face that had grown thin with fatigue and worry. He was a slight man, slender and shrunken without his biretta. His height always shocked Danforth, for whom his master grew in stature and dignity whenever he spent significant time out of his presence. He noticed that one of the Cardinal's hands trembled slightly, as though afflicted by a palsy. His clotted-blood robes danced with dark shadows in the firelight, burgundy and black smudges making odd shapes across the smooth red. He had always been younger in the face than his age – but no longer.

'My friends,' he said, his voice hoarse. 'It is good to see you after such a space. You do well, I trust?' Martin looked at Danforth, willing him to speak first. Danforth could sense that the Cardinal's appearance also shook his friend.

'Very well, your Grace.' The Cardinal held out his hand – the steady one – to them, and each bent in turn to kiss the sparkling amethyst on his finger. This was no ring denoting mere arms, as Dunbar had worn, but a pontifical ring, the symbol of the great authority invested in him by the Pope. 'We are come out of Glasgow, your Grace.'

'Ah, yes. I wrote you in Paisley some time back.' Beaton wrinkled his forehead as though trying to remember how long ago it had been. 'That seems a long time now. You were engaged in that business in Glasgow. Did you find the fellows who defamed my name?' Martin swallowed nervously. He had given all the papers into the custody of Danforth, who silently brought the Glasgow libels out of his pockets and passed them over. Beaton's eyes passed over them, his lips moving silently. As he read his pallor changed. 'There are men of evil minds in this world.'

'There are, your Grace. And these men are closer than you might suspect, as Mr Martin here has discovered.' He produced the scrap of letter written by Archbishop Dunbar's secretary. 'Please, look upon this and note the hand that put these words to paper.'

Beaton held the last of the slanderous bills in one hand and the scrap of paper in the other. His eyes slid back and forward between both. 'Whose hand is this? From whence did it come?' An edge had come into his voice.

'It is so,' Martin confirmed, finding his voice. 'I took this from the man's desk myself, directly outside the Privy Chamber of his Grace the Archbishop.'

'And now I employ thieves?' asked Beaton, but his tone was light and carried in it a little of his old energy.

'This is proof, your Grace,' said Danforth, 'that the Archbishop's man, his secretary, is the one who has slandered you in the most wicked way possible. His actions are contrary to the laws of man and God, to the laws of this realm. You might take this before the king, to prove that those who condemn your Grace's name and pour filth on your reputation are minions of the Archbishop. If they attack you now for what has happened on the border, they will be given no credit for it and the king will lend no ear to it. Further, I doubt the Archbishop will carry on long as Chancellor.'

'Dunbar *is* Chancellor no longer.'

Danforth and Martin looked at each other, thrown into confusion. Surely this was good news. 'Yet you might go further, your Grace. You have the libels and you now have this letter. The hand which wrote them is undeniably the same. You will once again be in the king's favour, as his unjustly dishonoured friend.'

'The king is dead,' said the Cardinal. His secretaries paled.

The sight seemed to rouse him a little, but hysteria had crept into his voice as he repeated, 'dead, dead, the king is dead!'

'It can't be,' said Martin. 'His Grace wasn't at the battle, wasn't wounded. Poison? Murder?'

'No gentlemen. He was ailing even before the battle, and the news of the girl-child hastened his decline. He has lain abed here these last days, since the news of the queen's delivery. On receiving it he turned his face to the wall and died.'

'No,' said Danforth, as though he could will the news to be false. A logical, reasonable part of his mind proclaimed that it must be so; it railed against it. 'That cannot be. Men do not turn their faces to the wall and expire, your Grace. I know death. It does not visit in that fashion.' Even Danforth's own father had taken time to pine away, refusing food, slowly settling his affairs before taking his leave of the world. 'Not unless there is some evil art in it.'

'Ever the English coroner-in-waiting,' said Beaton, attempting and failing to smile. 'I am afraid it is so. If he was broken before, the queen's delivery finished him. He believes– ' he corrected himself, 'he began to believe that every man both rich and poor had set their face against him, as had God. The Stewart kings began with a lass, quoth he – that lass as was delivered of her bairn in the Abbey of Paisley – and it might end with a lass – her born scarcely a week since.' Danforth shivered. The king's words had the ring of prophecy about them, and he feared that repeating them might make them come true. His hand wandered to his St Adelaide. Martin's mind had turned backwards, to the disorderly cry of 'murder', and the discovery of Agnes Blackwood's corpse. That had heralded the latest series of misfortunes that had befallen the kingdom. It had begun with a lass.

'I am undone,' said Beaton. 'We are all undone. The king's death will be blamed on the battle, and the battle laid at my door. Arran will now claim the regency unless … unless I can think of some other indication the king might have made.'

'Arran? That Hamilton boy? Sputtered Danforth, forgetting his place and Arran's. He and Martin had just come from the west, from where an absent Hamilton had owned the lands, only to find that soon the whole country would be ruled by one of that greedy clan. 'Why, he is a heretic. He calls the Holy Father a petty bishop.'

'And a very evil bishop at that. Yes, the Hamilton boy, half-brother to Paisley's absent Abbot, my own wretched kinsman. If he shows himself hot for reform then the Archbishop and I might have to unite in the face of a common threat. You see, gentlemen, how something bigger and more terrible than even the Archbishop's games can sweep the chessboard clean? James Hamilton, Earl of Arran, and little older than you, young Mr Martin. But what else is there, now that our king has been recalled to heaven leaving only a new-born bairn? Gentlemen, minorities can be troublesome enough, as generations of Scots can confirm. Now we have a regency in right of a six-day-old girl-child. Hail Mary, Queen of Scots.' Hysteria threatened again.

'Is all lost, your Grace?' asked Martin, his voice surprisingly cool.

'It might be; it might not be. If Hamilton assumes the regency, well ... he is but a young man. He might be glad of my experience and friendship. We can take nothing for granted. Presently I no longer trust looking further than tomorrow. But whatever falls, I shall see that you loyal gentlemen are not slighted, nor harried in the broils that are sure to come. There will always be a place for men of your faith and skill.'

'Can we do anything, your Grace? Can we be of service?' Danforth very much wanted to do something that might put some life back into his master.

'No. Thank you. You might leave me the letter. It might be of use, in some fashion. I would have it.' Danforth produced the papers from Dunbar's secretary and placed them on the little desk. Beaton did not bother to look down at them. 'Stay close, my friends,' he said. 'I might have need of good hearts and strong writing hands in the coming days. For now, you may go. Say nothing for the moment.' Danforth and Martin bowed, replaced their hats, and began to leave the chamber. Beaton caught them. 'Pray halt, gentlemen. Forgive me for being an oaf. I have not asked, Mr Danforth, how did you find the Abbey of Paisley? Did you complete the pilgrimage that has been on your mind these past years?' The pair looked at one another, Beaton giving them a bemused glance as he noted the strange silence.

'Your Grace, I thank you for allowing me leave to go. I found the Abbey a beautiful place. My pilgrimage is now complete: I have seen the best of Scotland, and all its holy places. I have found my peace.'

'Then it was worth giving you leave, sir. Mr Martin wrote me when I was at Haddington that you had fallen ill. Forgive me for not asking after your health. Yet I find you looking in better sort than when last I saw you. You have lost that drawn look that you once had. Good day to you, gentlemen. God bless you.' They strode out of the flickering room, leaving the Cardinal to stare back into the fire. He held his trembling hand by the wrist, and began slowly twisting his ring with a thumb.

On wavering legs Danforth followed Martin to another window casement, this one boasting a cushioned settle. Few servants moved around, most of them attending to their own masters, the royal household likely being gathered together to be told the news. Martin blew out a long, shuddering breath. 'The king dead,' he said. 'Another James to be buried, leaving a child to take the crown and others to rule.' Danforth could think of nothing to say. Eventually, he hazarded, 'well, Arnaud, we shall find out one thing at least.'

'What's that, sir?'

'We shall discover whether the Scots will accept a girl as their queen regnant, to rule them in place of a man.'

'And I don't doubt that we'll see blood spilled as minds are made up. No brothers for the little princess now, no prince to succeed.'

'No. The only prince now is England's Edward, and he shall be in want of a wife, and his father eager to give him one.'

'A worrying thought.'

'It is that. The times have been full of them of late.'

'Well, sir,' said Martin, turning to look at him. 'For all we've lost a king, we've yet gained a queen. The earth has not been rent, and we can pray that neither will Scotland. Across that courtyard life still goes on for hundreds. Across the country it goes on for hundreds of thousands. His Grace was wrong to say that the board's been swept clean. The king's gone, but the queen and the rest remain in play, a bonny new queen carved and set amongst them. But you'll have a friend to face it with. From an ocean of troubles might spring a little happiness and still more life.'

'As Pegasus and Chrysador sprang forth from the blood of a gorgon. That is pleasing, Arnaud. Thank you. Let us go. I am beginning to think that death stalks me as though he were Lelantos and I his mark.'

'You know,' said Martin, 'I may have to retract my friendship unless you learn to bridle your tongue.' Danforth turned to the animated, intense face, gave him an aggrieved look and then his own wan smile.

They rose from the cushioned window casement and began to make their way back to the servants' quarters, into bright, tapestried rooms where life hummed, buzzed and sang.

Author's Note

Though Simon Danforth and Arnaud Martin are not real, the world they inhabit is. One of the pleasures in writing this book was in researching it. Too often popular attention is focussed in this period on the antics of Henry VIII in England (at this time Henry had recently lopped off the head of the unfortunate Katherine Howard and was about to embark on military adventures in France and a largely one-sided romance with Katherine Parr). However, north of the border, events were tumbling into chaos, with the weak-willed but artistically-minded James V losing control of his magnates and leaning heavily on the clergy, both financially and politically. For interested readers, I recommend following up any threads in *The Abbey Close* with a selection of the interesting and informative works I was lucky enough to consult.

Central to writing this book was developing an understanding the personalities and events of the period. Although he remains off-stage, James V is an important figure in the novel. By far the most readable biography is Caroline Bingham's *James V, King of Scots* (1971, Harper Collins). Bingham offers not only an insight into the half-Tudor king's personality, politics and personal life, but a snapshot of the Scotland he inhabited, replete with lowland bourgeois wives decked out in copies of the splendour of the nobility.

In terms of the politics of 1540s Anglo-Scottish relations, Marcus Merriman's lively and frequently hilarious *The Rough Wooings of Mary Queen of Scots* (2000, Tuckwell Press) is invaluable reading. Merriman unpicks the complex politics, blasts apart many of the myths, and offers fair assessments of the key players. His book was crucial in painting as realistic a picture as possible of who knew what when. His book also helpfully acknowledged the phenomena of English exiles fleeing north of the border in the period after the Henrician Reformation. Useful also is Linda Porter's *Crown of Thistles: The Fatal Inheritance of Mary Queen of Scots* (2013,

Macmillan), which offers an overview of events before, during and after those depicted in *The Abbey Close*. Finally, J. D. Mackie's 'Henry VIII and Scotland' in the *Transactions of the Royal Historical Society* (Volume 29, 1947, pp.93-114) remains the standard short study of the infamous English king's aggressive, though inconsistent, policy towards the northern kingdom.

Although a staggering number of popular books exist regarding the everyday lives, beliefs and behaviours of those living in Tudor London (and Tudor-era England more widely), there is an unfortunate dearth of work on the everyday life of the sixteenth-century Scot. For that reason, Madeleine Bingham's *Scotland Under Mary Stuart* (1971, Allen & Unwin) proved extremely helpful in providing a general outline of how society functioned, from the administration of justice to the role of burgh baillies. For elements of Danforth's faith and superstitious belief system, Gordon Donaldson's *The Faith of the Scots* (1990, Batsford Ltd) was a great help.

Despite having grown up in Paisley, which reached the apogee of its fame during the industrial revolution, I knew very little about the importance of its Abbey in the early modern period. Here William M. Metcalfe's *A History of Paisley 600-1908* (2004, The Grimsay Press) provided a goldmine. The Abbey's great spire, mentioned in the novel, collapsed in the 1550s, and the building itself fell into ruin after the Reformation. However, thanks to the efforts of the gothic-minded Victorians, it was reconstructed and remains, today, a parish Church of Scotland church. The underground tunnels, or 'great drain' were excavated in the 1990s and remain a haunting reminder of mediaeval life.

The rivalry between Cardinal Beaton and Archbishop Dunbar was real, although the latter's campaign of libelling was my own invention. Nevertheless, I consider it plausible. In the early modern period, throughout Europe, political figures were subject to verse libels: pithy little poems attacking the famous, often nailed up in public places. For those interested in how these operated, I recommend James Daybell and Andrew Gordon's *Cultures of Correspondence in Early*

Modern Britain (2016, University of Pennsylvania Press) and Steven May and Alan Bryson's *Verse Libel in Renaissance England and Scotland* (2016, Oxford University Press).

Cardinal Beaton, like his near-contemporary, Cardinal Wolsey, is a figure about whom few have had much good to say. If it counts at all in his favour he was, however, an implacable enemy of Henry VIII. In her definitive, though densely-academic, *Cardinal of Scotland* (2001, Donald), Margaret Sanderson paints a complex portrait of a tempestuous, bloodthirsty man, generous to his servants and possessed, at his height, of a power greater even than Wolsey enjoyed in England. To date, no popular biography of this urbane, slippery figure exists. Someone ought to write one.

Giving your time to a book, especially from a first-time author, is a generous thing to do. Thank you to everyone reading this, and please feel free to get in touch via Twitter, where I waste time occasionally under the handle @ScrutinEye (a special thank you to anyone who gets the dated 90s reference). If you enjoyed *The Abbey Close*, you might be interested in the continuing adventures of Simon Danforth. In the upcoming *The Royal Burgh*, he will fall from the Cardinal's favour but find himself enjoying family life in Stirling. Unfortunately, it is to be interrupted by murder, as Scotland's criminal underbelly emerges in the wake of the king's death...

Printed in Great Britain
by Amazon

87472480R00140